Foreword

Rural Affairs is the second book ir
series. It follows on from Shop Talk ⌐... ...
Josie Carrington. The third title, Puppy Love Tales, is due out
later this year.

Drayton Beauchamp nestles in the Oxfordshire countryside, with
its Georgian Cotswold stone houses, impressive sprawling
Drayton Hall and quaint high street where Mel owns the Deli,
Charlie has the Drayton Bookshop and the Little Acorns hold
their annual Jamboree. The editor of the Drayton Chronicle
produces its weekly newspaper keeping the residents up to date
with village life, and Tina at The King's Arms always has your
favourite drink ready.

This edition introduces you to Alicia, Chloe and Matty, as well as
meeting up with old friends in Josie and Henry. I hope you enjoy
reading about their exploits, shopping antics and love lives.

Anna Hutton-North

Also by Anna Hutton-North

Shop Talk
Puppy Love Tales

Coming soon:
Finding Mr Write

Rural Affairs

Anna Hutton-North

This is a work of fiction. Names, characters, businesses, places, events and incidents are either the products of the author's imagination or used in a fictitious manner. Any resemblance to actual persons, living or dead, or actual events is purely coincidental.

First printed in 2012

V: 2012006

My thanks and heart-felt appreciation goes to Mark and Olivia for having to put up with me writing when I should have been cooking meals, ironing and tidying the house. Unfortunately I found Rural Affairs was just more pressing.

Thanks also to my parents, Margret and Richard, as well as to Lisa and Nick for the continued support and encouragement. A big vote of appreciation to Lucy Y for trawling through the rough edit; it was a huge help!

Once again thanks to Lynn and the team at Zimmer & Rohde for all their help with the Drayton Beauchamp Series.

And finally to everyone who bought, and hopefully enjoyed, Shop Talk. It was the spur to carry on writing about village life in Drayton Beauchamp.

Rural Affairs

Chapter 1

Slowly one eye peeled open, then the other as Alicia stared blinkingly at her watch; she tried to collate her thoughts ignoring the dull nag in the back of her skull, realising she was already late for her first meeting. Cursing quietly she rubbed her eyes feeling the dried mascara caked on the lashes, and taking in the strange surroundings of the bedroom, increased the cursing as she realised she hadn't made it home last night. There is only one thing worse than being late for an 8.30 meeting; and that's being extremely late with nothing other than your very skimpy party outfit to wear into the office. As quickly as her first class hangover would allow, Alicia slipped out of the bed and across the corridor into the small bathroom, where she failed to master the shower controls and ended up having an exhilarating but freezing cold dousing mid-way through washing her hair. The effect was not only an instantaneous wake up call, but persuaded her to hurry as nothing else could.

Creeping back into the bedroom she couldn't help but notice Zac's tousled blond head hadn't moved; it lay still and inert against the pale blue pillows. Cautiously, anxious not to make a sound, Alicia slid into her discarded skirt and eased open the wardrobe door and rifled silently through his suits and shirts until she found a pink and white check Charles Tyrwhitt shirt. Sliding it noiselessly off the hanger she pulled the soft cotton garment over her tingling skin; it hung down almost to her knees and her hands were obscured by the drooping sleeves. Deftly she rolled the cuffs up to a more reasonable length and knotting the shirt at the waist both removed the length and the bulk, leaving a more tailored look as a result. Spying an old sleeveless cricket jumper that was poking out of a kit bag, she pulled it on. Surveying herself in the mirror on the inside of the wardrobe door she decided that she might just get away with it; true it wasn't the look everyone was sporting on the high street, but at least she could go straight to the office and not have to trek halfway across London to get to her flat. Smoothing down her wispy skirt and combing back her wet bobbed hair she glanced around for her strappy sandals, making good her final escape. She finally located them in the sitting room under the red leather sofa. At what point had they managed to get there she wondered, and slipping them on realised her feet would be well and truly blistered and crippled by the end of the day. Resolutely she tightened the ankle strap and stood up ready to take her first tottering steps to the office.

Walking to the front door she noticed several large modern paintings hanging above the marble fireplace incongruous against the floral Colefax & Fowler wallpaper and antiques. She hadn't noticed them before in the dimmed lights and all the heady kissing. A sound from the bedroom roused her from her contemplations and sent her scurrying out of the flat and into the bright daylight of Belgravia Square, letting the door slam behind her with a satisfying finality.

"Good evening?" George asked cheerily, as Alicia slunk down behind her laptop. Slowly she raised her head. Somehow she had managed to get through the morning so far, a combination of strong black coffee, several doughnuts and two litres of cool fresh water meant that her headache had subsided sufficiently to allow her to do the most basic of tasks.
"Not bad." She admitted, thinking of Zac's extravagant wining and dining to celebrate his client's win in court.
"Well I hope you don't have to work too hard on the Solomon case."
"Don't try and dig for information George, that's bad practice, and shows that you really don't have a case." She replied with a wagging finger.
"Don't be too sure!" He asserted revealing that the prosecuting team obviously felt confident in the prosecution they were preparing. "We're going to win this one for certain. Just wait and see." She turned her nose up and spun her chair round so her back was facing him.
"I think I'll wait for the Judge to decide." She replied tartly.
"You do that!" he laughed. "Are you on for a drink tonight?"
Shaking her head cautiously she adamantly declined, counting down the hours before she could go home to sleep.

Phones rang shrilly and people shouted across the room demanding updates. The courier boys were delivering urgent files back and teams rushed off to meetings and gathered to go to court. Alicia focused on the case notes she was collating, her head was still heavy, but at least she had gone through the pain barrier of wanting to just slide under her desk and escape into a

2

blissful sleep. Hearing her name, she glanced up and saw the team's secretary hurrying over as fast as her platform heels would allow.

"Fort you'd wanna know," She puffed slightly from the exertion "They brought the client meeting for Van Plaza Clothing forward to this afternoon."

"What! But it was booked for tomorrow."

"Yeah I know but apparently they've gotta fly out to the States tomorrow on some kind of deal. It's all been moved forward."

With horror Alicia looked down at her outfit. There was no way she could go to a client meeting wearing last night's clothes.

"What time is the meeting?" Vague hopes of being able to dash across town to get something clean from home were totally dashed by Nikki's '*In an hour*'. Desperately she rummaged in her handbag, pulling her Amex card out from the motley assortment of discarded tickets, sandwich napkins and case notes. Holding it out she pleaded with Nikki.

"Can you run over to TM Lewin and get me a suit?" She toyed with the idea of putting an order in for shoes but knowing her card was maxed out and it was ages until pay day she decided against it.

"I ain't running nowhere today." Nikki warned, pivoting her ankle for emphasis, and shuffled away out of the office on her errand of mercy.

Palms on the desk, Alicia yelled across the banks of seating. "Larnie!" The petite Asian girl looked round. "Have you heard, the Van Plaza meeting has been called forward? We're going to need bound copies of that proposal we prepared pronto; and I need to find out where Simon is. He hasn't seen any of this yet."

The other girl uncharacteristically swore, swivelling on her chair she started to punch numbers into the phone. "It wasn't supposed to be until tomorrow." She swore again. "Printing are engaged. I'll go down and see if I can get them to push it through." She started to race down the corridor. "Simon wasn't in court was he?" Then still hurrying she twisted her head over her shoulder to make one final verbal volley. "You're never going into the meeting wearing that are you? Simon will flip!"

Alicia assured her with a casual wave of her hand. "All under control. Nikki's grabbing me a change of clothing. Now get going – we really need all the paperwork in order."

It was one of those crucifying 'just in time' moments; having snatched the newly acquired suit, grabbed the remnants of make-up that inhabited the dark recesses of her desk drawers and dashed into the ladies' toilets she managed to dress, powder and comb in record time. Meaning that she stepped out transformed just as Simon was ushering the two clients into the meeting room, indicating for Larnie and herself to join them. The obligatory platitudes were exchanged as Larnie served coffee and set out the plate of chef-baked biscuits onto the large boardroom table. Alicia took the opportunity to gather her inner composure with a few subtle deep breaths and a tug at the cuffs of the borrowed sleeves folded back over the jacket to give, what she hoped was, a Parisian look. Crossing her ankles inwardly amused at the sight of the strappy sandals she reminded herself that she really should make it home at the end of the night to her own bed.

The room they were in was one of the original parts of the building, dating back to the 1800s with high ornate ceilings, mahogany floor to ceiling glass fronted bookcases, detailed pediment above the door matched the furniture. Heavy damask curtains framed the two sash windows and thick cast iron heating pipes ran along the wall to the column radiators. The whole atmosphere was rarefied and comforting, seemingly cut off from the hustle and bustle of the modern day city. Its view stretched across the gardens down to the rhythmic flow of the Thames.

Without thinking Alicia leant across and helped herself to one of the shortbread delights, biting into the firm biscuit, savouring the sugary melting on her tongue. She was suddenly aware of the sardonic glance of the taller of the two visitors, watching hawk-like as her teeth expertly bit through, her tongue flicking the corner of her lips to catch the loose crumbs. For a moment she held his gaze, undecided whether to pointedly ignore or continue to simply look. In the end she gave a small self-depreciating smile and pushed the plate towards him. "Sorry I should have offered them first."

The man was off-balanced momentarily; he was used to controlling the situation rather than allow someone else to set the pace. His well-built fleshy frame stiffened before amusedly refusing the proffered plate. "Patrick Fernly." He extended a hand that engulfed hers and held it fractionally too tightly as an unconscious reminder of where the power lay. He turned to his companion. "And this is my brother Michael." Alicia shook his hand in turn, noting that the younger brother shared none of the natural assertiveness displayed by his older sibling. Simon shuffled the papers, catching Alicia's eye to indicate he was ready, and obligingly she turned her attention to him.

"It's quite a problem you've got here." Simon began. "We've taken advice from Counsel and it really could go either way. You have definitely infringed the contract relating to selling Brand XF over here. Now admittedly it was unknowingly, and the terms are fairly ambiguous, but that isn't an adequate defence in the eyes of the law."

"So do we contest it?" Patrick asked, one hand unconsciously thumping into the other.

"If we do then there's no certainty you'll win. You could end up with the legal fees for both you and Kudos Clothing. There'll also be a lot of heightened media pressure – these are the big boys after all. They won't care about the cost only about retaining the status quo."

"And if we were to admit liability? Would they settle out of court?"

"Maybe – but it's still going to be mega bucks." The three men stared disconsolately at each other. In the background Larnie's pen scratched on the legal pad as she took notes.

"Doesn't look like we have much choice." Patrick sounded annoyed and Simon grimaced in empathy. "Either way the business suffers."

Alicia felt her palms tingle with dampness, she tentatively cleared her throat and instantly three pairs of eyes swivelled round. *'This is it'*, Alicia thought *'This is where I dive into the unknown'* reflecting on the recommendations she and Larnie had provisionally worked up, but hadn't yet been able to run past Simon.

"Well there is one option." She started, her voice drying in her mouth. Taking a swig of coffee she tried again, shooting an apologetic look at Simon. "Simon mentioned that you were trying to break into the American market." Patrick inclined his head fractionally in agreement. "So you could of course look to buy into a company who is a distributor for the Brand XF range. That way you get round the infringement issue, as well as establishing a base for you to then get into the American High Street from."

"And you've identified a company?" Patrick was observing her with quickened interest.

She gave a quick nod. "If you turn to page 5 of the pack," They all obediently opened up the relevant page, and Larnie snuck a supportive thumbs up. "One of the high street retailers is divesting their portfolio so they can focus on the mid-market sportswear range. They asked us to help with the legal side of the disposals. One of their smaller JVs has the Brand XF distribution rights; the other shareholder is Kudos Clothing." There was a small silence as the men digested the information.

"So if we were able to buy into the company," Michael started "Then we would not only have the legal rights to distribute the Brand XF range…" Patrick cut in, already ahead of him. "But we'd also get the entry point into America – and we wouldn't have to go to court to settle."

"Because Kudos Clothing is hardly likely to sue someone they are in partnership with." Alicia agreed.

Patrick thumped the air in triumph. "Sounds like one hell of a good plan. How do we get the company?" Alicia pointed to Simon, who was sitting in stunned silence, wondering how they had managed to conjure up this victory from the salivating jaws of despair.

"Simon's the one who can help you on this." She replied diplomatically; not wanting to push her luck any further. "He'll be able to help you secure it."

When the meeting broke up Patrick shook her hand firmly. "Neat idea." He remarked and inside she felt a flame of triumph soar up. If the client was happy then Simon wouldn't complain too much about her presenting an idea he hadn't had the chance to approve. "Neat shoes as well" He complimented drily. "I don't see many lawyers wearing Christian Louboutin."

Work continued at a pace with no let up for anyone; days and evenings morphed into each other, everyone looking forward to Friday evening and a chance to relax. That night the din in the bar was deafening; there was a wall of bodies congregating around shouting orders to the barman; people were talking at the top of their voices. Alicia walked in and tried to make out where the others were; noticing her arrival, George detached himself and waved energetically to catch her attention. Fighting through the hordes she reached George. "You're late." He shouted into her ear.

"Tell me about it! I had to get the paperwork ready for Simon; he's flying up to Scotland first thing and needed the case notes with him." She pulled a face. "God I am so ready for a drink." George plucked a lone glass from a high table and filled it with a generous slug of wine.

"Here you go." They clinked glasses and Alicia took a large mouthful, enjoying the cool refreshing taste, and she felt some of the day's tensions ease away. Tossing her briefcase under the nearest chair, she saw the impromptu party was well underway. In one corner Nikki, in her lime green city shorts, was holding court with several of the messenger boys. Larnie and several other of the trainees were practicing drinking games remembered from Uni days amid spills and spluttering laughter.

"Have you heard about New York yet?"

George shook his head. "I thought I might have heard this week; but you know what it's like. Trying to get anything organised through HR is awful. I swear it should be renamed Human Remains – they never seem to get anything resourced."

Alicia smiled sympathetically. "Any plans for the weekend?"

"Thought I might head down and see my folks in Oxford on Sunday. My sister and her brood are going to be there and we're in for one of Dad's famous roasts." He considered it for a moment and then added. "I could always go via Drayton Beauchamp if you wanted."

She held up her hands in mock horror. "I don't think so. I'm not expected to do the dutiful daughter bit for ages." Her plans were for a lazy breakfast sitting on her balcony with fresh coffee and a catch up on the newspapers before heading across to Bond Street and a look at clothes. Maybe if she was lucky Zac would be able to get away and they would spend the afternoon together. It was so rare to get a whole weekend free that she was going to enjoy it to the full, the last thing she needed was some obligatory trip out into the country.

The carousing intensified as the evening wore on; someone had found out how to turn on the music system and now the background was filled with the beat of punk rock and classic 80s. The wine was flowing quickly, discarded bottles and glasses littering every surface. George was trying unsuccessfully to hold a conversation with his latest girlfriend, a model for the glossy weekend magazines. Alicia marvelled at George's effortless ability to attract beautiful women. They pursued him with the same dogged determination of a Boxing Day Sale aficionado. Leaving him shouting at the phone in an effort to be heard, she wove her way to the ladies toilet passing by a group of Senior Partners and out into the corridor. When she returned one of the men had detached himself from the group and was leaning nonchalantly against the wall. With a studied indifference, borne out of long practice, she said hello and went to move on, but he stood upright blocking her way. He was tall and slender, with a Grecian profile and sleek blond hair, beautiful to look at and totally aware of it.

"I seem to be missing a cricket sweater." He joked in a low voice.

"Are you?" Alicia replied archly, enjoying the parry.

"You didn't even say goodbye." He chided as though wounded by the omission.

"Far too busy." She said breezily. "Too many people to see, contracts to write. You know the type of thing."

He surveyed her and then pushing back a lock of her short bob, stroked her cheek. "Simon's been singing your praises." He said conversationally. "Apparently you impressed him over the Van Plaza deal. Pulled a proverbial bunny out of the hat and increased our fees into the deal." A shot of pride ran through her body, if she kept this up then they would definitely consider her as Partner material. She could envisage it now: name on the door, office on the 8th floor and her own personal assistant.

"You could have come back to celebrate." Zac was saying. "Only Marcie's insisted on coming up this weekend for a show."

Some of the elation sapped out of her. "That's the problem with wives." She snapped. "They never do what you want them to."

◆◆◆

"Ohhhmygoshhh!" Alicia dashed across the polished stone floor as fast as her heels would allow. "I'm so late I know – can you ever forgive me?" Skidding to a halt she hugged her friend hard, ordered a drink from a waiter and plumped herself down in the chair. In the background the lively chatter of evening diners and the soft playing piano circulated around them. "I really did mean to leave on time." Alicia was insisting.

"You say that every time." Josie pointed out good humouredly. "I have yet to meet up with you and not be at least one drink ahead.

It does my figure no good at all, particularly when it is compared to yours. What's the secret? GI, Atkins, Ford?"

"Hardly! It's the *'I'm too busy to eat; have to work late'* diet invented especially for aspiring lawyers."

"Is it really that busy at the moment?"

Alicia grimaced and nodded. "I only got away this evening because I promised I'd go back afterwards. It's going to be an all-nighter I can see."

"How come?"

"We're working on a high profile divorce case that involves splitting a business up. The husband wants to push all the paperwork through before his wife can object."

"Doesn't sound very fair."

Alicia shrugged, viewing it all in a detached way. "He says she's having an affair and planning to do the same with her mystery lover."

"And is she?"

"No idea. We can't find out if she is actually playing away from the marital bed, they've had all sorts of attempts to find out – but so far they've drawn a blank."

"But the husband's going ahead anyway?"

"His motto is attack is the best form of defence; look out for it in the papers tomorrow – it's sure to make some kind of stir."

"And apart from that – is everything ok?"

"Yes couldn't be better. I'm starting to get involved in the larger clients and I'm even in charge of some of the smaller ones on my own." She glowed with pride.

Josie leaned in and with a stage whisper asked. "Anyone special on the scene at the moment?"

An image of Zac floated into her brain; but theirs was a purely convenient set-up. She gave him the guaranteed discretion required to keep his wife in the dark, and he gave her the opportunity to further her career. It was satisfying to a point, but it was hardly the heady stuff of true romance. "No," she said. "I'd never find time to date someone properly."

"That can't be good." Josie was shocked.

"It's fine." Alicia assured her. "As soon as I've made Partner then I can start thinking about Mr Right. Until then I need to concentrate on work. It's a tough place out there – there's always competition. I need to make sure I'm being noticed. George has just got a secondment out to the States with the firm he works for. He's a such lucky thing. It would be great to go out to the New York office."

Josie agreed. "Oh yes! There's Bloomingdales, Central Park and Neiman Marcus." She said dreamily.

"There's rich clients!" Alicia replied cynically taking a swig of wine and absently-mindedly reaching out to scoop up a handful of cashews. "So how is life with you?" Popping one of the salted delights into her mouth. "I can't believe you've ended up back in Drayton Beauchamp. Aren't you bored out of your mind yet?" She thought of Matty and the emails she hadn't responded to that were filled with village gossip.

A knowing smile played round Josie's lips; she knew her friend's aversion to the village and its provincial rural affairs. "Not at all. The shop's doing really well. I've got a new girl helping out a couple of days a week, which means that I can go out to see clients and not have to shut the shop. That was why I came up. Lots of clients want new ideas and it's London Design Week, so I wanted to go round the collections at the Chelsea Harbour showrooms to see what the new season's looks are."

"And to do a bit of shopping as well?" Alicia asked drily pointedly gazing at the assortment of LK Bennett, Whistles and Jaeger bags that lay sprawled around their feet under the table.

"Well I had to take the opportunity while I could." Josie explained reasonably. "And as I knew you would be late – yet again - I thought I'd make use of the time."

"And that's how you're going to explain it to Henry? Tell him it's all my fault for not being here."

"Exactly!" Josie grinned. There was nothing like using a good friend as an excuse for spending.

Chapter 2

The words *'ring Alicia'* stared out from the post-it stuck on the telephone. Mavis had written it three days earlier to remind herself to do it. Since then she had carefully averted her gaze every time she walked past the phone. Calling Alicia was something Mavis steeled herself for, writing the note was part of the routine of preparation. Every so often she would feel a pang of maternal guilt at not having checked that her daughter was ok, and so she would write a note to try and encourage herself to face the unenviable task. The note would then sit forlornly on the telephone, abandoned and unwanted, until Mavis would finally take the plunge and call. The fact Alicia rarely phoned her mother illustrated the status of their relationship; it wasn't that they loathed each other, deep down they definitely cared. The simple fact was they were very different people, they always had been, and probably always would be. When Alicia had been growing up it had amazed Mavis and Bill that their daughter was actually related to them. She and Bill were both easy going, believing life was for the quality of the moment and not becoming part of a ferocious rat race. They had met at horticultural college where a shared love of dahlias and brassicas had sealed their relationship. After graduating they had returned to Bill's family nursery where they worked during the day and lived with Bill's parents in the evenings. It had been a cramped muddled existence but they had been happy, knowing they would never be rich, but working quietly alongside each other in a companionable silence.

When Mavis had discovered she was pregnant they were both delighted, they talked constantly of how their baby would be able to be part of their working lives. They would be able to use the ancient perambulator Bill's mother had used, so that the baby could doze under the shaded boughs of the old apple trees. They talked about where they would create the child's first garden so they could grow big cheery sunflowers and tasty strawberries, then later when their child had grown up they would be able to pass on the nursery and keep the eternal circle flowing. Except it never happened. From the first Alicia made it plain that she detested the outdoors, every time they tried to leave in the dappled shade of the ancient boughs she had promptly screamed and screamed until taken back in doors.

When they had tried to encourage an interest in gardening, she had studied their faces hard asking intently why she had to get all dirty and when they tentatively mentioned careers, Alicia had already fully made up her mind. She had read enough of the 'At home with...' feature articles in Bling & Boudoir to know that City lawyers had money and partied hard. So as soon as she had the required A level grades Alicia had fled to university and the temptations of London, to the secret relief of her parents. As much as they loved her, there was only so much advice one could take from their capitalist offspring. Her constant enquiries into profit margins, pension funds and growth plans had begun to wear the couple down. They were only too happy with their home, working companionably side-by-side, beetling around in their old van – after all they said, what did they need with a flash new car, holiday home in Spain or a fashionable wardrobe?

The phone rang and Mavis held her breath almost wishing her daughter was too busy to answer, but luck was out and Alicia was in. In clipped tones she answered with a curt "Yes?"
"Ali, it's Mummy. I thought I'd just phone up and see how you are."
"I'm fine, just finishing off in the office, I had some things I needed to get finished tonight." The conversation was following the normal limited script, soon someone would ask about work, maybe discuss the weather and chat off-handedly about the possibility of meeting up.
"You sound tired." Mavis commented. "You're not working too hard are you?"
"No more than usual. It was just a bit of a late one last night."
"Oh what did you do?"
"Went to a party with a couple of friends after work."
"Anyone in particular?"
"No, just the usual crowd."
"So no man in your life at the moment then?" Alicia uncharacteristically blushed at the thought of Zac – her mother would never approve.
"No mum there's no-one. How's the nursery?"
"Oh the same as usual, we're trying a new brand of compost at the moment."
"Really." Alicia tried to keep the note of boredom out of her voice. "How is it working?"

"Oh fine, the legumes are really blossoming though I'm not sure about the roses and the pansies. They don't seem to be doing as well, but that might the bout of greenfly we had." She stopped abruptly realising she was wittering on and a tiny pause expanded.

"Lovely weather we're having." Alicia said in an attempt to get the conversation kick started again.

"Yes, isn't it."

"Mum have you thought any more about getting a financial adviser?"

It was Mavis' turn to blush down the phone, however well her daughter's intentions were she preferred to ignore the attempts to get her finances sorted out, believing firmly in the school of thought of 'what you don't know, can't hurt you'.

"Mmm, a little." Mavis said vaguely, and in attempt to draw Alicia's attentions away from money suggested. "Why don't we meet up soon, it's been ages." Alicia felt a pang of guilt, since her father had died she hadn't made any effort to make sure her mother was coping. "I can't do next weekend though – it's the local horticultural show."

"And I've got things on the next few weekends after that."

"Oh well, maybe we'll fix something up a little nearer the time." Mavis tried to keep the relief from escaping. "Now I'll let you go, I know you'll have work to do."

"Bye Mum."

"Bye Alicia."

Putting the phone down her stomach rumbled, glancing round Alicia wondered whether it had disturbed any of the others, but it appeared not; she realised that the time had stolen into late evening. Selecting one of the take away menus that lived permanently on her desk, she speed-dialled the first one and ordered a bento box special to be biked over. She turned her attention back to the screen, concentrating on the words. As her eyes began to throb in protest at the prolonged stare she rubbed them wondering if she needed to get them checked. Heavens knows where she'd find the time for that. She turned back to the screen; if she worked hard then she should be out before midnight. Checking her watch she hoped the food wouldn't be too long, her stomach was really starting to distract her.

Chapter 3

Matty looked down at the small homemade flyer she had picked up at the village shop. It had been printed on flimsy pink paper that crimpled immediately at the touch. In the centre an almost childlike drawing of a flower dominated the page, around it were details of the Drayton Hall fete. It lay innocently amongst the clutter on the kitchen table whose scrubbed pine surface was no longer visible. The strewn debris that had originally been confined to the table had virulently spread so that almost every ledge and surface in the cottage was covered. Back copies of Vogue and Viva, old calendars, money-off coupons that were now out of date and unopened post. Matty couldn't remember how it had escaped out of the control, it was something that she only seemed to notice once it had successfully taken hold. She had kept this afternoon free to try and start clearing, planning to make a start once lunch was over but she was distracted by the flyer, deciding to suggest to Tom that they went. It would be fun to go out together, they hadn't done anything like that for absolutely ages. She heard the Landrover chug in the drive, heralding Tom's arrival and a few moments later the back door opening as Tagger, Tom's black and white collie scampered in, followed by Tom.

"Good morning?" she enquired as he washed his hands.

"Yes, we've got all the sheep into Home Farm field, so we'll be able to worm them this afternoon and get the job done in a reasonable time. Might even finish early and we could go for a drink at the pub." He sat down pleased with the progress. Matty felt a chill of ice run down her spine, she paused dishing up the jacket potatoes as she recalled Tom asking her to collect the wormer on the way home from work. She had completely forgotten about it until now, reluctantly she realised she would have to go into town after lunch to pick it up, all thoughts of spring cleaning abandoned.

"Erm, I haven't got the wormer." Matty admitted in a small voice.

"What?"

"I plain forgot."

"Oh Matty," He sounded disappointed. "I did remind you yesterday."

"I know you did, I don't know how it happened but it went clean out of my mind." She set the food down and sat down opposite him. "Don't worry I'll go to the vets and pick it up this afternoon."

"But why didn't you get it yesterday?" Tom persisted.

"I don't know, I just didn't ok."

"Alright, calm down." He said, recognising her agitation. The phone rang distracting them.

"Hello." Tom answered in between mouthfuls of food. "Oh hold on, I'll just ask." He covered the phone with his large broad hands. "Mum wants to know if there's anything you want from the shops." Matty shook her head, she never felt comfortable asking Barbara to do her shopping.

When she and Tom had first been married she had thought how kind Barbara was offering to pick up things when Matty was too busy, but one day she had come home to find the shopping put away, her wet washing out on the line and the dirty breakfast things washed and dried. Upon seeing it she had promptly burst into tears; it made her feel of no consequence in her own home, insignificant and worthless. The problem was that she didn't seem to be able to make Tom understand, to him it was perfectly natural that his mother would still want to do things for him. She always had when he'd been living at home, so why should it change now? Privately he thought Matty was over-reacting, particularly since Matty had insisted on carrying on work at Saunders once they were married which meant they hardly had any time together, especially when farming wasn't exactly the typical nine to five job. Matty had felt too awkward to let Barbara know how she felt, so instead she had carefully avoided Barbara's offers of assistance and concentrated on doubling her efforts on being the perfect wife, housekeeper and farming gofer.

She listened to Tom carry on the conversation: "Where are you going...oh right, you couldn't go via the vets could you? Matty forgot to collect the wormer. You can? Oh great. Yes brilliant – thanks Mum. Tell Dad I'll see him down the field." Matty sat rigid with anger, her teeth clenched tightly together and her hands gripping the chair forcibly. How unfair was this – true, she had forgotten the wormer, but she, Matty, had been going to collect it, and now Barbara was seen as the super-Mum because she was coming to the rescue.

"Mum's going to pick up the wormer."

"I said I'd get it." Matty spat through clenched teeth

"Well Mum was going out anyway, so she was more than happy to pick it up." Tom's voice was calm and reasonable, as though he was explaining something to a small child.

"I bet she was." Matty's voice was snide, and her face showed an open loathing.

"What's that supposed to mean?" Tom was beginning to feel exasperated. "I thought you would appreciate not having to go into town on your afternoon off." He threw his knife and fork down onto the plate. "What's wrong with you Matty? You never have a civil word to say about my family these days. We should be grateful for everything they do. Instead you just seem to resent them." He shoved his chair back so hard that it toppled over backwards, falling onto the vinyl floor with a loud thud, causing Tagger to jump out of his basket and start barking loudly at imaginary invaders. "I'm going back to work." He called the dog sharply, striding to the backdoor grabbing the Landrover keys.

"What about your cup of tea?" Matty called after him.

"I'll have one at Mum and Dad's." He continued walking, not bothering to turn round.

"Tom!" Matty's voice was full of contrition. "Tom." But her calling was drowned out by the rattling of the Landrover as it sped out of the drive and down the lane to his parents' farmhouse. A slow silence descended on the cottage, the only sounds were the distant drone of a lone combine harvester cutting the barley stalks and a fat bloated bluebottle buzzing against one of the window panes. For a moment Matty just stood rooted to the spot, transfixed by the mix of emotions that had been poured and folded together that lunchtime, like the ingredients for an elaborate cake. Slowly she stooped and righted the fallen chair, before clearing the table of the lunch plates. She noticed the pink flyer had become splattered with bean juice from Tom's knife and she tried wiping it off, but it only smudged, causing the paper to sag and wrinkle. Seeing it aged and dirty saddened her, it had held such promise before. Carrying the plates over to the sink she filled it with hot water, squirting the lemon scented liquid so that instantly thousands of iridescent bubbles appeared. In a state of trance she mechanically washed the plates and cutlery, leaving them to drip their soapy suds onto the draining board. It was so second nature that her eyes remained staring out of the window across the garden. Beyond the low yew hedge sat an old bench; she had been meaning to create a small private area where she could sit with friends and serve elaborate afternoon teas ever since she had moved in, but like so much else she hadn't managed to do that either. With a sinking feeling of drowning under the day-to-day tasks, she realised suddenly there were no more objects to wash up. Pulling the plug out there was a schlerp and the water began to disappear down the plughole. Watching it Matty felt a pang of recognition; it was just like her life being sucked away into some deep cavernous pit. Where had it all gone wrong she wondered, when had all the dreams and expectations she had so firmly believed in been so cruelly crushed underfoot. With a small sigh she filled the kettle and set it down on top of the Aga patiently waiting for it to boil. Opening the cupboard door to reach for a mug her eye was caught by the tiny pink rosebuds on their wedding crockery; its delicate pattern always made her think of long lazy summer days. Deciding to use it, she made a cup of camomile tea and made her way out into the garden, over to the bench by the yew. She sank into it gratefully and felt the same wave of safety and protection that a duvet brings. Detachedly she sipped her tea and observed the garden as a stranger would; noticing the outbreak of weeds along the edge of the small paved path, the shed that needed repainting and the bed of shrubs that needed trimming before they became one large homogenous tangle.

Matty wondered where the past ten years had gone; how could one minute she be a carefree student only interested in fashion, parties and Leo on the Titanic (convinced he would marry her if only they could meet) and the next moment it seemed she'd collapsed into a boring caricature in a dead end job, continually bickering with her mother-in-law and not having a clue what she was doing with her life.

Somehow over the past decade she'd lost touch with friends, as everyone else moved away, seeking the excitement and thrill of the city; starting their careers amongst the bright lights of London, Manchester and Edinburgh. A series of half-forgotten memories flickered through her brain like an ancient whirring slide projector – of big hairstyles, white stilettos and denim shirts, or dancing endlessly to REM and not giving the future a second thought. The flitting affairs with fellow students - young, intense and somehow doomed from the start by naivety; of all the energy expanded on analysing every conversation, dissecting every reaction and replaying every pleasurable moment over and over again in her mind; of the intrepid expedition to Mexico, walking along the Inca trails with a boy she couldn't even recall the name of, and of the girls-on-tour holiday in Greece where they had drank, swam, slept and partied for two whole weeks. She and Alicia had danced so late one night that they watched the newborn sun rise over the shimmering Aegean sea as they made their way back to their rooms, their high heels in one hand, bags in the other. In the aftermath of the club the slumbering countryside had been like a magical place, transported from a wonderful fairy tale. Matty had tried to express the feelings, to share the mystical magic, but Alicia had been tired and distracted, not wanting to listen; still silently grieving for her father. Matty wondered where she was now; how could friends who had been so close now drift so far apart?

Examining herself she wondered how life had become so muddled; unsuccessfully juggling the roles of working woman and farmer's wife, never the easiest option because of the decidedly irregular nature of the farm. It wasn't unusual to get roped into helping Tom and his father with the harvesting and be out collecting bales in the dark at two in the morning, only to be in the office for nine o'clock. Taking turns on the lambing duties during the night or tending a sick calf before work. She remembered how Tom had vociferously wanted her to give up work when they were first married, citing their plans for a family and the help he needed round the farm. She knew Barbara disapproved of her not being at home playing the doting housewife, but her job gave her a little bit of independence, defining who she was, giving her life a semblance of structure. At the moment especially it felt like the only part which kept her sane as everything else crumbled.

Chapter 4

The courtroom was filled with a cacophony of noise. Voices from all over the room were raised in an attempt to be heard over the din. The defendant in the dock, a normally mild mannered elderly man, was calling for justice; one of the spectators in the upper gallery, a VAT inspector who had been pursuing Mr Solomon for alleged outstanding taxes was screaming for vengeance, his ill-fitting nylon suit looking crumpled as though it had spent the night stuffed in a carrier bag and his shirt showing darkened stains under the arms. The two barristers were verbally abusing one another, while the twelve faces of the jury were confused and uncertain, not knowing how to react to what was quite a normal set of proceedings in the courtroom. The judge, resplendent in his thick red robes and carefully manicured grey periwig watched impassively Alicia noticed, looking distant and disdainful; even though it was a baking hot summer day the impervious face was cool and collected. It was how Judge Goodwin always appeared, in every season and every occasion and she wondered how he did it. She was warm and sticky in her charcoal grey suit, the material prickling her skin; the wooden bench was uncomfortable, causing her to constantly shift her position. Then as quickly as the noise started it stopped; three sharp raps and a regal 'silence in court'.

"Any more noise from you Sir," Judge Goodwin pointed to the nylon clad spectator, "And I will hold you in contempt of court." He turned to Mr Solomon. "And I think you will find that there is always justice in my court, have no doubt about that." His tone was aloof and withering, causing Mr Solomon's eyes and mouth to droop at the rebuff, conscious of the ludicrousness of his outburst. "While you Mr Perry and Mr Osborne." He stared hard and long at the two barristers like a stern Sergeant Major to two squabbling squaddies. "You two should know better than to engage in a round of verbal sparring in my court." They both dropped their gaze keenly feeling the professional rebuke. "Let us continue; the time is getting on, it is getting warmer and I am sure we all have plans for this evening." Alicia bit her lip and tried not to smile, everyone knew it was the Annual Judges' Dinner, which meant Judge Goodwin would definitely finish on time, and probably require a slightly later start the next morning. The Judges' Annual Dinner was a splendid affair, a veritable feast held amongst the gilt and silver within the Inner Temple. The proceedings continued, the prosecution barrister, Mr Perry, demanded that Mr Solomon told them where the half a million pounds of savings he owed in tax had been transferred to. Mr Solomon, who had been totally over-excited by the whole event, finally cracked.

"Savings, schmavings." He cried, gesticulating wildly with his arms. "I don't have any money for savings. I have a wife and three daughters, do you really think they wouldn't have spent it if I really had it? Huh!"

The jury burst out laughing at the indignant man, and once again Judge Goodwin was forced to call for silence.

"Mr Solomon, please just answer the question. Where is the money of…" he consulted the notes "two million pounds."

"Objection My Lord." Mr Osborne shot to his feet.

"On what grounds Mr Osborne."

"Of the leading question; as my client has never had this money it is trying to force him to answer an impossible question."

"Objection over-ruled Mr Osborne, I wish to hear what Mr Solomon has to say." He turned back to the defendant who was unhappily wringing his hands.

"But it's true, Mr Judge, Sir… I have never had that much money coming in. I am a dentist, how could a dentist ever earn that much? Do you have any idea how many gold teeth it would take to earn that much?" Again the jury gave a snigger until quelled by a look from the judge.

Alicia was really beginning to enjoy the case, it all seemed so ludicrous, one of those cases that actually should never have come to court. It had all started ten years ago when Mr Solomon had submitted his tax return as usual to the Inland Revenue. When the letter came from the Inland Revenue requesting a tax payment of £100,000, Mr Solomon had merely presumed it had been sent in error and just discarded it – which was the fatal mistake. By not prompting the Inland Revenue to investigate they had started to hound him over the payments and when these weren't forthcoming they had pursued him for the interest as well. The culmination of all this was an inspector who wanted to make a name for himself to secure swift promotion to the higher echelons of HMRC, who had single handedly started a campaign to get the payment out of Mr Solomon.

"Let me get this straight." Judge Goodwin said slowly. "You are claiming that is was an original error in the tax return you submitted." The defendant nodded his head so emphatically that his curls became all tousled. "Let me see his original tax file." Judge Goodwin instructed Mr Perry. Mr Perry flushed, his cheeks matching the judge's robes. "Erm, well we don't actually have the tax file." Mr Perry quietly admitted. Alicia leaned forward with anticipation, if the prosecution didn't have that then the case was going to be hard to prove. Mr Osborne slyly turned his head towards her and gave a subtle wink, he then majestically stood up and reminded his learned friend that a copy had been sent through to the Inland Revenue when they had presented the error in their assertions over a year ago.

"It was a fake." The inspector screamed from the gallery, his face red and angry, spittle forming on his lips. Mr Perry looked confused and embarrassed, Judge Goodwin fixed a glaring eye on the errant inspector and glacially declared. "You have been warned; another word from you and I will have no hesitation in ruling you in contempt of this court with a recommendation for a sentence in jail." Norman Clive could not believe what was happening. No one was taking any notice of his carefully constructed case, instead they were listening to the gibbering old man's excuses. How could they? Mr Solomon was guilty of not paying his taxes, why didn't they all see it. The rage was rampaging through him, making every muscle tense and every nerve twitch. It was all encompassing, except for one tiny rational section linked to self-preservation, which nagged away telling him this was not turning out beneficially for his future career. He remembered how triumphant he had felt putting the case before his superiors and overcoming their reticent to support the legal pursuit. What was he going to tell them when he returned to the office? His hope of a fast track promotion was dissolving like salt sprinkled on ice. He jammed his hands between his knees trying to ignore the shaking sensation reverberating through his body.

"Mr Osborne," Judge Goodwin was saying. "Do you have a copy of this return?"

"I do My Lord, it is exhibit 12 in the pack." Everyone waited with baited breath as the Judge studied the document intently, his icy blue eyes reading the words fully, line by line, page by page. There was no other sound apart from the rustle of the turning paper, then the judge looked up and after a moment's contemplation requested for Mr Perry and Mr Osborne to join him in his chambers. The clerk's imperious voice rang out *'all rise'* and the attendants rose as the three men departed. A general hushed chatter broke out and swelled, speculation over what was happening with conjectures and prophesies being bandied backwards and forwards like a metaphorical tennis ball. George slid across the wooden bench towards Alicia with a gloomy countenance, trying to ignore her look of hopeful triumph.

"Stroke of luck your side having a copy of that return." He complained, almost as though it had been a feat of magic.

"George – you should have had all the info from your client." She laughingly retorted.

"Reckon he must have shredded it. He swore it had been lost five years ago."

"We did present all the correspondence to you before trial."

"But old Stormin' Norman was so adamant that it all made sense to us."

"Next time perhaps you'll look at the evidence rather than just the client's opinion." Her tone dripping with patronage.

"How did you suddenly come up with a copy of the tax return after ten years?" George asked suspiciously; Alicia smiled knowingly before tapping the side of her nose and saying "Client confidentiality – we couldn't possibly comment."

"Hah!" Disbelievingly he slid back to his original place to await the return of the trio.

Fifteen long interminable minutes passed by before the men re-entered the court room. All their faces were impassive, devoid of any emotion. Alicia tried to catch Mr Osborne's eye but his gaze skated away like a ballerina. The judge settled himself once more in his chair and re-arranged his wig. Clearing his throat he began judgement, his words clipped and tone crisp.

"Ladies and gentlemen of the jury; you have heard the case for and against Mr Solomon with regards to his outstanding tax. The course of events has been highly unusual; in fact I think I can safely say it is an unprecedented case. Having spoken to Mr Perry and Mr Osborne it would appear that this case should never have been brought to court. I am therefore relieving you of any passing of judgements. Instead I am recommending that the Inland Revenue ceases this claim against Mr Solomon immediately…"

Alicia saw Mr Solomon's wrinkled old face look stunned, as though not daring to believe what he was hearing.

"Plus," Continued Judge Goodwin, "I am ordering that the Inland Revenue pay Mr Solomon's legal costs." He stood up to leave and the clerk once again demanded 'all rise'. The retreating figure acted as a catalyst for a sudden cacophony. Mrs Solomon, Miss Solomon and Mrs Abraham (nee Solomon) all burst into emotional tears, hugging each other and clasping one another to their large well-endowed bosoms – an amorphous mass of Chanel and Boodles bling. Mr Solomon continued to look stunned even as one of the clerks slowly led him from the dock and back to his barrister – unable to believe the fear of prison was no longer a reality. Mr Osborne looked across at his Tuesday night squash partner and gave Mr Perry an indiscreet V sign which Mr Perry shrugged off and returned with a smiling single finger retort. The jury all relieved at not having to make any decisions were reliving the case and discussing which pub to retire to and enjoy the rest of the summer afternoon. Only Norman Clive was oblivious to the general bonhomie; he was seething at the indignity of losing. His carefully researched case had been smashed by some upper class twit of a judge who obviously didn't recognise a tax fiddler when he saw one – but he thought savagely, the judge was more than happy to keep having the advantages of the taxes gathered. Well serve him right if his pay was suddenly cut because of all the tax fiddlers he let off. Grinding his teeth he watched as Mr Perry and George approached; Mr Perry resplendent in his voluptuous black cape and grey wig, George every inch the lawyer in grey suit and sombre tie.

"Bad luck." Mr Perry muttered in consolation, uncertain what else he could bring himself to say since his client had obviously disposed of any evidence that hadn't suited his view point.

"Oh piss off." Norman spat, uncharacteristically, before pushing roughly past them and storming out of the court room, bumping into people wildly as though blinded by rage. Mr Perry and George glanced at each other, they were used to sore losers but Norman Clive seemed almost fanatical.

Alicia joined Mr Osborne and Mr Solomon, the latter who was continually shaking his barrister's hand in gratitude, outside the court room. Mr Osborne was speechless for once – overwhelmed by the verbal praise being plied on him and feeling somewhat like a working water pump. Just as he was going to beg for a let up Mr Solomon transferred his attention to Alicia, enveloping her in a hug before holding her face between his hands and tilting her oval face up, kissing her resoundingly on the cheek.

"Mensch – you helped to keep me free." Alicia smiled and squeezed his hand.

"I'm just glad Judge Goodwin had the sense to see that the case should never have been brought to court. It was always a ludicrous claim – I can't believe they took it this far."

"Well that's probably to do with my father. He managed to avoid paying any tax." He had the good grace to look sheepishly as he revealed the dubious fact. "You see for many years he…" but they were destined never to know what Mr Solomon senior had done as the shouts of Mrs Solomon, Miss Solomon and Mrs Abraham drowned out his voice and diverted his attention. Alicia stepped back to allow the rumbustious family reunion to take place amid much kissing, hand patting and twittering chatter. It reminded Alicia of a family of noisy robins who inhabited her mother's barn welcoming back a fledging who had been out of the nest too long. Mr Osborne realised that unless he took charge of the situation they would still be standing in the street for the next hour, so he began moving them along. Mrs Solomon, riding on a wave of emotion, cried out that they needed champagne and triumphantly they went to swarm across the road.

Looking back later Alicia couldn't pinpoint why she had turned round at that exact moment, but whatever the reason she registered an old Escort bearing down on them. The engine was screeching as the gears were dragged into place; the tyres unable to grip on the dusty cobbled path. The driver was leaning menacingly forward, filling the windscreen with a manic grimace. Instinctively she realised the driver was purposefully aiming at their group with no intention of slowing down and primeval self-preservation kicked in – shouting a warning to her colleagues she pushed them to the right out of the line of the racing vehicle. Everything then became a blur, with a sound of squealing brakes and a dull crunch before a commotion as people rushed round to examine the accident. Alicia lay pinned to the ground, dazed and winded, aware of bodies on top of her moving off and lightening the weight to allow her lungs to mercifully refill. The outraged voices of the Solomon family began to ring out until they noticed her form still lying there. Caring hands reached down and started to help her up until an involuntary cry stopped them. Faintly she tried to move her wrist, but the joint was awkwardly offset and a dull pulsating pain began to throb. Climbing to her knees and clumsily supporting her broken arm she stood up. The crowd that had gathered round the crashed car obliterated their view, but Miss Solomon having forced her way to the centre for a ring-side view excitedly headed back.

"It was the tax inspector, can you believe it! Someone's saying he's hopping mad he missed. They've got an ambulance crew there trying to sedate him. Apparently the police reckon he's flipped." She breathlessly repeated, unable to believe her luck at being involved with a real-life drama.

"No." Her parents were aghast at the way things were turning out; they watched in horror as the handcuffed man was manoeuvred into the back of the ambulance. A remaining paramedic singled out Alicia and deftly set about creating a temporary sling before putting her into the second ambulance. All the excitement and jubilation fizzled away, like a bottle of pop that has been left open too long. A rather sad blanket descended as Alicia was driven away; the victory now but a distant memory.

It was late afternoon when Larnie found Alicia, her right arm clad in plaster and her face scored, sent on the mission of mercy by the office. Alicia's normal smooth olive complexion had taken on a green tinge where the bruising was starting to work its way out and her immaculate short fringe had been shaved away to allow a row of neat sutured stitches to the right of her forehead.

"Poor you." Larnie consoled – shocked at her friend's appearance. "I came over as soon as we heard in the office. I didn't know if you'd need some help getting home."

Alicia nodded, one cheek was swollen, making it difficult to talk without sounding as though she was chewing cotton wool pads. "Think I'll be finished here thoon." She lisped. "The doctor is just checking the plaster has thet properly." Larnie took in the shoes that had been kicked under the bed out of the way of toing-and-froing doctors, the suit jacket with its ripped sleeve and her friend adjusting her position as if trying to get comfortable. Either side of the narrow bed was a cabinet, its surface cluttered with medical instruments and discarded debris while overhead the

25

florescent light flickered, buzzing intermittently as a fly hit the casing.

The other side of the party curtain was a mournful drunk who seemed to have spent the last six hours either tunelessly singing, shouting abuse or vomiting copiously. Alicia felt she had reached the point of suffocation, she desperately wanted to get out of here. Hospitals were detestable at the best of times, but having been stuck here, a virtual prisoner, had made it far worse – it had brought back unbidden memories of her father's death that she had tried to close off as she moved up to London.

"So how long have they signed you off for?" Larnie asked, secretly envious of anyone who could wrangle time off work in the summer.

"They thaid about three weeks, but I've got thome holiday I need to take as well."

"Lucky you! So are the doctors much cop?"

"Hardly." Alicia managed a small smile. Thinking of the combination of studious, geeky trainees and the tired overworked consultants. Their dedication to work obviously prevented any mortal considerations such as occasionally remembering to book a haircut, take the suit to a drycleaners or nourish dry skin. One of the registrars returned, his large owlish glasses peering round the lurid green swirled curtains. Unconsciously he pushed the spectacles back up the bridge of his nose and wiped away his flopping fringe.

"Miss Connor?" Hesitantly he stepped into the cubicle, tripped over his undone lace and almost joined Larnie sitting in the chair. His cheeks flushed crimson and flustered he took a moment to shrug himself back into his white coat. Pointing to her arm he indicated for Alicia to hold out the plastered limb.

"That all seems fine. You can go now – we'll expect to see you in six weeks." He walked out of the cubicle, narrowly avoiding a collision with a medicine trolley.

"You were right – that was no George Clooney."

"Let's get going." Alicia pleaded but her vision of a speedy exit was hampered by her body. Gingerly she knelt down to retrieve her shoes from the bed and noticed one of the heels had been scratched – thank goodness they weren't her favourite Jimmy Choos. Pushing her feet in it felt clunky doing everything with her left hand; she had never appreciated how dependent she was on using her right hand. After a short struggle with the jacket, Larnie

26

took it and draped it over her shoulders and ushered her friend towards the exit.

As they left the building Larnie's phone rang.

"How's Ali doing?" George demanded.

"Fine, considering that run-in with the batty tax inspector. We're just leaving the hospital."

"Great. Come over to Vinopolis, I've got us all invites to some event my lot are putting on. It's just the thing to make Ali feel better. Company may be dull but the drinks will be fabulous."

"Will do – let me just tell her the plan." Larnie turned and Alicia saw her friend's eyes were sparkling with excitement. "George has got us invites to Vinopolis for tonight. Isn't that great?"

"Tonight?" Alicia said weakly, the thought of going anywhere other than home seemed far too much of an effort.

"Yes; and there will be loads of booze. You'll soon feel better." Hearing George's voice tinny and distorted down the phone, Larnie put it back to her ear. "What was that? Zac's hosting it?" Slyly Larnie threw the apple of temptation at Alicia's feet. "Still unsure?"

Alicia couldn't believe her friends were seriously expecting her to party. She hadn't seen her reflection yet, but she was certain it wasn't the sort of look you wanted the guy you most lusted after to see. Plus the painkillers were beginning to wear off and the dull ache of torn muscle was making itself known. Feeling tired, dirty and crumpled she was ready to descend into a vortex of self-pity when her phone beeped, indicating a voice message. Playing it Mavis' voice came through.

"Darling, it's Mummy. I got your message. I'm on the train and I'm going straight to your flat. Take care sweetheart." Never before had she needed her mother's presence so much. Clicking the phone shut she realised Larnie was still waiting for her response. Spying a taxi she raised her left arm and flagged it down.

"Think I'll give it a mith and just go home. Have a great time though and say 'hi' to George."

"If you're sure." Larnie edged slightly away, hoping Alicia wasn't going to become all clingy and want help getting back. She'd been dying to go to Vinopolis for ages, plus if Alicia wasn't around then she'd stand a much better chance with Zac.

"Yes, my mum's coming over so I'd better get going or she'll be thitting on the doorstep." Getting in the taxi she gave a half-hearted wave and sank back gingerly into the seat. "43a West Albion Street please."

The taxi was stuffy, the summer evening was clutching on to the heat from the earlier mid-day sun, making the skin feel prickly, the seats itch against the back of your legs and clothes to cling damply. Outside the world appeared unchanged, it was only Alicia whose world had turned upside down. Everyone else was carrying on with their normal humdrum routine, aware only of the monotony of the narrowing vista of their lives; too scared or too bored to break out. The streets looked the same, with the milling crowds interweaving. Mothers with children, commuters and overactive teenagers, all oblivious to the others, just following the time honoured rituals of the day. The roads were no different, the lanes were clogged with vehicles each burping out fumes. Yet to Alicia something had subtly shifted, like a photographer using a filter to change the hue she felt she was viewing the world from a new set of eyes. A set of eyes that were watchful and afraid; she had always loved London and its buzz and vitality. It attracted her like an iridescent prism which was always dancing and intriguing. Now it was a jumble of chaos, a tangled rope that was pulling tighter and tighter, so that she couldn't break free.

West Albion Street was a row of converted wharf buildings that were now executive apartments on the south bank of the Thames. Although the flat was tiny, it was a foundation stone amongst the flotsam of a changing life. The views from the sitting room were out across the flowing pewter of the river, lit up at night by a myriad of glows and lights. In the summer dusk she would open the picture windows leaning against the open frame to catch any passing breeze, with a cold beer grabbed from the fridge. Catching sight of an upright figure striding along the pavement Alicia yelled for the taxi to stop. Tumbling out ungraciously and calling to her mother, Mavis was taken back as Alicia leaned in for a motherly hug.

♦♦♦

They spent the night in Alicia's flat, agreeing it would be better to travel the next day when they were feeling more refreshed. Alicia spent the evening quietly watching TV while Mavis used the few ingredients in her daughter's meagre store cupboard to conjure up omelettes followed by ice cream, food Alicia could eat despite her aching jaw. There wasn't a repeat of demonstrable emotion but Alicia trailed behind Mavis as she prepared the meal, reminding Mavis of the early years, whenever Alicia had been poorly she had become a second shadow, clinging to her mother for comfort. It seemed that underneath her tough urbane exterior Alicia was still her little girl.

The sun was high above the office blocks on the opposite side of the Thames when Alicia woke up. Although she had slept soundly, unlike Mavis who had lain crunched up on the sofa listening to every strange noise and unable to get comfy, Alicia woke up to increased pain as the hospital administered pain killers had worn off. Where yesterday her muscles had nagged, today they screamed. They were reluctant to move and her wrist, unused to being in one position, throbbed mercilessly beneath the cast. The pain made her grouchy and snappy, ready to find fault with everything and everyone. Her mother recognised the change and drew up the drawbridge, trying to sound relaxed and unperturbed by her daughter's behaviour to prevent it escalating any further. Alicia padded through to the kitchen and slumped down at the small table.

"Would you like some croissants?" Mavis asked brightly having been out to the local Cost-Saver on the corner while Alicia slept. "Or I could do you a boiled egg. You need to keep your strength up."

"I'm not hungry." She responded irritably.

"But you must have something darling." Her mother rationalised. "After everything you went through yesterday your body's going to need some sort of substance; besides your painkillers need to be taken with food."

"I said I don't want anything. Don't keep on about it." She stormed off towards the bathroom. "I'm going to have a shower." Mavis bit back the mixture of anger and pity; it was obvious that Alicia was in pain but did she really have to use that tone? The slam of the bathroom door was followed by the sound of running water before abruptly turned off and the flat became deathly quiet. Concerned Mavis stood poised, uncertain whether to go and check or to stay out of the way; eventually she gingerly walked over to the door and pressed her ear against it; there was a faint muffled sobbing. Immediately Mavis knocked sharply on the door.

"Alicia, what's wrong?" Her voice was unnaturally high through tension. "Darling, open the door and tell me what's wrong. You're scaring me." A tense moment passed before the sound of the bolt being drawn back and Alicia's tearful face with its intricate grazes and colourful bruising appeared. "What's wrong? Is it your arm – have your hurt yourself?"

Despondently Alicia shook her head, her bottom lip quivering in an attempt to stem the crying. Piteously she held up the plastered arm; "I can't even have a shower."

With a sense of relief Mavis hugged her and putting a guiding arm around her led her back to the bedroom. "Don't worry – let's get you home and you can have a long bath there. Now pull on some clothes and I'll help you pack. If we're quick we can be in Drayton Beauchamp in no time."

Chapter 5

Chloe stared out of the window by her desk and felt the hot tears well up inside her. She wasn't sure how she had ended up in this state; but something had changed inside her and suddenly the thing she wanted more than anything else was a baby. At first she presumed it was just a passing phase; the same as she had each season when new clothes lines were launched; and like that expected the longing to become tempered with reality. How could she have wanted the puff-ball skirt with her legs or the jumpsuit with her hips. But this seemed to be different, somehow it was deeper, almost as though it were a primeval longing, something that she couldn't function properly without. Initially she had started smiling at the neighbour's little boy, then she started walking via the baby clothes section in department stores just to see what was available.

This had been the start of her downfall. How could anyone be immune to the sweet little outfits, the miniature collection of designer jumpers and teeny-weeny denim jeans. She had become totally and utterly hooked on babies, guiltily sneaking round the baby shops hoping not to be noticed, pretending to be 'one-of-them'; a mother. The only trouble was she wasn't; she wasn't a mother, she wasn't even a wife; heavens she wasn't even anyone's girlfriend. The whole situation was just hopeless. It was just like when you diet; all you can think about is food; all you can see when you are out is food; all anyone talks about is food. Which is how Chloe felt, like everyone around her was busy having babies and she couldn't take part.

This morning had been the worst; she had logged on for some cyber-gossip to see what everyone was getting up to, only to find three of the girls she had been at school with were having babies. One of them was even on her second. Why couldn't it be me, she'd raged silently at the computer screen; I want a baby more than they do. It was upsetting when girls you remembered as gangly teenagers were now married pregnant women. Desolately she opened a packet of Rolos and munched unhappily through them, it wasn't until she had eaten the last one that she realised she'd devoured the whole packet. Horrified at her lack of self-control she quickly threw the empty wrapper, disposing of the incriminating evidence under a pile of old receipts in the bin. She needed to get a hold of herself, otherwise she would end up some fat lonely singleton, then the fact hit her, maybe she wasn't really fat, but she was a lonely singleton. Her life was officially dire.

She cast around the tiny space she and Pete called an office, it barely had room for two desks, so all their papers and files were stacked on desks, on window ledges and on the floor. It was a relief they didn't get many people visiting as there were only narrow walkways to each desk. But that was the beauty of being a letting agent, people only wanted to see the houses they didn't want to keep visiting you. Which reminded her, she was due to do a quarterly check on one of their smaller properties. Her heart sank thinking about it, Wisteria Cottage should, from its name, have been an idyllic rural retreat; instead it was a pebble dashed 1960's bungalow that had previously been inhabited by an old gamekeeper who insisted on letting his ferrets run around indoors whenever he had visitors. She shuddered at the memory and fervently hoped the new tenant wasn't of the same inclination, but with such a hideous building who of taste would choose that over the sweet thatched cottages just down the lane?

She scrawled a note and stuck it on Pete's screen telling him Natalia had phoned yet again and would he call her back urgently, which probably meant she needed help choosing which nail varnish colour to apply. She was supposed to be helping them out on some of the viewings, but Chloe was dismissive of the whole scheme. She just couldn't envisage the Brazilian Barbie being happy showing people round in her Jimmy Choos. Every time Chloe met Natalia she felt like some lumbering heffalump compared to the diminutive but full chested South American beauty who had perfect chocolate brown hair, matching eyes and permanently tanned skin.

Leaving the office she wove her way through the streets to where her car was parked by the green and opened the door in trepidation. A blast of hot air hit her face and she winced as she gingerly lowered herself onto the mini's vinyl seats. Turning the key she hoped the car would start, she wasn't in the mood to cope with enticing life out of the ancient engine; it started on the second attempt and Chloe revved the pop-popping engine as she pulled out into the traffic.

As she drove down the country lane it became a little cooler. The breeze caught at her hair through the open window and the bowing trees either side filtered out the glare. Beyond the verges Chloe could see the fields, each one being prepared for harvest in its own way, the hill top ones had sheep dotted around like dabs of escaping cotton wool, the meadows near the farmhouses held the black and white dairy cows dozily munching their cud as they patiently waited for the next milking and the chance to relieve their bursting udders. Interspersing these were the arable fields – statuesque stretches of majestic wheat and oats glowing golden in the sunlight. Occasionally the low rumble of a tractor could be heard above the mini; the slow steady progress of the farmer as he cut the hay leaving long straight green ridges behind him where the grass lay in lush heaps. There was something deeply satisfying in watching the seasonal rural affairs, the continuity where life begins, blossoms and fades only to reappear again, like hope eternal.

Driving on, past the small garden nursery on the left and the dotted collections of neat cottages which were set around the deserted cricket green, she turned in to Wisteria Cottage. Pulling into the weed infested gravel driveway and coming to a halt behind an old Landrover she put the handbrake on and surveyed the garden. It was, if possible, worse than ever. The front garden that had once had a central neglected flower bed was now obliterated under piles of chippings and pebbles; looking along the narrow path to the back garden, Chloe could see discarded logs, sleepers and railings. The whole thing looked a mess, as though a child had grown bored with them and carelessly dropped them. Sighing Chloe reached for her folder and went to open the car door when suddenly a huge animal hurtled forward furiously barking, jaws snarling. Quickly she slammed the door shut and panicking wound the window up as fast as her slippery fingers would allow. The dog threw itself at the mini, its front legs pawing at the window, causing it to rock slightly. '*Oh help*' Chloe thought '*I'm not just looking like a dog's dinner, I'm going to end my days literally as its dinner*'. A figure came out of the house and, taking in the scene, piercingly whistled; the dog immediately dropped down and obligingly

33

trotted over to her master. As Chloe calmed herself down she watched the muscular physique of the man striding over to the car. As he stooped down to open her door, she was aware of his tanned calloused hands; taking in his unruly hair and piercing blue eyes.

"I hope Bertha didn't scare you too much." He was saying as he helped her out.

"Not at all." Chloe lied, as she tried to coax her shaking legs to co-operate. "She's a very effective guard dog I'm sure."

"She is," He was rueful, "Which is exactly what I need out here with all my stuff." He laughed noticing Chloe's look of disbelief. "Perhaps I should explain. I'm a landscape designer. All of these," He circled his arms to encompass all of the garden piles, "Are en-route to clients. If I lose them it means I make a loss on the job." They started to walk towards the side door, access to the front door being blocked by a mound of stone chippings. He opened the door and ushered her in. "After you." Stepping inside Chloe felt she had walked into the wrong building. Gone were the dank dingy rooms with the oversized furniture and piles of out-of-date newspapers; in their place were white washed walls and a few bits of pine furniture. Mutely she followed him through to the sitting room, two mis-matching armchairs sat invitingly either side of the table holding the TV, along the other wall was a bookcase full of horticultural titles, and on the floor a rag rug of reds and golds blocked out the nondescript brown carpet. It was a room that was completely devoid of any character or features, it was plain and functional; not a cushion or photo in sight. Obviously no woman had taken any part in setting the room out, giving Chloe a surge of hope. Clearing her throat she dug out one of her business cards from her cavernous handbag. "Mr Williams, I'm Chloe Palmer. Here's my card with all my details on. I just need to check over the cottage to make sure everything is ok; it shouldn't take more than about 15 minutes."

"Please call me Rob, everyone else does." He took her card and placed it in his jeans pocket; she couldn't help noticing how well they fitted. "Is there anything else you need me to help with?" A number of scenarios whizzed unbeckoned into her mind, most of them involving a great deal of naked flesh.

"Erm, no thank you. I'll just go through the rooms." Chloe retreated in a fluster while Rob sunk into an armchair, one booted foot resting across the other knee causing a sprinkling of fine dust to fall against the faded denim and awaited her return.

Efficiently Chloe opened her folder and started to run though the inventory and notes for each room. The dramatic clearing made the process easier and she quickly found herself in his bedroom. It was decorated in the same utilitarian style as the rest of the house, a double bed with faded duvet cover and odd pillowcases was between a wardrobe and chest of drawers. There was no other decoration in the room apart from a small shaving mirror and a plain roller blind at the window. Walking across to check the back garden she caught sight of a navy sweatshirt sitting on the chest; without thinking she picked it up and held it to her face breathing in the musky aroma of pine needles and Calvin Klein. Could this be the man of her dreams? Blushing furiously as though suddenly aware of a million sets of eyes watching her, she guiltily replaced the sweatshirt and turned away. How could she have done that, she'd never acted like this before, invading a client's privacy. Supposing Rob had walked in and found her hugging his clothes; what kind of uproar would there have been. She finished the rest of the check in double-quick time, ashamed at her behaviour, stopping only to request Rob to sign and date the check form for forwarding on to Wisteria Cottage's owners as proof of inspection.

"Would you like a cup of tea before you go?" Rob had politely offered.

"Oh no, I must get back to the office." Chloe fibbed still embarrassed, then kicked herself for not taking the opportunity to get to know more about him. "Well, thank you for sparing the time – I know it can seem intrusive but we do promise our clients that houses rented through Sherborne and Sherborne will be regularly inspected."

"I assure you it's no problem." He jokingly mocked mimicking her formal tone. "And next time I promise Bertha will be safely shut away."

"Wonderful." Chloe managed a weak smile. "Any problems though, please give the office a call."

Rob patted her business card. "Don't worry I will." Watching her walk out of the door and out to her car.

The house was big, but that's all that it had going for it. Natalia sauntered her way room to room, opening doors to allow Charles Pennington-Smythe to wander past and examine the sitting room with the large oak fireplace, the dining room that could seat twenty and the kitchen with its double sinks, prep area and large double Aga.

"This is becoming quite a regular thing – meeting like this;" He had said one eyebrow arched as Natalia had opened the door to welcome him in. "I thought it was Pete who was due to show me around."

"It's your very lucky day. You get me. Besides he would try and make you rent this place." She said boldly, her head on one side as she appraised him with her liquid brown eyes, heavily outlined with long luxurious eyelashes.

He was amused by her forthright manner. "And you're not?" People automatically assumed he would be paying, because he could afford to, whether it was a round of golf, a round of drinks, or around town for the night. It was refreshing to have someone showing such candour.

She returned his disbelieving stare. "Of course not. It's horrible and dark, and far too boring for you."

"But it sounds perfect; and from the outside it looks just right." He refused to be wrong, pointing to the details held out in his hand.

"Come!" She ordered, strutting across the parquet floor. "You'll see that I'm right." With a sceptical harrumph he followed, unused to being ordered around by anyone, particularly a diminutive Brazilian beauty. Women normally just smiled and simpered when they were talking to him; this was a whole new experience.

They went in silence from room to room, until they had toured the whole house and were back in the sitting room. Gracefully Natalia draped herself on one of the squashy sofas, watching Charles' attempt to manoeuvre his bulky frame into the low seat.

"So!" she demanded, going in immediately for the kill. "Was I right?"

Uncomfortable at being wrong, and awkwardly perched on the fashionable low sofa, he was aware of being at a disadvantage. All he could manage was a slight nod.

"Hah! I told you it was a horrible house." She clapped her hands in delight at having been verified right. "This isn't you at all. You need something far more stunning that has a real wow factor.

Not some ordinary boring house. Besides," she added. "You need to be thinking about whether the house reflects the woman you will be living with as well."

"Why? I'm not involved with anyone."

"Not yet." She flashed, her eyes glinting with temptation. "Now let me think." She closed her eyes in concentration, the fingers of her clasped hands running slowly down her nose in an unintentionally erotic way. Charles watched mesmerised; sensing a charge in the atmosphere, and feeling totally overwhelmed. He drank in her creamy tanned skin, slender legs, and provocatively arched feet housed in killer heels. Suddenly she opened her huge chocolate drop eyes, having had a revelation, and pointing towards him declared. "What you need is space and light, and lots of rooms for parties and entertaining. You don't need a house at all – you should be looking for a flat."

"A flat! I don't think so." He said as dismissively as though she had suggested a cardboard box under the arches.

"Yes it is!" She flared back, unperturbed by his outburst. "A glorious penthouse flat with views to die for. Something you can show off to your friends, and have some real fun in when they go home."

"But I want a house." He persisted doggedly. "And why would I want to hold lots of parties."

"Because they are such fun!" Her eyes were shining with such certainty that for a moment Charles wondered whether she could be right.

"But I need a house." He continued, however his voice held a small note of wavering, as the thought began to catch and grow.

"No you don't!" Natalia told him firmly. And that was that; the decision had been made.

◆◆◆

Pete was struggling with the accounts as Chloe walked back in, he continued to stare at the figures and without lifting his head he greeted her.

"I'm glad you're back, I had a double booking; the Fletchers wanted to look round the barn conversion and Charles Pennington-Smythe was due to look at The Old Rectory over in Drayton Parson. I ended up having to get Natalia to show him over the house, but it was no good. He says we need to find him

37

an apartment now. Can you try and conjure up the something for him."

"Yes of course."

Pete waited expectantly for Chloe to continue with her customary run-down on a new client. When it became clear she wasn't about to give her usual witty profile, Pete prompted:

"So what was the new tenant at Wisteria Cottage like then? An improvement on Bert?"

Chloe felt her cheeks glow with a spreading blush, but acting unconcerned she shrugged her shoulders. "Oh yes, he was fine."

"Oh. Fine." Pete echoed.

"Yes, he's a gardener or something." Chloe continued. Pete studied her intently, in the three years she had been working for him, she had always come back from meeting a new tenant full of details from personal circumstances, star signs and critiques on décor. At first it had both amused and exasperated him that she spent so much time in seemingly trivial conversation, but over time it had shown its worth. Tenants and clients had begun asking for her to handle their account because she remembered their grandchild's name, partner's birthday and complete inventory of the house from memory. After having had a long supply of gorgeous but useless assistants, it had been refreshing to see Chloe's efficiency.

"Where's the family history? The Lawrence Llewlyn-Dooda's run-down on his decorating taste?" Pete queried then stopped. "You did go didn't you?"

"Of course I did." Chloe snapped back. Then flopped into her chair, she shouldn't take it out on Pete, it wasn't his fault she was without a boyfriend. "I'm sorry." She rubbed a hand over her face, it felt damp from sweat. "I think it's the heat, this weather is really tiring. I can't wait for some cooler weather."

"Shall I get us an iced smoothie from the deli? They've just started doing pineapple and passion fruit."

"Definitely – it looks like the only way I'll be getting any passion this summer." The thought of the icy drink was too tempting to resist, well she could always start her diet tomorrow. "Did you phone Natalia back? I left a note for you on your PC. I think it must have been important."

"It was." Pete agreed mock seriously. "How do you think I know about the smoothies." He said wryly giving her a wink as he left the office.

Chapter 6

There was a crash, cursing and then silence. Mavis held her breath and tried to count very slowly to ten. A week had passed since Alicia had arrived at Apple Trees and it seemed that every minute had been spent on a knife edge. Alicia had set about proving her independence, defiantly trying to show everyone she could carry on as normal; which was how Mavis had ended up cringing in her bedroom having had Alicia shouting at her to *'leave her alone and that she was perfectly capable of doing the washing up'*. The crash gave Mavis a guilty feeling of smugness; she had been right; Alicia couldn't do everything with one arm in plaster; tempered with regret at the loss of a plate. On the first evening they had spent at Alicia's flat Mavis had thought that maybe this would be a turning point for the two of them, that with Alicia being incapacitated and vulnerable that she would need her mother more. The opposite had turned out to be true; her daughter, in her own unique indomitable style had gone all out to prove her independence. It was as though she had planted a prickly hedge to stop anyone getting too close, guarding her privacy with razor sharp blackthorn.

Mavis walked downstairs and into the kitchen, finding Alicia trying to sweep the broken plate up, the brush held awkwardly in her left hand, the dustpan propped up in the corner of her plaster cast and upper arm. Each time she tried to brush the remnants up the dustpan would slip away, so that nothing was collected. Mavis bent down taking the brush and pan and quickly sorting out the mess before depositing it with a clatter into the bin.
"It just slipped out of my hand." Alicia was defensive. It was on the tip of Mavis' tongue to retort that was exactly why she was going to do the plates before Alicia had rudely insisted, but she kept quiet not wanting to face another argument. Instead she picked up her gardening gloves off the table and lightly said. "I'll be out in the greenhouse if you need anything." Knowing that Alicia's contempt for the outdoors would at least provide a safe haven.

Alicia watched her mother wander through the nursery, tenderly checking plants as she went. The self-anger slowly abated; leaving frustration and misery in its place. The days seemed to be a downward spiral. The first few had been spent almost in a drugged daze, a combination of painkillers and the body's way of healing. Since then boredom had started to set in, apart from watching daytime TV there was nothing to do in her mother's house. The only books were either plant notebooks or historical romances with unlikely tales of milk-maid heroines being swept off their feet by the dashing young Lords. All highly implausible for a girl bought up on Bridget Jones and Lara Croft. Throwing herself down on the sofa she flicked on the television and resigned herself to an afternoon of Countdown and some obscure Antipodean soap that seemed to have no real story line. Picking up the phone she stamped in George's number, there was nothing like a good moan to start feeling better.

Outside, in the fuggy warmth of the greenhouse Mavis peacefully worked her way through the potting up of her seedlings, gently removing the tender young sproutings with infinite care. She had stopped to help a newly married couple select a few plants for their new marital home, but there weren't as many customers these days. People seemed to prefer the large impersonal DIY stores or the commercial nurseries that had coffee bars, garden furniture and shops stuffed with ornaments and clothes. No one wanted good quality healthy plants, or to find the flowers, trees or shrubs that would prosper in their kind of soil. Nowadays, influenced by a constant diet of instant garden makeover programmes people bought to fashion. Out were the delicate scented traditional cottage garden flowers and in were decking, terracotta and Italian olive trees. Where once customers had selected small saplings with a view to watching them grow over the years, now they selected monolithic stones or tortured steel sculptures that conflicted with the tiny suburban surroundings. She couldn't understand why everyone didn't appreciate the simple virtues of flowers and shrubs. Even Adam, Lord Beauchamp, had asked for more exotic plants for the Drayton Hall fete. "It's not that I don't love your delphiniums and hollyhocks," He had said half-apologetically, "But you know how it is, everyone's doing Italy at the moment and they want their gardens to be included. So if you could do some olive cuttings and rosemary we should be able to sell a few more." So Mavis had set out cultivating a new range for Sunday's fete. She and Bill had always provided the plants for the plant stall, taking over from Bill's mother. In the early days it had been a wobbly trestle table and a few left over cuttings that stood next to the WI stand with its orange juice, tea and Victoria sponge cakes. Now it was a full blown money raising event – she had even heard Adam was ordering a bouncy castle for the children, co-ordinating the canapé caterers and setting up a website to attract people from outside the village. All the money raised went to helping good causes in the village; the scouts had a smart hut, the football team fashioned their latest strip, and the Little Acorns had their annual jamboree. It was all terribly worthy, yet Mavis hankered for the yester-years when locals would wander along to Drayton Hall to catch up and bag a bargain. But the village had changed. When she had first come to live here most of the villagers were working one way or another for the Drayton Hall Estate, whether directly employed as farm labourers, working in service at the house or helping out on a casual basis. As the Estate had changed so did the village. Now the few left who worked on the Estate lived to one side in the old tied cottages. The rest were incomers whose husbands worked in town and whose wives shopped in supermarkets. For a moment Mavis felt a wave of sadness pass over her, for the things lost in the name of progress, but she shook the feeling off and carried on methodically transplanting. Above her the lazy drone of a captured bee bumping itself against a pane of glass caught her attention before being drowned out by the sound of an engine. Listening she heard a vehicle pull into the car park, and taking off the worn leather gloves she walked out to greet the potential customer.

Alicia had subconsciously heard the car pulling up, but as she left everything to do with the nursery to Mavis she didn't pay any attention to it. She carried on watching the black and white film and flicking through an old copy of Bling & Boudoir. She was only vaguely aware of a movement in front of the window before hearing the back door slam shut. Incensed that one of the nursery customers had presumed to come into the house, despite the very large 'Private' sign on the door, she stormed into the kitchen and found a tall bear-like man about to sit down at the table.
"Who are you?" He growled, incensing Alicia even further with his presumed impertinence.
"I should be asking the same of you." She glared at him ferociously. "What are you doing in my house? This is private property – as you would have seen from the very large sign on

the door if you had managed to read it." Sarcasm dripped venomously from her words.

"I thought it was Mavis' house not yours." He replied pointedly and Alicia noticed that the scowl he was wearing had set into a permanent feature. She was about to order him to leave when Mavis walked in and felt the shooting rays of hostility.

"I see you two have met." She ventured cautiously.

"But without introductions." Rob said pointedly. Inwardly sighing Mavis waved a hand at Alicia. "This is my daughter, the one who lives up in London. Alicia, this is Rob, he's one of the landscape designers I work with."

"I'd never have guessed," Rob addressed Mavis. "She doesn't take after you in looks or manners." Alicia felt her blood boil, how dare this stranger calmly walk into here and start throwing insults around. Even as she tried to find a stinging retort Mavis was beckoning Rob to sit down while she retrieved the planting plans from her study.

"I'll put the kettle on in a moment." She promised calling from the other room.

"I'm sure Alicia can do that while we carry on working." He drawled. Alicia flushed scarlet, the thought of the embarrassing fiasco with the washing up flashed through her brain, there was no way she was going to repeat it in front of this brute. Like a stroppy teenage she brandished her plaster cast. "I can't. And even if I could, I'm not here to wait on you." Turning on her heel she stormed back out.

It was some time later Alicia heard Rob's vehicle leave and another fifteen minutes before Mavis popped her curly head round the door to let Alicia know that dinner would be ready soon.

"Pork chops ok for you?" She enquired as though it wasn't the thing they had eaten every Thursday all the time Alicia had been growing up. Occasionally Alicia had previously wondered what Mavis' response would have been if she had asked for something else. She had asked her father once why they always ate the same food, and he had genuinely looked surprised at the question. "But why would we want to eat anything else?" He had asked. "We like the food – don't you?"

"Yes, it's fine, but don't you long to try other things."

"Not really." Her father had admitted "If we like it why would we want to change it?". The simple logic had confused her because it was at such odds with her outlook. She believed life was for living and everything was for trying, all around were new sensations waiting to be savoured.

"Who was that oaf?" Alicia asked as they finished their supper.

"Who? Oh you mean Rob? As I said he's one of the landscape designers who uses some of the plants I grow for his clients. He's only just set up on his own and he's finding it tough to get established."

"I'm not surprised with those kind of people skills. Is he as rude to his clients? I can't imagine they would like his form of customer care."

"Actually he's always been quite nice to me. I expect you just caught him off guard, I'd forgotten to tell him you'd be here."

"Why should he know whether you had company or not?" Alicia demanded.

"No reason." Mavis blustered unconvincingly.

"You're not romantically involved with him are you?"

Mavis burst out laughing at Alicia's shocked expression. "What would a strapping young man like that see in an old woman? I'm sure he has no problem finding someone of his own age."

"Hardly. He's not exactly Brad Pitt." She thought longingly of Zac's exquisite chiselled features.

"I think he's rather dishy in a rugged kind of way."

Alicia stared at her mother in disbelief; they couldn't be talking about the same person could they? Rob had appeared little better than a bad mannered lout, she compared him, unfavourably, with the men she knew in London who knew how to charm, had intelligent conversation and proper grooming regimes.

"And he's a brilliant designer." Mavis continued. "Look at these plans." She pushed the rolled up papers across and Alicia saw an outline sketch showing a series of winding paths fanning out across the page, each one ending in a different space: one with a fountain, another with seating, a third to a dining area. Along each path the labelled flowers which were replicated in a central bed. The resulting design was a carefully divided garden that held surprises at each turn, keeping the view hidden until the last moment so that someone walking through would come across a secret place almost by accident. "I told you he was good."

Alicia couldn't bring herself to compliment him giving only a grunt of agreement. How could someone so Neanderthal-like in appearance prepare such imaginative work?

◆◆◆

"Have you seen my work trousers?" Tom bellowed from the bedroom.
"They're in the wash." Matty yelled back from the kitchen "There's another pair in the airing cupboard." The dull thud, thud, thud as he walked along the landing overhead before the expected cry for help. Sure enough Tom's voice bellowed out again.
"Where Matty, I can't find them?" With a rueful smile playing on her lips she went upstairs and joined her husband by the packed shelves in the airing cupboard.
"Where they always are." She softly chided, laying her hands on them immediately. He took them gratefully and kissed her on the cheek.
"Now what would I do without you?" He wound her arms round his neck and she whispered.
"Probably have to go to market trouserless." He pulled her tighter towards him feeling her body supply fit into his.
"Well I'm not wearing any at the moment, so we could save some time undressing if you fancied popping back to bed and reminding me of the other reason I married you." He suggested lustfully.
"You're incorrigible. Let me tell you that I'm a respectably married woman, who unfortunately has to leave for work any moment now."
"Couldn't you phone in sick?"
"No I couldn't!" She protested laughingly, and disentangling herself from Tom watched as he good naturedly resigned himself to putting his trousers on.
"We're never going to have a baby if we don't practice." His voice had a wistful note to it.
"Can I remind you of last night, or have you forgotten so soon?" They shared a smile at the memory of the intimate moments.
"Of course I hadn't forgotten." He protested. "It's just that I thought you'd be pregnant by now. When we started talking about having a family I imagined it would happen much quicker."
Matty kept the smile fixed on her face, not betraying the sinking

feeling she was again experiencing. The last thing she wanted to do was to get into a discussion on babies.

"Well, these things take time, you can't just click your fingers and make it happen. Babies don't really grow in the cabbage patch all ready for you to collect."

"I know that!" He lightly spanked his wife's buttocks. "Now out of the way woman, I've got work to do."

They went back to the kitchen and Tom tucked into his breakfast cereal as Matty made fresh tea. She sat down opposite him cradling the brew, savouring its delicate scent.

"What are you up to today?"

"Dad and I have to start cutting the hay down in the meadows, we need to get it in while the weather still holds otherwise we'll lose the lot and there won't be enough come winter to feed the sheep."

"Will it be a late one?" Matty knew that harvesting took no notice of normal working hours.

"Probably, we'll keep going till we've done it all. Don't worry about cooking for me tonight, Mum'll probably make something up."

"Right you are." Her eye caught the pale pink flyer, twitching it out from the rest of the pile she re-read the words. "There's a fete at Drayton Hall. It's this coming Sunday, I thought we could go along."

"But we always go to Mum's for Sunday lunch." Tom sounded surprised Matty had suggested it. Taking a deep breath Matty continued.

"I thought we could have a Sunday to ourselves," She outlined, trying to tempt her husband. "We could have a lie-in just like we used to before we got married." She looked at him coyly from beneath her lashes and was rewarded with his enthusiastic response. "And then we could go to Drayton Hall and then even go for a few drinks at the pub. What do you think?"

"I think I'm a lucky man. I'll tell Mum we won't be there this week." Matty didn't let the flush of success show, but mentally she did a high five in triumph. Some people might have called it pitiful that she couldn't just tell her husband that she wanted to spend a Sunday without having to go to his parents, but to do so would just spark an argument, with Tom seeing it as a snub against his family; which it wasn't. It was just occasionally she wanted her husband to herself. Clearing the breakfast things away swiftly and grabbing her keys she realised she was late for work, but somehow it didn't matter, she was suddenly feeling far more optimistic.

◆◆◆

Driving down the high street to Saunders office, Matty passed the offices of Sherborne and Sherborne and noticed a blonde woman hanging out of the window waving madly to someone. Amused by the scene she walked into the office still smiling. The elderly receptionist, who was renowned for her penchant for whiskey breakfasts and gin lunches snapped. "It's all very well you waltzing in here like Julie-Bloody-Andrews, but I was the one who had to tell Mr George you weren't in for your nine o'clock meeting."

"Thank you Rose." Matty called ignoring the implied criticism. "I'll go and tell him I'm in now." Before adding as an after-thought: "And perhaps we could have two coffees?"

The woman leaning out of the window was Chloe. It had all started so innocently; she had rushed to answer the phone as she entered the office.

"Sherborne and Sherborne." She puffed

"Am I interrupting something exciting between you and my son?" A deep throaty voice rasped hopefully.

"Lily! How can you say that, you know Pete's devoted to Natalia. Besides there's not enough room for a cat to perch in this office let alone enjoy a quick romp."

"Humph, ever hopeful he was starting to be impulsive and just throw you on the desk."

"Not this morning; I think he and Natalia are choosing her outfit for the Drayton Hall fete."

"So the Latin dwarf still hasn't found her decision-making brain cell then." Chloe burst out laughing, it might be disloyal to Pete, but it was so good to have someone to share her bitchy thoughts with. "I keep telling that waste-of-space son of mine to come to his senses and grab you while he has the chance, but does he ever listen to me?"

"He's desperately in love."

There was a loud snort down the line. "He's desperately in lust. Anyway are you coming to the fete?"

"Nah, don't think so. It's not my sort of thing. You know what it's like, all well-to-do-women in tweeds and DINKY couples." *'Not to mention all those babies,'* she silently added then continued. "Think I'll just have a quiet day at home with a bottle of wine."

"Oh no you don't." Lily instructed. "You're not getting out of it that easily. There's no way you're leaving me alone with the Mexican Minx. You can come along and keep me company, otherwise I swear I'll brain that bimbo with one of Lord Beauchamp's priceless statues."

"Put like that I can hardly refuse. If only for the tempting chance of seeing you wielding some masonry."

"I take it from the stream of abuse towards my future daughter-in-law that Pete still hasn't arrived."

"Correct; you know Lily for an old dear you seem to have kept all your marbles."

"Ha! Less of the old. When I was your age I was running that office, looking after Pete and still finding time to have three men on the go."

"I know, I know." Chloe conceded in admiration It was strange to think that Lily, with her larger than life character, could have spawned the quiet reflective Pete. "Oooh," she called excitedly "I've just seen him across the road."

"Well open the window and yell for him to come in, I need to speak to him."

"Ok, hold on a mo. I've just got to undo the catch, they get so stiff. Aaahhh."

"What is it?"

"I've broken a nail." Chloe wailed.

"Bugger the nail, get my son for me." So Chloe wiggled onto the narrow window ledge and with the telephone clamped between her shoulder and ear she held precariously onto the open window and waved the free hand wildly in the air.

"Pete! Cooeee! Pete!"

"Don't shout so loudly." Lily complained into her ear.

"Pete!" But oblivious of her calls he carried on walking down the road, however the crowds around the office began to notice the unusual behaviour and turned to stare at the buxom woman who was gesticulating madly. As she decided to give up on attracting Pete's attention, one of the crowd walked over, and Chloe suddenly realised she was the central focus, but even worse she was almost level with Rob Williams. Staring into his craggy features she felt her cheeks perfuse pink as it dawned on her the spectacle she was making. She decided the only way to retain any vestige of dignity was to bluff it out. "Hello there."

"Hi, erm, do you need any help there?"

"No I'm fine. I was just trying to speak to someone. I don't usually hang out of the window." She went on hurriedly. "In fact I'll just get back in." It was then she realised she was stuck. Her body was perfectly counter-balanced between the open window and the sill, one arm in front of her, one leg behind her. Any attempt to adjust her position to crawl back in would result in her falling ungraciously out of the window down onto the pavement. "I'm stuck." She wailed and down the line Lily exploded.

"Do you want me to call an ambulance or maybe the fire brigade – they have much sexier uniforms."

"Can I help?" Rob offered, Chloe would have liked to refuse, but the consequences were too dire to contemplate.

"Yes please." She muffled.

"Here, let me take this hand." He took the hand off the window and kept hold of it. "And then if I just lift you up." Somehow he managed to pick her up by the waist and manoeuvre her back into the office and onto her feet. In the ensuing tangle the phone slipped and the handset clattered onto the pavement. They heard Lily squawk indignantly. "Sorry about that." Rob apologised into it, as he retrieved it. "But you'll be pleased to know the mission of mercy was successfully completed." Then handing it back to Chloe he gave a quick nod goodbye and walked back into the crowd. Watching his long purposeful stride, Chloe felt a tinge of lust returning until she become aware of Lily's squawks increasing.

"Sorry about that Lily. What were you saying?"

"Who was that?" Lily demanded. "He sounded very masterful."

"The tenant at Wisteria Cottage." She went for casualness.

"And obviously one of the more handsome ones." Lily said shrewdly, not fooled for one minute by Chloe's nonchalance.

"Now you come to mention it, he is quite good looking." She admitted, hoping Lily would now drop the subject, but Lily sensed the weakness and was ready for the kill. Down the line her cackling sing-song voice rang out.

"Chloe's got a crush; Chloe's got a crush." Indignantly Chloe slammed the phone down – really; Lily was the limit.

Chapter 7

The day of the fete dawned fair promising a beautiful English day. The sun was roaring away in a cloudless blue sky, moving slowly higher and higher so that by early afternoon the plants were beginning to droop and Lord Beauchamp's army of staff and helpers were beginning to wilt. The normally perfectly manicured lawn had been covered with marquees and stalls, much to the concern and chagrin of the gardener, whose only role in life (he felt) was to tend to the grass and ensure the levelness and lushness were better than any bowling green. The gates had been open for fifteen minutes, but already visitors were milling around, the women dressed in floaty summer dresses and the men more self-conscious of their city-pale legs poking out from khaki shorts. They toured around like a swarm of bumble bees, greeting each other, couples they only ever saw in passing cars, getting a yearly update of how awful the English tax regime was, where the best places to stay in Italy were *'Tuscany is getting so chichi, you really should try Umbria'* and deploring the state of the education system. The women declared how quaint the whole fete thing was, and this was exactly why they moved out of their cramped Fulham flat so that the children could grow up in a healthy countryside atmosphere, while the men tried to play down the commute that had doubled through the move and focus on the joys of local cricket teams, real beer and no mobile phone reception.

Mavis' flower stand nestled in the only shade afforded by the fronded leaves of the large ornamental maple; a young sapling that Lord Beauchamp's great grandfather had planted over a century before to mark the birth of his son. The trestle table had been covered with a white plastic tablecloth; Mavis knew only too well that linen ones would be ruined by the leaking pots and trails of soil. The array of geraniums and pansies cheered up the sedate olive tree saplings, bobbing lavender heads and swaying bamboo canes. On Rob's suggestion Mavis had also brought along a selection of herbs so that the air was filled with the delicious fragrance of rosemary, sage and mint as she sat on her deckchair in between helping the various customers. Alicia had scoffed at Mavis' suggestion that she might want to bring along a seat and a hat but it had been a futile victory, her legs ached from standing up, and her forehead was beginning to feel tight with sun burn; she was also conscious of wearing the wrong clothes and looking totally out of place. In London she lived in her skinny jeans, tight vest tee-shirts and strappy high heeled sandals; here it looked out of place against the Paul Costello and Betty Barclay outfits. She was also beginning to lose count of the number of her mother's friends who had declared how much Alicia had grown since they had seen her last, then went on to ask what she was doing now, did she have a boyfriend, and was it difficult in London with all those strangers on the underground. 'No' she had wanted to shout 'it's alive and interesting' but instead she had simply ground her teeth and sold them another nameless plant.

The afternoon wore on and the heat increased; the WI tea tent was doing a thriving trade with their chilled frappuccinos and fruit smoothies, it seemed no-one could get enough, although the chocolate rice cakes had melted to such a degree that they had been declared totally inedible by the visiting vicar. The children drank orange squash whilst avoiding the diving wasps, flapping ineffectively at the buzzing enemy, and the men supped their beers. The heat was doing nothing to improve Alicia's temper; when Rob arrived she was hot, tired and extremely irritable. Mavis, spotting him, had gaily waved her huge sunhat to catch his attention. He strode over and Alicia saw he was wearing a pair of faded chinos and polo shirt, both emphasising his muscular frame which didn't seem affected by the heat. Alicia on the other hand was fully aware that her face was glowing and that small rivulets of sweat were intermittently trickling down her back between her shoulder blades.
"Afternoon Mavis, how is it going?" He leant down and kissed Mavis lightly on her weather beaten cheek, giving Alicia a derisory nod which incensed her so much she turned on her heel and stared in the other direction.
"The herbs are selling well, it was a clever idea of yours. How on earth did you think of it."
"Well everyone seems to be talking about that Oliver chap's Mediterranean cooking, and you can't cook without fresh herbs so it made sense to offer them here. Then all these yummy mummies can conjure up those holiday meals they discovered in the tavornas last year."
Alicia scoffed. "What would you know about cooking?"

"Quite a lot actually." Rob responded coldly. Alicia sniffed her disbelief and stalked off to get a bottle of Evian.

"You'll have to excuse her, she's not herself at the movement." Mavis apologised. "I don't think she's very happy being stuck down here with no friends and nothing to do."

Rob bit back the comment that Alicia should consider herself fortunate and not hard done by to be looked after, it would only upset Mavis further. Instead he suggested:

"Why don't I stand in for you for a bit, you could go and wander about and see some of the other stalls." Mavis' face lit up, she'd hoped Alicia would offer to man the stand, but she hadn't been brave enough to suggest it.

"If you're sure, I'd love to have a quick look. I always stock up on my books, everyone donates their holiday reads so I get my fill of romantic slush." She undid the zipped pocket apron from around her waist and handed it over. "I won't be long." She fibbed happily as he settled down in the vacated chair and dropped his peak cap forward over his nose settling in for a snooze.

"Why would anyone be wearing stilettos to a fete?" Lily hissed to Chloe as they trailed behind Natalia and Pete, watching as her razor thin heels drove into the dry crusted earth occasionally trapping them so that Pete would have to gently prise them free. "She should have known better. Honestly what can he see in her."

"Shussshhh. She'll hear." Chloe chided, although whole heartedly agreeing. While everyone else had dressed for comfort and coolness, Natalia had chosen what seemed the tightest dress possible. It clung to her body like a sheen of water, causing her chest to be raised and pumped and her buttocks to be two firm peaches. She clung to Pete, whispering into his ear, snuggling into his hold and sluttishly, in Chloe's opinion, running her hand down his inner thigh. They had spent ten minutes at the bookstall waiting while Natalia pondered between two books, unable to make up her mind.

"Just choose the one with the most pictures." Lily had brightly suggested, adding in an undertone to Chloe. "It's not as though she can actually read." From there they had traipsed to the tombola stand where Natalia had insisted Pete select the tickets for her, which he duly did, winning a large orange teddy bear.

"Oh how wonderful. Look we won Mr Teddy; isn't he sweet." She giggled, ignoring the Vicar's wife's disapproving scowl having just seen Natalia's hand creep towards Pete's crotch. "Here Pete, carry him for me." Which meant due to the largeness of the teddy and the petiteness of Natalia it looked as though he had a girlfriend on either arm.

"I'm not sure I can stand much more maternal mortification." Lily confided. "Let's go and get a strong drink, I need some sort of reviver." To Pete and Natalia she called out. "We'll catch you up later, you two young things don't want us playing perpetual gooseberry." As they headed off to the beer tent Natalia's voice floated lightly across. "Your mum is a wonderful lady; for someone of her age."

Chloe watched as Lily went an unflattering shade of purple. "Did you hear that!" Lily bellowed. "For someone of my age. Good God, she makes me sound like some decrepit ancient octogenarian. I bet they're looking at retirement homes for me in their spare time."

"Calm down or you really will burst a vessel or something."

"Arggghhh. How could my son have got involved with such an airhead. Didn't I bring him up to know how to enjoy himself?"

Chloe hid a smile; Pete had once confided some of the more unusual surprises Lily had arranged over the years, including tandem-bungee jumping, free-fall parachuting and survival training in Thailand. For someone so full of life and verve she couldn't believe her son wasn't the same, but where Lily was impulsive, Pete was thoughtful and where Lily enjoyed the thrill of the risk, Pete considered the cost.

The crowds of people made it difficult to get to the bar, sheens of perspiration appeared on their foreheads, but finally they were served by a man who appeared to have studs and bolts attached to every visible orifice.

"Two extra-large gin and tonics, and don't spare the ice." Lily ordered with an extravagant movement indicating the vivid blue bottle of Bombay Sapphire. "And something for yourself. It's sweltering in this tent."

"You're not wrong there." He agreed, deftly pouring their drinks and selecting an ice cold can of coke for himself.

Their drinks were cool and refreshing, quenching the thirst and revitalising the body.

"I needed that." Lily drained her glass while Chloe sipped, unused to such generous measures. "Right onwards and upwards, where's the next stall?" The next one was the plant stand, resting in the shade of the tree; as they got closer a pair of male muscular legs poked out from one end; in unison their eyes ran up the body, noticing the toned stomach where the polo shirt had ridden up, on up to the peaked cap.

"Now that's what I call a body." Lily admired. Her voice stirred Rob out of his doze, and stretching his arms, unconscious of the fascinated audience, he twisted to get more comfortable and then pushed back his cap. Chloe took a sharp intake of breath and instantly looked round for somewhere to hide, only to realise they were marooned on a sea of grass. There was no protection anywhere, other than behind Lily. Surreptitiously she fell into step behind Lily who was now bearing down on the plants with the perennial excitement of an avid gardener. Any hopes that it would be a quick purchase so they could leave without Rob recognising her where cruelly dashed as Lily pounced on a gaudy geranium and turned to her grinning. "It's a good specimen isn't it? Just like the perfect man, healthy limbs, good colour and a pleasure to look at."

"Is that right?" Rob was amused at Lily's flirtatious manner. Something in Lily's brain pinged. The voice sounded familiar, but she couldn't quite place it...

"Oh yes definitely, don't you agree Chloe?" Buying time while the memory she was seeking could be found and caught. Chloe glowed red from shame and heat, and mumbled an indistinguishable reply that took Rob's attention from Lily to herself. Automatically he gave a friendly hello and enquired if she had leant out of any more windows recently. The ping went off in Lily's brain again. Of course this was the man who was renting Wisteria Cottage, the one she suspected Chloe of having a crush on. Slyly she glanced at her young friend and saw she was obviously torn between wanting to be friendly and toe-curling mortification at meeting like this. A small surge of sympathy swept through Lily, it was obvious that Chloe needed a love-life, and here was the perfect specimen, a healthy if somewhat rugged featured man. She wondered if there was anything she could do to kick start a budding affair. She had always pictured herself as Cupid trying to bring Pete and Chloe together, but as they had continued to remain only friends maybe she should find her an alternative. The only question was how. Aware of an embarrassed silence having fallen over them she enquired:

"So are these your plants Mr....?"

"Williams, Rob Williams. No they're not mine. They belong to Mavis Connor of Apple Trees Nursery. I'm just helping out today."

"So you're not into horticulture then?" She was disappointed that he was going to be green-fingerless.

"In a way I am. I'm a landscape designer. Mavis helps me source plants I need for my commissions."

Lily raised her head slightly skyward and sent up a quiet thank you, it seemed this man really was perfect.

"Really! That's such a coincidence. I'm looking to do something with my garden at the moment. Do you have a card or something with your number on? Then maybe I could give you a call."

He padded his pockets but they were empty apart from a pack of chewing gum and crumpled petrol receipt.

"I don't." He looked crestfallen at having to let this potential client slip through his fingers, then inspiration struck, turning to Chloe he eagerly asked.

"Could you pass on my details to your friend? You should have them on your file."

"Yes of course no problem." Chloe smiled through gritted teeth, uncertain what Lily was up to, but definitely not trusting her. Since when did she let anyone touch her garden?

"Well that's settled then. How much do you I owe you for this?" She handed over the money. "And I'll be in touch." Giving a beaming smile she followed Chloe's quickly retreating figure.

"Lily how could you!" Chloe groaned, as they sat on the grass waiting for the other two. "You aren't thinking about getting your garden redesigned. You hate anyone going near any of your herbaceous borders and you even yelled at me for picking something from your flower beds."

Lily sniffed archly. "That shows just how little you really know me. I've been planning it for ages actually." She lied airily not quite meeting Chloe's glare. "It's up to me isn't it who I ask to help? I don't think it really concerns anyone else. So if you can just let me have his number on Monday…"

"You're not really going through with this charade are you?"

"It's not a charade." Lily defended herself but mentally she realised she may well end up having to have something done to her beautiful garden if she was ever going to get Chloe and Rob together. She thought of the tiny bit of waste ground to the side behind the garages, maybe she could just focus on that for a bit, after all it was in the name of love.

Pete and Natalia appeared from behind the 'guess the weight of the pig' with the huge teddy dragging behind them.

"What's not a charade?" Pete asked having heard the tail end of the conversation.

"I'm thinking about getting some help to get the garden redesigned." Lily explained with a saccharine sweet smile directed at Chloe's disbelieving face.

"How sensible." Natalia congratulated. "It must be getting a bit much for you, having to look after such a big garden by yourself at your age."

Lily's indignant look at her potential daughter-in-law made both Pete and Chloe burst out laughing, any animosity disappearing like small popping bubbles.

Further down the garden, by the cascading fountain, Matty and Tom had paused to watch the chubby koi carp greedily nudging the surface of the pond, hungrily seeking out morsels of food. There was a silent companionship between them as they stood gazing down at the fish and as Tom felt for Matty's hand he gave it a small affectionate squeeze. It had been an enjoyable day, similar to the early years of marriage when they had spent every possible moment together.

"Shall we go and get a drink, I'm parched."

"Good idea." Matty agreed.

They walked over to the WI tea tent and ordered two frappuccinos, as they looked for somewhere to flop down and enjoy the drinks, Matty caught sight of two women sitting opposite each other making desolate small talk. Riding on her wave of bonhomie, she gave rein to her instinct and rushed over to say hello.

"Alicia!"

Alicia turned round and a vacant look passed through her eyes until she recognised her old friend.

"Matty, what are you doing here?"

Mavis pulled out one of the spare chairs and beckoned them to sit down.

"Hello Mrs Connor, I can't remember when I last saw you. How are things? Alicia and I were at school together." She reminded her husband.

"No, it was '*Drayton's version of a finishing school*'. Alicia corrected her, mimicking the over-annunciated tones of their form teacher, causing both women to giggle and suddenly they were transported back to their teenage years, swapping stories on mutual friends, half-forgotten teaching staff and humorous recollections. Mavis turned to Tom, recognising him from his days of Young Farmers who would annually be sent to the nursery to borrow her warming lights for the greenhouses if a sick lamb needed to be kept warm, and asked after his parents before glancing at her watch and realising how long she had left poor Rob manning the stand. Apologetically she stood up and Alicia, taking a cue from her mother followed.

"It was lovely to see you both again." Matty enthused

"Yes, why don't we meet up for a drink?" Alicia suggested, anxious to try and cling to any semblance of a social life.

"Give me a call, we're under Gregson in the phone book." Matty tried to contain the fizzing of excitement at the thought of dressing up for a girl's night out. Inside she was eighteen again, the world suddenly had limitless possibilities; gone were the worries about over-bearing mother-in-laws, lost dreams and the drudge of the job. Instead everything had been put through a hot wash, leaving it clean, fresh and exciting.

"What a small world it is." Matty said when they were alone. "I can't believe it's nearly ten years since we were at school, time seems to fly by. I remember Alicia being sent out of class for impersonating our teacher. She hasn't changed at all, I recognised her straight away." Tom watched his wife and felt a small sliver of impending doom seep into the atmosphere; she was like an overwound train chugging round and round the track, getting faster and faster. He didn't know why, but he felt she was moving away from him, that she wasn't the girl he had married. Secretly he had hoped that having a baby and staying at home would give her back some of the joie-de-vive that had drained away, but Matty still wasn't pregnant. He didn't know what else to do, he just hoped it wasn't too late to save their marriage.

Chapter 8

In mute desperation Alicia watched as her laptop died for the tenth time that morning; all her work disappearing into a mass of pixalated gibberish. It was enough to make her want to drop her head into her good hand and weep. How was it possible that in this day and age she couldn't even get a connection to the internet. She thought longingly of her flat with its state of the art wireless connection and her large zinc desk overlooking the Thames. A far cry from the cramped space she had here; sandwiched in the dining room between her mother's archaic filing system one end of the table and the growing collection of back copies of Gardener's Delight at the other. Even the sun had conspired against her; glinting into her eyes every time she stared at her screen so now the ancient plum velvet curtains had been drawn across in an attempt to shield out the light. As work environments went it wasn't terribly conducive. With a forced patience Alicia wiggled the telephone wire that now sat plugged into her machine and tried to reconnect; the static bleeps as it dialled out grating on her nerves. How could she be reduced to an ancient system like this, especially when she was working on the Van Plaza paperwork? Simon had been keen for her to still be involved despite the fact she was supposed to be on holiday. The last thing she needed was a technology meltdown. The screen sprang back into life, and willing it to stay online she recommenced her slow painful typing.

Finally deciding to call it a day Alicia logged off, no doubt her mother would be in soon to cook dinner before another interminable evening watching some landscaping series her mother was addicted to. The shrill ring of her phone interrupted her thoughts. Answering it George's cheery salutations rang out.
"So how are you?" He boomed; in the background Alicia could enviously hear the chatter of happy hour drinkers.
"Bored! Frustrated! I don't know how anyone sticks living in the country. They don't have proper broadband connections, no decent clothes shops and I have to half lean out of a window to get any chance of a mobile signal." She complained bitterly.
"So you're missing us all then!" George asked wickedly and heard her sigh in response.
"If you saw the natives here you'd understand why." She said waspishly. "They are obviously the missing link evolutionists

have been looking for." George burst out laughing. "Seriously! I'm telling you they are all a bunch of inbreds. There's one who's working with my mother and I swear his knuckles drag on the floor everywhere he walks!" She was rewarded by another guffaw of laughter down the phone but her neck prickled and she had a strange sensation of being watched. Spinning round on the chair she saw Rob standing in the doorway, his face glowering and anger burning in his eyes. A momentary pang of guilt seared her as she contemplated how much he may have overheard; then remembering how overbearing he was decided that it served him right. He shouldn't be eavesdropping into a personal conversation, she thought. Pointedly she turned her back on him and carried on chatting to George, asking about work, who was out partying and getting an update on his secondment and latest girlfriend.

When the call came to an end Alicia clicked off and stalked into the kitchen, expecting Rob to be waiting, already with a biting comment. The room was empty though; he had gone and all that remained was a pile of drawings on the table addressed to Mavis.

"Mum! Mum!" Alicia shrieked with all her might from the backdoor across the garden. The lack of response increased her frustration. Where on earth was Mavis hiding. Her muscles were tense with anger, she couldn't believe her beautiful Karen Millen cargo pants had been so thoroughly destroyed. With the limp, lifeless fabric clutched in her good hand she swept out of the house and into the strange hostile garden. She had never enjoyed being outdoors, her memories of it were being cold, muddy and wet. While some adored the smell of damp earth and catmint lingering in the early morning air, of watching the slow unfurling buds in spring and admiring the russet landscape as the trees turned in the autumn, Alicia always wanted to remain inside in the warm where you could keep control of life and there were no sudden surprises. Her parents had always thrived outside, whenever she thought of her father it was swathed in layers of jumpers to keep out the chill, his beaten up old cap slightly askew, carefully tending to plants as though they were the most precious thing alive. It was strange to unexpectedly recall her father, she hardly ever did in London, but being at home there were constant reminders. Small things such as his discarded boots at the back of the store cupboard that would catch her unawares and cause an uncomfortable mix of emotions to boil up unexpectedly.

She continued up the stone path past the wicket fence which portioned the nursery from the small gravel car park where Mavis' old, but beloved, car sat in state watching over the area, and on to the orchard where the ancient gnarled apple trees and pear trees had once borne fruit to help sustain the household and whose harvest now fell unheeded each year to the floor helpless to the scavenging intents of wasps and mice. The three large greenhouses ran down the right hand side of the path, their wooden frames looking uncared for, the once gleaming white now faded to a dirty grey, patchy blisters revealing bare wood. Green flecks of moss grew along the window panels and a wiry stem of unbidden weed appeared along the brick base every few feet. The annual repainting of the greenhouses was something that stuck in Alicia's memory as a yearly reference point, like the start of school term or Christmas. It had taken her parents weeks, carefully sanding the wood, treating any minor problems and then painstakingly painting the wood around each panel, making sure they didn't get any flecks on the glass.
"Why don't you get one of those nice new aluminium framed ones?" Customers would ask, seeing the huge operation underway, but her parents had looked knowingly at one another and shared a smile.
"These do us just fine." Her father would say patting the wood as though it was a living object.
"What about all the work though, all that hassle just to make it look tidy."
"It's no hassle." Mavis would explain. "We like looking after them, they are part of our nursery." Customers would shrug with incomprehension, not understanding the deep bond Mavis and Bill had with the nursery. To them it was the most precious offspring; it was their way of life and their reason for living; it was something Alicia had never felt and never shared, had only ever felt excluded from.

Behind her stomping feet faint dust storms trailed in her wake, overhead the unmerciful sun slipped behind the tall structural poplars that bordered the land and although shielded from the cruel harsh rays the air was still hot and humid, causing everyone to be short tempered. Hearing a sound in the farthest greenhouse, Alicia wrenched the door open and screamed shrilly.

"What did you do to my trousers?" She brandished the limp frayed rag that had once been a beautiful satin outfit. "Look at them!"

As though captured on film and played back in slow motion, Alicia saw her mother turn from the bench where she was working replanting the new seedlings into individual pots, her face crumpling as she recognised the garment. She had prayed Alicia wouldn't find them until she'd replaced them.

"I'm sorry." She started to apologise profusely.

"How could you, they were my favourite trousers."

"I'll buy you another pair." Mavis offered conciliatorily.

"I doubt you could afford them – they are £150." Alicia spat nastily.

Mavis hung her head lower and mumbled: "Don't you have any other trousers you could wear?"

"I wanted to wear those." Alicia raged; a small movement to the right of Mavis caught Alicia's eye and she saw Rob step forward.

"I suggest you stop acting like a spoilt brat and be grateful you have others to wear." His voice was cold, obviously highly unimpressed with the behaviour towards Mavis. Alicia pointedly ignored him and carried on berating Mavis.

"What did you do to them? It clearly says they need hand washing on the label."

"I didn't think it would matter, I put them in with my gardening shirts and they sort of shrunk a little." Mavis admitted.

"Why didn't you hand wash them – it's not difficult."

"Then why didn't you do it then?" Rob interrupted his tone scathing. "Your mother is running a business, she is not here to wait on you hand and foot." His face was glowering, the contempt made him look even more unattractive.

"Rob..." Mavis intervened, but he put up a silencing hand, his eyes never leaving Alicia though.

"So why don't you start to help out a little?" He challenged.

"Because of this Einstein." She spat back holding up the plastered arm, brandishing it like a trophy. "I didn't exactly ask to be sent down to this back water. I was perfectly happy looking after myself in London." She carried on. Rob harrumphed disbelievingly and turned his back on her, ignoring the glare of her olive shaped eyes, showing that he considered the conversation to have ended.

"Why don't you go and find another outfit." Mavis suggested, "And then maybe I could run you into town instead of you having to order a taxi." She tried out an encouraging smile at her daughter, desperate to re-establish communication. With bad grace Alicia acquiesced, turning on her heel and pointedly ignoring Rob as she stomped out, her head held high and imperious.

"Why do you let her treat you like that?" Rob asked, riled by Alicia's remarks.

"She's having a rough time." She saw his look of disbelief and continued. "I know it's no excuse, but deep down she's still my little girl. The trouble is we just don't know how to deal with each other – unfortunately we never really have done. I can't believe someone so fierce, clever and determined can really be related to Bill and me. Somehow it feels like we failed her in a way, that we didn't give her the environment she obviously needed. We loved living here, running the business and we just assumed she would too, but you can't make those assumptions."

"I think you're being a bit hard on yourself. I reckon you gave Alicia the type of home that most children would crave. So what if you didn't live in the lights of London, there are greater hardships going on in the world than living in Drayton Beauchamp."

"Maybe, but there is such a disconnect between us; I'd hoped it might get less when her father died, but if anything it's just got worse." Mavis' shoulders seemed to droop a little and her eyes wrinkled, causing her skin to pucker further.

"It's her loss Mavis, she obviously isn't able to recognise a good thing." Rob said brusquely.

"Thank you for being so sweet about it, but enough of my troubles. Have you got the final plant list for that new garden yet?" He nodded and pulled a wad of paper from the back pocket of his jeans and unfolded it carefully, it was already looking grubby and worn from being constantly referred to. He handed it over to Mavis who scanned the list mentally ticking off what was in stock and what she would need to buy.

"I've got most of these; the delphiniums are doing well in the other green house and there's a gorgeous Acer that will look just the part. The azaleas are a bit small still, but once you plant them and give them a good feeding they'll double in size." Rob nodded approvingly. "I'll need to order in the box trees, I've just sold the last ones, so they will be ready probably a week on Monday. How does that sound?"

"We're starting on site in a few days, it'll be a bit tight, but we should get it done. The owners want it ready for a fiftieth birthday party." They exchanged a look that said '*some clients*' both had experience of people who wanted to buy a ready-made garden, rather than enjoy watching it develop slowly over time. They were interrupted by an earnest earthy looking pair who Mavis recognised from the fete still in matching cardigans and sandals.

"You mentioned that you had an organic vegetable section. We wondered if you could show what you have, we want to restock our allotment." Before Mavis could respond a distant, but distinct, shriek came from the house.

"Mum, it's time to go."

Mavis gave the astonished couple a tight smile and quickly explained. "It's just my daughter, I'm supposed to be giving her a lift." The pair's faces fell at the thought of being deprived of being able to revel in a discussion on organic horticulture. "I'm sorry..." Mavis started to say, feeling guilty at having to let her customers down when Rob interrupted.

"I'm all finished here Mavis and I've got to go that way. I'll give Alicia a lift for you." His voice sounded resigned, more at having to put up with Alicia's company than helping Mavis out.

"Are you sure?" Mavis was taken aback by the suggestion, envisaging World War III breaking out in Rob's Landrover. "It's not too much trouble?"

Before he could answer Alicia's voice, louder and more insistent, shouted for her mother.

"It's no trouble, you stay and look after these two, I'll take the precocious princess to the ball." He said a general goodbye and walked out of the greenhouse and back down the path towards the house. He could see Alicia impatiently moving from one foot to another, now dressed in a wrap-around dress, the pale blue showed off her olive skin that still held a hint of pasty office tan about it. She astutely ignored him as he walked towards her, glancing behind him trying to see if her mother was finally coming. He came to a halt in front of her, blocking her view completely.

"What do you want? Is my mother coming yet?"

"Your mother is dealing with customers, so she won't be able to take you. I'm giving you a lift."

She stared at him, the loathing clearly glinting in her eyes. "Why would I want a lift from you?" She demanded haughtily as though he had suggested she cleaned the toilet with her toothbrush.

"Because you've no other lift, and it will be an hour's wait for a taxi." He pointed out. It was on the tip of her tongue to tell him where to shove his lift when she realised the truthfulness of his statement. She could easily end up waiting half the night for a taxi, and she didn't have Matty's mobile to let her know she might be late. Another evening trapped in the house would be unbearable. Taking a deep breath and gritting her teeth she uttered a defeated 'ok'.

Rob walked across the path and out into the car park to where the Landrover was parked under the shade of a cedar tree, its swaying boughs casting shadows across the bonnet and roof. Striding over to the driver's door, his feet scrunching on the gravel, he unlocked it and climbed in not bothering to turn round and check on Alicia's progress. Alicia was following on behind silently cursing his large bear-like back, trying unsuccessfully to bury her anger. Walking to the passenger door she put her left hand on the handle to pull it down and release the catch only to find the combination of using her left hand and standing awkwardly away from the vehicle to protect her sling meant she couldn't get enough leverage to open it. In frustration she tried again, but she still couldn't manage it. Tears of infuriation suddenly threatened, the embarrassment of not even being able to open the car door unaided.

Unable to look at Rob who was testily sitting tapping his fingers on the wheel, their rhythmetic beat forming an impatient tattoo. She gently knocked on the window, for a moment he sat staring at her, not understanding why she hadn't got in. *'Surely you can't be expecting every man to wait on you hand and foot. In the age of equality women should be opening their own doors'*. He thought angrily before noticing her averted gaze and pitiful effort to try and open the heavy door. An emotion, similar to a pang of guilt, twinged inside his rib cage as he realised that she couldn't get in, not that she wouldn't. Leaning across he pulled the clasp inside and pushed open the door, awaiting a tirade of verbal abuse from her. When nothing was said he turned abruptly to watch her gently manoeuvre herself into the dark tweed seat and shut the door. She was studying the dashboard, a faint crimson stain on her cheek as she reached for the seat belt and brought it across her body to try and fasten it. It obstinately refused to click shut. Leaning across Rob took the offending seat belt and with dexterous care clicked it shut for her.

"There you go. Are you ok?" He arranged the webbing of the strap under her sling so that there was no pressure directly on her arm. "Is that comfortable?"

"Yes thank you." There was a hint of humility in her voice that took him unaware, he didn't know how to cope with an Alicia who wasn't shouting abuse at him. It was rather like seeing a hedgehog shorn of its spikes and an uncomfortable feeling of pity crept under his skin. He didn't know what to say, how to respond to this almost vulnerable woman, so he said roughly.

"We'd better get going or you'll be late for your date." He revved the engine and the car pulled out onto the village road.

As they made their way through the country lanes that surrounded the Drayton Hall Estate, Alicia noticed the stubble fields where crops had been harvested, thinking she must get her hair cut, unconsciously her left hand crept up, wisps of growth were appearing that refused to stay neatly in place, instead they kept breaking into soft waves like the placid foam on an English sea. Rob noticed the parched fields, dry and arid and worried about how he was going to keep the new garden watered to make sure everything survived. No client was going to be happy if their new plants turned their toes up to shrivel and die.

"Where do you want dropping off?" Rob asked breaking the silence for the first time since their journey had begun.

"We're meeting at Zanzibar. Matty said it was just behind the old clock tower off the High Street. Do you know it?"

"I've been there a couple of times, it's got a good lively atmosphere, though it's probably not a patch on what you're used to in London." Alicia's head spun round and stared at his profile, trying to determine whether that had been an intentional snub, but she couldn't tell, his face remained expressionless. They came to a stop in the cobbled street with a clock tower on one side and shop frontages on the other where a Moroccan sign and windows half covered in ornate fret-worked shutters indicated where Zanzibar lay.

"Here you go." Rob said as he pulled the handbrake on, and then seeing that she was about to undo the seat belt hastily moved to undo it. "Let me." He unclicked it and held the belt as it slowly wound back in, shielding her arm as he did so.

"Thank you for the lift." She sounded as awkward as Rob was feeling.

"No problem. I was coming this way anyway." He lied smoothly. "Hope you have a good evening." She climbed out and gave a self-conscious half wave as he pulled away down the street.

Zanzibar had been the brain child of an aging London club owner who had made his fortune during the 1990s and wanted to dabble at something in retirement. As his latest wife fiercely protected her time as her own, the last thing she wanted was a bored husband hanging around the house, watching each time she went out for lunch or counting the shopping bags she returned with. So she encouraged him to channel all his energies into the new venture. Luckily the employment of the bar's manager had tempered some of the owner's original designs, so out were the leopard skin sofas and heavy gold chandeliers, and in were the ethnic influences of the Middle East and the bazaars. Deep red felt armchairs squat to the ground level with the low dark solid wood tables, large square cushions in orange were scattered around to give more seating. The walls were rough plastered and washed white so that the fabrics stood out like exotic jewels. The place had become a hit overnight with the ex-Hammersmith husbands and former Wimbledon wives who still hankered after a smart wine bar to head off to after a hard day in the office.

By the time Alicia arrived it was already crammed with commuters dropping in for a quick chardonnay before going home to the overworked au pair and hyperactive children. She jostled herself to the bar and waited to be served. Around her there was a buzz as people loudly greeted friends across the room, cheerfully complaining about interest rates and the price of shares. She recalled other evenings in places like this which Zac would whisk her off to whenever he had time, but he was obviously busy. There had still been no contact from him still; she realised how awkward it was for him to explain any absences to Marcie, but she had still hoped that he would at least phone or email. There had been nothing though which made her question what she actually meant to him. They had been together for two years, and yet it felt as though they were still strangers.

The barman caught her attention and in an Auzzie twang asked what she wanted.
"A bottle of pinot grigio and two glasses."
"Right you are."
Adeptly he pulled the cork out of the wine bottle with a satisfying pop, and let her taste the wine. It was cool and fruity, and as the first glass of alcohol since the accident it tasted like nectar. Juggling the bottle and glasses with one hand, she made her way over to a recently vacated table by the window and sat down to watch the door. A slight breeze came through the open window, cooling her hot flushed skin; pouring two glasses of wine she settled down to wait for Matty.

Matty couldn't believe it. The only night she was going out and the office had conspired to make her late. Between Rose and Mr-sodding-George, they had managed to prevent her doing any work all day, only to announce at five o'clock they had things booked for the evening, and shouldn't Matty get a move on with the wage packets, tomorrow was after all pay day. With a clamped jaw and a lot of ungracious thoughts she had ploughed through preparing the pay ready for the morning. She had been planning to go home after work and get changed. Now she was having to run across the road, still in her boring grey suit, her hair a mess and all vestiges of make-up completely gone. Arriving slightly breathlessly, she walked in and spotted Alicia straight away. Slumping into the chair opposite her, she wailed about her day.
"I can't believe how it turned out. Lord George strutted out as soon as the clock struck five, leaving me to do the salary packets for the men." She paused to gulp her wine down and appreciatively showed a smile. "I'd planned to get changed before coming out, but that didn't happen. So you're stuck with me in this old thing."
"Don't worry about it." Alicia reassured her. "You look fine; most people are still in work gear."
"But theirs is Agnes B, it isn't Dotty P."
Alicia topped up her friend's glass. "Have another drink and then tell me everything. I haven't seen you properly since your wedding. I thought you might even have had a sprog by now."

Matty gave a pitiful sigh and grimaced.

"Oh not you as well, perrrlease. Why does everyone automatically assume that just because you get married you are going to start popping babies?" Alicia raised an eyebrow realising she had obviously touched a nerve. "I mean it's not as though I don't want one, but not yet. I'm far too young to be tied down with a baby. I've got things to do."

Alicia looked interested. "What things?"

Inwardly Matty groaned. That was the problem, what did she really want to do? Somehow she had lost her way so badly that she couldn't work it out. "Oh just things." She said lamely.

"Does Tom want a baby?" Alicia asked, guessing that the outburst was a venting of pressure. Dumbly Matty nodded.

"But you don't?"

"Yes. I mean No. Well, of course... just not yet."

"Why don't you tell Tom then?" Alicia couldn't see the issue.

"I can't." Matty wailed again as she finished the wine off with another huge swig. "He's so excited about it, and if I did say anything then his mother would know and she already thinks I should be giving up work and staying at home like a good little wife."

"What's Tom's mother got to do with this?" The conversation was starting to get confusing.

"Oh God. You have no idea just how much. You wouldn't believe it. First of all she still treats Tom as though he was her little boy, cooking him lunch every day, phoning up to see if there's anything he needs from the shops, or the market, or the farm suppliers."

"Well most mothers do that; it's part of the rule of parenting, you don't recognise your offspring is a grown adult with their own thoughts and lives until they are drawing their pension. And even then it's a painful process."

"But that's only half of it. The other thing is she keeps telling me what to do. She thinks I should have given up work when I got married, and she thinks that I should have had a baby by now, she thinks our house is too untidy. Of course it bloody well is. I spend all my time working or helping out on the farm, I never get any time to worry about starting to tidy up."

Alicia pulled a sympathetic face. "I'm not sure I can give any advice. I don't exactly have much knowledge about mother-in-laws."

"I envy you so much." Matty's voice was heated with emotion. "It's so much simpler being single." Alicia thought of the snatched nights with Zac only when they could be certain his wife was out of town.
"Actually, it's not all it's cracked up to be." She admitted heavily.

With the phone clamped between her ear and shoulder; typing awkwardly with one hand and trying to quell an insistent itch above the plaster cast on the other by rubbing it against the table edge, Alicia ended up leaning back slightly too far in the chair. The inelegant scramble to right herself resulted in the phone clattering onto the mushroom pink carpet and a jarring sensation shooting painfully up her arm. With a curse she clambered under the dining table to retrieve the phone from where it lay on the dusty carpet, bumping her head as she stood up too soon. Irrationally angry at the bumps, bruises and breaks, she stormed into the kitchen deciding it wasn't too early to start on a bottle of wine. The husband in the divorce case was arguing over the substantial fees, and Simon with his Teflon shoulders had sloped it onto her. Meaning she was now trying to show where their time had been spent working to the client's ridiculously tight deadlines. It was an unfulfilling and thankless task, no-one in the team appreciated her querying hours and activities, even though it was instigated by the client.

Irritably she walked across the hall and into the kitchen, hearing the sounds from within she expected to see Mavis there; instead Rob stood by the oven, saucepan bubbling on the hob and finely sliced vegetables sitting on the chopping board.
"What do you think you are doing here?" Alicia demanded.
"What does it look like?" Rob replied flippantly, not bothering to disguise his dislike.
"Why are you cooking – don't you have your own home to go to!"
He gave a look of sheer loathing.
"I often cook for Mavis if we've been working late, she enjoys the company." Alicia ignored the snide jab at her absences.
"Very cosy!" The irony dripped from the words. "But I do have to warn you that if you've any intentions towards my mother then I have to tell you that she's got far better taste than you." She told him nastily.

He didn't bother to respond, instead he turned back to concentrate on the saucepan so that Alicia was left looking at his broad back dominating the already small kitchen space. Giving a frustrated scream and clenching her fists she stormed out. Throwing herself into an armchair in the sitting room she turned the TV up loud to block out the culinary clinks and chinks, grinding her teeth and trying to ignore the unfairly tempting aromas which were wafting into the room.

When Mavis popped her head round the door half an hour later and announced supper was ready, Alicia considered refusing, but her stomach rumbled disloyally. With mutinous thoughts she went into the kitchen. Chicken breasts, plump and succulent, sat in a white wine sauce surrounded by sautéed vegetables and a carrot mash. Mavis, sitting in the middle, smiled encouragingly as Alicia drew back a chair to sit down. Rob ignored her but did at least condescend to pour three glasses of wine.
"This looks lovely." Mavis enthused, trying to thaw the chilling atmosphere. "Doesn't it Alicia?"
Alicia forced herself to give a quick polite nod of asset and then took a large gulp of wine. It was surprisingly good, she had obviously underestimated Rob's knowledge of wine. Mavis served them both, cutting Alicia's chicken quietly and efficiently without comment, so that her daughter could eat the meal with a fork, before starting on her own.
"This is delicious as always Rob." She complimented with a twinkling glance. Alicia took the first tentative forkful, a subtle maelstrom of flavours burst onto her tongue. The sweetness of the honeyed parsnips contrasted with the chicken and the herbs within the sauce. Neither she nor Mavis was that interested in cooking, it was always functionally rather than flamboyant. The meal tasted heavenly – but there was no way she would be admitting that to Rob.

Chapter 9

"Mr Williams?" A husky female voice enquired down the phone. "It's Lily Sherborne here. We met at the Drayton Hall fete." The mental cogs started whirling and Rob remembered the flamboyant character.

"Hi, how are you?"

"Very well thank you. I mentioned about my garden I think. Well, I need some advice, some new ideas. You know how it is, you roll along happily designing and then suddenly you come up against a blank and you find you've run out of ideas. At least I have."

"And what sort of garden do you have?" There was a warmth in his voice that showed he was amused by the unusual address.

"Oh you know the type, lots of grass, lots of flowers and lots of trees."

"Grass, flowers and trees! Sounds wonderful – why are you changing it?"

Good gracious Lily thought, this man had flair, he was almost flirting with her. "Sometimes I just want a complete change. I have a very low boredom threshold, I warn you now."

"Then I'll make sure I keep introducing new and interesting things." On the other end of line Lily blushed, she hadn't been spoken to like this for years!

"Make sure you do." She said faintly.

"So when shall we start?"

Lily almost dropped the phone at his presumption; she squeaked "Sorry?"

"I meant," He said slowly, his voice conveying his grin. "When do you want to meet up and discuss your garden?" He added with mock seriousness. "What else could I have meant?"

"I really have no idea." Lily replied, deciding two could play the game. "But if you could come on Thursday evening – say about six o'clock. You could run your expert eye over it." She heard him flicking through a diary.

"Thursday's fine. What's your address?" He wrote it down.

"And your girlfriend won't mind you working in an evening?"

He laughed. "No danger there, I'm a fully-fledged bachelor."

"I'll look forward to seeing you on Thursday then." Lily said, rubbing her hands gleefully.

As she replaced the handset, Lily flicked back her hair with a self-satisfied smile. It was good to know that she still had *'it'*. She licked her forefinger and ran it across her heavily plucked eyebrow. Not that she was interested in Rob for herself, oh no there were far greater plans for him. She picked up the phone and dialled the office number for Sherborne and Sherborne. Immediately it was answered with a cheery: "Good afternoon, how can I help you."

"If you are that chirpy then my waste-of-space son has obviously left for the day." Was Lily's introduction.

"Wrong! Actually we've just been discussing his forthcoming wedding plans. Apparently they want to theme it around a Country House weekend, you should see the outfit they've chosen for you. It's a lovely tweed two piece with matching flat brown brogues and Fairisle stockings. Oh and there was talk of a trilby with a pheasant feather dyed to match."

"There is no way I am wearing that. I'll boycott the wedding." Lily trumpeted loudly down the phone.

"Gotcha!" Chloe said with gleeful wickedness.

"Chloe how could you subject me to such horrors, and I thought you were such a nice girl."

"Shows how wrong you are." Chloe said happily.

"Well I'm going to overlook your idea of fun and still invite you round for supper on Thursday."

"Why? What's the special occasion?" Chloe asked suspiciously.

"Chloe, really, does there need to be a reason other than I wanted to see a friendly face and catch up over a bite to eat. But if you're too busy..." She let the sentence hang in the air long enough for Chloe to bite like a tempted trout going for a fisherman's hook.

"No of course not. I'd love to come over, what sort of time. Seven thirty?"

"Could you make it a bit earlier, say six thirty? Come straight from the office, but make sure you wear something smart."

"Why do I have to wear something smart?"

"Oh just in case we end up going out somewhere." Lily answered breezily.

"But I thought you said we were having a bite to eat."

"We are. Look be a good girl and just get here for half past six, and when you see Pete could you ask him to give me a call. Thanks. I'll see you Thursday." She hung up before Chloe could pose any more questions and rubbed her hands once again.

Now all she needed to do was put the final piece of the plan into action.   Picking up the phone for the third time she dialled Barbara's number grinning excitedly at her plan to play Cupid.

◆◆◆

Not everyone was having such luck that day, across the village Natalia was sitting amid a pile of papers sobbing her heart out as Pete entered. It had been a good day in the office; he and Chloe had managed to let three properties and had two new ones on the books, and driving home he had been buoyed along on a wave of euphoria. As he stepped into the front hall the bubble slowly sagged like a sodden ceiling, the euphoria melting away leaving him fraught and anxious. Hurrying into the sitting room, he waded across the sea of glossy magazines, skating on some as his leather soles failed to grip.   Bending down he took Natalia's tear stained face in his hands and tilting it up so that he could see her swollen eyes asked. "What's this all about?" His voice tender with concern, and he wiped away the trails of tears that lined her cheeks with the ball of his thumb. Incoherently she tried to speak but the only sound was a strangled sob. Concerned at what could be troubling her, he held her tightly until the convulsing sobs subsided leaving an occasional whimper.
"Now tell me what's wrong? Is it something someone's said?" His thoughts flew immediately to Lily, for someone who could be so kind and generous, she certainly had a darker side.
"No. It's the wedding." Her voice was small, choked with emotion.
A chilled hand squeezed his heart. "What about the wedding?"
"It's not going to be able to happen, we're not going to be able to get married."
"Why can't we? What's happened Natalia, tell me what's going on." He watched as her lower lip continued to tremble and the tears threatened again. "Come on. What's so awful that our wedding is threatened? Tell me about it." He gently cajoled.
"It's the wedding planner, she's just told me I'm the worst client to work for and she's quit. Now we'll never get everything ready, and we're going to have to call it all off." Her clenched hands showed white knuckles. "I can't believe it. We've only got three months to go to the biggest day of my life and all I wanted was to make it all perfect. How could she say I was too demanding?"

Laughing with relief Pete pulled away. "Is that all? Darling we can sneak away to the registry office one lunch time and get married. We don't need some huge fancy wedding. In fact if you're so worried about it, why don't we do just that? We'll invite close friends only and go out for a meal afterwards. Doesn't that sound better?"

It didn't to Natalia, in response she screwed up her face and proceeded to scream abuse at Pete, hitting out at him with clenched fists. "No way José. This is supposed to be the best day in a girl's life. I want a proper wedding, not some back street affair that no-one will remember. You've obviously been talking to your mother; she never wanted us to get married in the first place. All I wanted was a real wedding, and now you won't even let me have that." Her face had become flooded with red, and her usual doe like eyes bulged unbecomingly. Fearing something would rupture, Pete grabbed her pounding fists and said slowly.

"Calm down! Ok. Ok. We can have the full works if that's what you want." She ceased screaming and eyed him suspiciously, wary of his sudden acquiescence.

"With another wedding planner?"

"Yes with another wedding planner if that's what it takes." He said suddenly worn out from the histrionics.

"And we can still have the chapel in Tuscany decked out in candle light."

"If that's what you'd like." He said indulgently kissing the top of her head.

"And I can have the Vera Wang wedding dress? The one I showed you in the magazine." Her voice had dropped into a gentle coax. Pete gulped, he had seen the price tag and questioned whether there should be a decimal point somewhere between all those noughts. "Oh please Pete." Her hand moved to the buttons of his shirt and began to play with one. "Because then Miss Goldilocks could show big Daddy Bear just how grateful she is." Try as he might Pete felt his resistance dissolve. "Go on then." He said gruffly, wondering whether he could manoeuvre Natalia up to the bedroom so she could fully show her gratitude. Climbing onto his lap, she kissed him responding with a whispered: "Shall we go upstairs and get a little more comfortable?" She gave a little wiggle and another extended embrace before slipping off his lap and drawing away. "Why don't you go up and get out of your suit. I'll join you in a moment."

"Don't be long." Pete instructed as he hurried to the stairs.

"I won't." She called after him, watching his departing figure and listening to the sound of him climbing the stairs. Calculating when he would be out of ear range she pulled out her mobile and dialled the number of the bridal boutique.

"Hi, this is Natalia De Bueni, I'm phoning up about the Vera Wang dress I tried on earlier. I'll take it."

Lying in bed, Pete couldn't remember when his masculine bachelor pad had morphed into this feminine concoction. Where it had once been sleek straight lines of glass and steel, with manly colours such as British Racing Green and Jaguar Red; it had somehow been transformed; glass tables were covered in delicate cobweb doilies, walls had been repainted soft yellows covering the stripes, the denim bed covers exchanged for Diary of a Country Lady. When he had asked if she was planning to re-decorate him to blend in with the new look, she had simply thrown back her head laughing, showing off pearl white teeth that contrasted with her luscious red lips.

Now her head leaned on his shoulder, her hand stroking his smooth chest and Pete knew he should have been revelling in the attention but he felt distracted and edgy. He was aware that Natalia had been chattering away happily for some time about her plans for the wedding when he suddenly realised she had ceased talking and was looking expectantly at him, obviously waiting for an answer. He had the grace to look shamefaced and tutting she said.

"Don't you listen to a word I say?   All this avoiding any conversation about our wedding, I'd have thought you wanted to be involved in the big day decisions." His mind flew back to the early concessions and he looked like a hurt schoolboy at the injustice of her allegation. "It's important," she carried on. "After all some people don't like fruit cake, and sponge seems so boring. It's so difficult to decide what kind of wedding cake to have.   Unless we go Italian, maybe a panettone style cake drizzled with white icing and candid fruit cut in the shape of hearts."

Pete's mobile bleeped, announcing a new text message, and leaning over he opened the flashing envelope.

"Are you listening to me?" Natalia demanded.

"Of course I am." Pete murmured as he waited for the message to appear. It was difficult to feel enthusiastic about the ongoing nuptial discussions when it seemed the only thing they ever discussed. Natalia had turned into a 'woman with a mission' filtering everything else out; confused at what was happening Pete had asked Chloe's advice. She had told him to be patient, trying to explain the stress every bride-to-be felt as the wedding loomed nearer and how it would all go back to normal once the wedding was over.

"At least that's how I think it feels." Chloe admitted at the end. "It's not as though I've had much of a chance to enjoy getting stressed, I can't seem to find anyone who wants to settle down with me."

"So what do you want to do about the cake?" Natalia's voice interrupted his thoughts.

"Just choose whichever one you want." He suggested, then laughed as he read the text from Chloe. She had sent a picture of a sequined tee-shirt with the embroidered words 'Too posh to push (the hoover)'. *Just right for Lily's b-day!* was her accompanying message. He showed it to Natalia. "Look what Chloe's found for Mum's present."

Natalia sniffed and climbed out of bed, pulling her dressing gown on and tying the belt tightly. "You seemed to have more time for that fat blob than you do for your own fiancé."

"Chloe's not fat! She's just curvy."

Natalia continued as though not hearing, her voice conveying a combination of outrage and hurt. "And if you want any dinner you'll have to order takeaway. I've been far to busy to go shopping." She stormed out of the bedroom. Pete sighed, and wondered how the earlier euphoria had managed to disappear so effectively.

Chapter 10

"Alicia!" Mavis called up the stairs. "Phone for you. It's Josie." Alicia raced down and took the outstretched handset. Breathless from the exertion she exchanged pleasantries until Josie asked. "And how are things now between you and the gorgeous Rob?" "Fine." Alicia said cautiously noncommittally. A tense truce had been called between them, and although the verbal sparring and explosive arguments had ceased, temporarily, both were still watchful for any signs of re-ignition. It was unspoken, but it made life easier to rub along with only a slight abrasion, especially for Mavis who no longer felt trapped in the role of referee, counsellor and constant mediator. In fact Rob had even gone so far as to lend her a couple of the latest murder mystery novels when he heard her wistfully long for something other than Mavis' slushy romance.

"The reason for phoning is I need to go over to Oxford tomorrow to check out a new furniture supplier and wondered if you wanted to come along for the ride?"

"Definitely, if I'm not going to be in your way."

"Not at all. I thought I could drop you off for a wander around the shops and the covered market, and then I could meet you for lunch at Browns."

"Sounds great! I could do with some new clothes - I hadn't bargained for all this glorious weather. I can't believe we're having a proper summer." For someone who usually lived extensively in an air conditioned office, with two weeks in the Caribbean or Far East, it was a novel experience to be able to work outside in the orchard, the network cable trailing through the grass. Her wardrobe though needed some attention, she'd been living in a an old pair of Mavis' gardening shorts and some tee-shirts she'd left at home years ago. She might not be going into the office every day but that was no reason to let her standards slip.

"I'll pick you about nine tomorrow morning." Josie instructed as she rang off with a cheery goodbye.

Returning back to the kitchen, Mavis was still sitting at the table, her small glasses balanced on the end of her nose.

"Josie's invited me along to Oxford tomorrow – you don't mind if I go do you?"

Mavis tried not show any surprise at being consulted. "Of course not. Have you got any work on though?"

Alicia shook her head. "I phoned into work this morning and Simon says that the client at the clothing company I was telling you about seems really pleased with everything I've done so far. Hopefully it will mean they'll ask me to work on more of their projects."

"Sounds exciting." Mavis agreed gently squeezed her daughter in encouragement.

"They're planning a number of overseas acquisitions, so I might even get to do some travel."

"My daughter – the jet-setter." Mavis declared proudly.

Alicia ducked her head self-conscious of the praise. Then changed the subject with: "Do you want a coffee, I was just about to make one when the phone rang."

"Great. Actually the kettle's just boiled."

Awkwardly Alicia slowly used her left hand to scoop the coffee granules into the mugs, a fine trail followed the spoon where her unsteadiness had caused small landslides. It was tricky adjusting to being dependent upon her left hand. Everything took twice as long and it felt like she was doing everything back-to-front.

With infinite care she placed a cup in front of Mavis without spilling any of the hot liquid and gazed across at the printed sheets.

"What are you doing?" She indicated to the pages with a tilt of her head.

"Working out the plants Rob's going to need for his project and trying to get them ordered. But every time I get through to any of the suppliers a customer turns up and I end up having to hang up."

Examining the pages closer Alicia could see a list of plants which Rob had obviously produced, and by the side in her characteristic spidery handwriting were Mavis' notes on how many, rough size and which supplier.

"I could have a go if you want, if it's just phoning the suppliers."

"No, don't worry. You just rest and get your strength back." Mavis reassured her daughter.

"Honestly, I mean it. It can't be that difficult can it? It's just a few phone calls, and I can still manage that with my arm in plaster." She pointed out ruefully.

Mavis looked undecided, weighing up the benefits of having some help while cautious about whether the right plants would be ordered from the right suppliers. Having worked on her own for the past five years, she found relinquishing control scary. In the distance the ting-ting of the brass bell above the entrance gate could be heard faintly travelling on the still summer air. Alicia raised a questioning eyebrow to her mother and waited for the verdict.

Mavis sighed. "Here is the list of plants that Rob needs, just phone the supplier I've written by the side – all the numbers are on the back of the calendar behind the bread bin. If there are any problems just tell them I'll call them later." Again the metallic ting of the bell floated through the open window.

"Seems straight forward enough. Now go and help your customers otherwise they'll end up going to the nearest DIY centre and buying some sickly excuse of a plant." She urged.

Mavis hesitated before standing up. "Are you sure you'll be ok?" She asked anxiously.

"Mum, just go. I'll be fine."

Mavis scuttled out grabbing her thick leather gloves from the side as she did so hurrying out of the dim kitchen into the bright summer morning. Alicia shuffled the papers round and leant across to the battered breadbin to tweak out the 1988 RHS Chelsea Calendar from behind it. Sure enough the whole of the back page was covered in columns of telephone numbers. Scanning down the list Alicia was amused to see there was number for almost everything, cacti farmers through to organic compost, Mavis obviously knew someone for everything – well except mending hearts broken by a non-appearing Law Partner, there wasn't anyone listed as 'miracle worker'.

Picking up the phone she dialled the first number.

"This is Apple Trees Nursery," Her voice trembled slightly. "I'm looking for some Acers to be delivered next week if that's possible."

"It certainly is." A thick Somerset twang boomed back. "Now just give me a few details."

◆◆◆

The afternoon sun was streaming into the kitchen when Mavis and Rob walked in. The strong rays captured the floating dust motes kicked up from the dry parched earth, casting long shadows over the cabinets where piles of outstanding paperwork continued to sit patiently waiting for Mavis to deal with them before the annual visit to the accountant.   The cabinets had originally been put in by Bill, lovingly chosen when she was expecting Alicia, but today for the first time a small chink of dissatisfaction caught her unawares.   Suddenly the kitchen no longer had the pristine cupboards she had carried around in her memory, now she saw them as they were – old and tired.   A bit like herself, she thought sadly.   The style looked dated with their dark wood Formica and metal edges, and one drawer hung lopsidedly as though it had just got back from a night out on the town.   The vinyl floor was intermittently faded with tracks showing where it had worn thin from countless tramping feet.   Pushing these unwelcome thoughts to the darkest, furthest corner of her mind, she refused to dwell on it.   Having to change anything without Bill around to share the excitement and adventure didn't hold any appeal; she didn't seem to have the energy or enthusiasm to embrace updating anything at the moment.   She wondered if she ever would again.

Alicia looked up at the sound of their approach; stretching her arms and yawning, trying to relieve the stiffness that had set in from the lack of movement.   Glancing at her watch she realised that she had spent most of the day working on the plan list.   "I didn't realise what the time was." She exclaimed shifting the papers up into one pile to clear the table. "The day seems to have flown by. Does anyone else want a cup of tea?"
Mavis ushered Rob to sit down and walked over to the kettle. "Don't worry, I'll make it.   Tell me how you got on.   Is there anyone I need to phone back?"
Alicia ran her eye down the list. "Nope. I think it's all under control, everyone was really helpful. Although a couple of people are having to phone back tomorrow once they've had a chance to check what they have in stock."
Privately Rob wondered if that would mean poor Mavis would be charged extra for sub-standard plants.   The nursery suppliers were notorious for passing on their more sickly plants to naïve buyers.   As though reading his thoughts Alicia tartly said. "I told them that you would want to examine them before we paid, and I checked the prices for you Mum between suppliers so we got the best price."

"You didn't!" Mavis sounded impressed. "I never like to ask for a price if I know I'm not buying from them."

"That's why it took so long. I had to keep waiting for people to call me back. I'm not sure if you'll be able to read my writing, but I've jotted all the prices down." She passed the sheaf of papers to Mavis who paused from making the tea to look through.

"These prices look good, I've never managed to get them so low. You have written them down correctly haven't you?"

"Of course I have! I just reminded them of how long you've been using them, and suggested they might want to retain your custom in the future by being a little bit more competitive in their pricing."

"But I would never have been able to leave them." Mavis was horrified.

"Of course not, but they weren't to know that were they!" Alicia pointed out with a wicked smile.

"Let's hope they don't send us their rejects." Rob said darkly, running his huge shovel hands through his hair, anxiously imagining his client's face as their new garden died in front of their eyes. Alicia was stung at the implication.

"I did check the sizes that Mum had given me, and I did ask for the details of who to contact if we were mistakenly sent plants that couldn't be considered fit for purpose." She retorted.

"Well done love. You seem to have considered everything, doesn't she Rob." Mavis was beaming with maternal pride.

"Yes" He agreed, grudgingly wishing it hadn't been his project that Mavis had decided to use as a reconciliation tool with Alicia. As far as he could see it was just going to end in tears on Mavis' part.

"Do you want to stay for supper?" Mavis started to rummage through the fridge for something more edible than a wilted lettuce and a rind of brie.

"I'd love to, but I'm on my way to a client meeting. It was one of the visitors at the garden fete who gave me a call. Wants me to look at her garden. It seems a bit strange though, she obviously knows loads about gardening, so I'm not sure why she wants to see me."

"Probably having an old-age crisis and is just after your body." Alicia said with a hint of former spite, still rattled by his derogatory comments. "It's not as though you've got a girlfriend to worry about."

"You're looking very smart." Mavis assured him, slipping into the role of mediator, noting the pale blue short sleeved shirt and cream chinos that were totally different to his normal working attire. "I hope the lady appreciates the effort you've made."

"Somehow I know she will." He was grinning, causing his craggy face to become even more creased. "She seems to be a real character. Well thanks for organising the plants Mavis. I'll speak to you later in the week about exact delivery times." He turned awkwardly to Alicia. "See you around." In response she nodded a goodbye.

It was just the two of them, and a restful atmosphere seemed to waft over them.

"Thank you for your help today love, it's a load off of my mind I can tell you. I just hope you weren't too bored."

"Actually it was quite nice to be busy. It's boring not being able to do much. Although Rob didn't seem too impressed I'd been helping out."

"I don't know why the two of you don't get on."

"Because he's annoying, rude, stubborn, argumentative..." She ticked each fault off on a different finger.

"Some people might say the same about you." Mavis quietly pointed out. Alicia flew to defend herself, but the honesty in Mavis' face checked her, and she realised the futility of trying to defend herself against the obvious.

"Maybe." She half admitted and Mavis felt a small soaring victory, she couldn't remember the last time Alicia hadn't just launched into an argument at the smallest excuse. Looking down at the expiring salad she swept it up and unceremoniously dumped into the bin.

"After all our hard work today I reckon we deserve a slap up meal. How about heading over to The Leather Bottle for something to eat like we used to?" A picture of her parents bearing her off to the pub on a warm summer evening when she was little popped into her mind. Where had that sense of belonging dissipated to; how had it been lost? She clamped down on the intruding reminiscences of her father; it was still too painfully to think about him gone.

"Can we have scampi and chips?" She asked, in exactly the same way she had pleaded as a ten year old.

"Definitely and chocolate sponge to follow." Companionably they got ready to go out, chatting about their day.

◆◆◆

Lily heard the doorbell ring while she was still in the kitchen busily preparing a refreshing jug of Pimms. Distracted, the lime she was squeezing spurted out and straight into her eye. Howling with pain she heard the doorbell being pressed more urgently this time. "Wait a minute." She shouted. "I'm coming." Cursing her visitor for being early, she tried to wipe away the juice but instead only succeed in making it worse. Half blinded she felt her way to the front door and yanked it open. Rob was taken aback by the snarling greeting of: "You do realise you're early." That replaced the usual 'hello', and the alarming sight of the odd eye make-up and bloodshot pupil. Starting to step backwards in retreat he began to apologise and was determining whether a sedate walk or swift sprint was the safest option when Lily suddenly beckoned him in. Cautiously he stepped through the front door into the large atrium with dark parquet flooring that was furnished with what Rob guessed were expensive antiques. He followed behind the swishing long skirt and floaty scarf walking into the kitchen where Lily fished around for a paper towel to try and mop up the tears that were gushing as a result of the juice.

"Erm, I don't mean to pry, but is there something wrong with your eye?" Rob asked eventually, unable to bear the look of the bloodstained eyeball much longer.

"I got lime juice in it." Lily complained as she dabbed away with a piece of kitchen roll.

"Well I think you need something more effective than that. Come here." He took her hand and led her over to the sink and turned the tap on. "Put your head over the sink and I'll wash it for you." He instructed as though she was a young child, and obediently she bent her head forward. With the utmost care he began to gently douse the eye, surprising Lily that a man of his stature could be so careful with his administrations. The stinging pain began to recede and shortly she was able to blink without it feeling as though a thousand tiny scorpions were stinging her lid. With dexterity he turned off the tap and then as Lily stood up, he tilted her face towards him and slowly wiped away the water and running mascara so that she ended up with one eye fully made up and the other looking denude and startled. They were within a few inches of each other, and Lily took full opportunity to gaze at his features and enjoy the proximity of his muscles. In any other situation she would have expected the man to sweep her into a full embrace, and while it was a pleasant thought, she didn't want to jeopardise her plan. Stepping backwards with an artful laugh to put some space between Rob and her raging hormones, she hoped Chloe would appreciate the sacrifice made on her behalf. The thought of her young friend immediately chilled any ardour, and she reverted to her usual chatty self, urging Rob to pour them both a Pimms so they could take them out to the garden.

The garden was a riot of colour, it looked like the palette of an over enthusiastic artist, dabs of bright colours intermingling with one another. It was based along the lines of a cottage garden with large blowsy flowerbeds throwing up hundreds of happy smiling faces towards the sun. What stopped it looking too twee were the vast tracks of lawn that intersected the beds, carving their way through, leading the casual walker onwards with the half-promise of the unknown. Rob and Lily strolled along the grass avenues, occasionally Lily would stop and remove a dead head or pluck an incongruous sprouting weed, past the winding stream and decaying decorative bridge. They talked generally about plants, their favourites and their failures, of the changes in fashion and the seemingly unexhaustive passion for decking, water features and Japanese gardens. Finally they turned towards the house and Lily steered him over to the neglected patch of earth between the house and the garage block.

"So who designed this garden for you originally?" Rob asked.

"I did." Lily said simply but with pride. "Of course it hasn't always been like this. I did make a few mistakes along the way." She cringed at the thought of the thousand begonias and bedding plants she had regimentedly planted only to have the whole area look like some municipal park.

"You've certainly got an eye for detail. The way you've got the essence of a natural cottage garden, but with the linear structure that keeps tempting you to explore." He sipped his Pimms, enjoying the fizzy fruity taste, and thoughtfully said. "But I don't understand why you need me. I hate to do myself out of work, but you seem more than capable of designing." Lily eyed him appraisingly, wondering if he was just trying to soft talk her into declaring his designs were so much better than anything she could have come up with. Did he, she wondered, have an ego that needed constant massaging. If he did she'd have to warn

Chloe. "It is a funny area though." Rob continued musingly as though speaking half-formed thoughts. "It's almost like a garden within a garden, because you can't see it from the house. Is that why you didn't include it with the rest of the work on the garden?"

"Sort of. It's so much more secluded here, and its far more shady, I thought I'd end up with moss for lawns and no living plants apart from brambles."

Rob assessed the space with a professional eye, it was about twenty foot square, hemmed in by the side wall of the garage block, the corner of the house and a row of tall horse chestnuts. The grass looked flaccid and the earth felt crumbly underfoot. He couldn't think of many encouraging points.

"It's certainly a challenge." He declared, rubbing his hand through his cropped hair as though hoping to stimulate his imagination.

"I've been toying with ideas on and off for the past ten years, but somehow I've never managed to come up with anything that seemed to fit."

Rob pulled out his notepad and made a few sketches to help him remember the plot once he was at home.

"Have you thought about an Oriental style garden? That wouldn't need much planting." He mused, scratching behind his ear thoughtfully with his biro as he envisaged gravel broken up by small square blocks holding red leafed Acers, their fronds casting dancing shadows over the a pool running through the centre. "And it would be very peaceful."

Lily scoffed. "I don't need peaceful!" She threw her hand to indicate the sprawling house. "I rattle round in this every day by myself. The one thing I don't need to create more of is solitude."

He wrinkled his brow as he concentrated, but no sudden flash of inspiration would come. Disappointed with himself he put the book away. "I'll try and come up with some designs." He promised, watching as Lily kept checking her watch.

"What was that?" She lied looking towards the house. She had been expecting Chloe fifteen minutes ago, if she didn't arrive soon then the whole plan was going to fall to pieces and she'd end up having to take both Barbara and Chloe to the Drayton Beauchamp WI meeting. Just as Rob began to speak again they heard a car pull up.

"You've obviously got company, I'd better get going." Rob said politely, preparing to move.

"No, stay where you are I'm sure it's no-one." Lily fibbed. They heard the slow footfall of footsteps on the gravel crunching away, then a figure appeared round the corner. A middle-aged woman with short grey hair dressed in a matching coral jacket and skirt. Lily's heart sunk. The plan she had so carefully devised was falling apart as each minute progressed. Forcing herself to show some natural pleasure at seeing her friend, she gaily greeted Barbara with an air kiss and linking her arm through her guest's walked back to where Rob was standing. At the back of her mind a struggle was forming, torn between anger and concern for Chloe, which she didn't dare show; instead she chatted and regaled stories non-stop for fifteen minutes, after which her energy began to sap and Rob and Barbara began to fidget.

"Lily we really ought to be going." Barbara gently chided. "We can't be late for the guest speaker."

Taking his cue Rob politely began saying his goodbyes. Stricken with disappointment Lily followed them back into the house, leaving their empty glasses in the kitchen and walking to the front door. Bending down to pick up her handbag, Lily opened the door still crouching and came face to knee with a long cotton skirt. Glancing up she saw Chloe's beaming face.

"I'm sooo sorry I'm late. I had the tenant from hell looking over the penthouse in the Old Windmill. You will never believe what happened." She brandished a bottle of wine. "Let's open this and I can tell you all about it, I mean it was..." Catching sight of Barbara and Rob behind Lily's crouching figure her flow of speech ceased. "Oh I didn't realise you had company." She finished lamely.

Lily straightened herself up. "Hello Chloe. What a surprise." She said unconvincingly.

"No it isn't. You invited me over for dinner. Remember?"

"Did I?" Lily replied vaguely.

"Yes." Chloe pressed. "You said wear something smart."

Barbara intercepted. "Lily if we don't get going we are going to miss introducing tonight's speaker." Lily watched Chloe's face fall as it became clear she was being stood up, and her resolve almost weakened.

"Well I could come with you and Barbara." Chloe suggested hopefully.

"No you can't." Lily blurted out as Barbara opened her mouth to accept, putting on her most beguiling smile she turned slowly to Rob. "I appear to have made some mistake this evening. I don't suppose you would take pity on us and take Chloe out for something to eat, especially as she has made such an effort to get dressed up." She fluttered her eyelashes at him and he couldn't help notice the twinkle in her eyes. Inside he let out a small laugh, he realised she was setting them up. There was no way, he thought, that a sassy lady like that would ever double book. He'd bet his life that she would be able to keep several lovers on the go without ever slipping up, but he decided to play along, the recollection of Alicia's comments about the lack of love life niggled him, and judging from the low cut top Chloe was wearing he could always sit back and admire the view.

"Of course, it would be a pleasure." He stepped past Lily and taking Chloe's elbow lightly steered her towards her car. "I'll be in touch with the designs, although presumably they aren't too pressing now." He said mockingly as he waved goodbye. "Follow me to the pub." He told Chloe when they reached her mini.

"Oh no I can't." Exclaimed Chloe embarrassed at the way Lily had foisted her onto this poor unsuspecting man.

"Have you got anything else planned?"

"No of course I haven't." Indignity rang in her voice. "I was supposed to be having dinner at Lily's."

"Then let's both go and get something to eat. I don't mean to hurry you but I've missed lunch and I'm absolutely starving. The strength of that Pimms would have felled an elephant, and being on an empty stomach isn't helping. So let's get going." He was so plainly going over the top to conquer her embarrassment that she couldn't help giving a nervous giggle and agreeing to a quick bite to eat at the pub.

The two cars drove out of Lily's gates leaving dust trails hanging above the gravel in their wake. The remaining two older women got into Barbara's Peugeot and buckled up before Barbara turned on Lily and with a questioning arched eyebrow asked: "So are you going to tell me what that little charade was all about?"

Lily had the grace to look discomforted but tried a nonchalant "I've no idea what you mean." In case she could get away with it.

"Lily Sherborne! I've known you more years than I care to remember and I have never known you to forget a single date. You're famous for having the memory of an elephant, and a skin as equally as thick."

Lily tried to look affronted but failed. "Am I?"

"You know you are. So what was that farce all about, because I don't believe you actually want to go to this WI meeting about trekking through Wales any more than I do. So what was it all about?"

The tension of the planning became too much, Lily knew she was dying to tell someone all about her plan, after all if she was playing Cupid she wanted the recognition.

"It's a long story, but it started with Chloe falling out of the window, only she didn't, she was saved by Rob. I didn't know it was Rob at the time, all I knew was Chloe was obviously smitten by him. Then she and I met him at the garden fete and the poor lamb went scarlet every time he spoke, so I knew she was never going to do anything about it. I decided that if they were ever to get together it would be through a little nudge, so I planned for a 'chance' meeting to set them up. It was easy really. I had Rob over to discuss garden designs and then organised for Chloe to turn up only to find…" she paused dramatically, "that I had double booked, at which point I appeal to Rob's chivalrous nature not to abandon Chloe to an evening of TV meals, and instead whisk her off to the pub."

"So you've just used me to help you play Cupid?" Barbara pointed out drily.

"If I remember rightly your mother used the same ploy to get you and Joe together, and that it was me who was left helping her deliver the Christmas edition of the Drayton newsletter." Lily reminded her playfully. Barbara conceded with a smile at the recollection.

"So why didn't Chloe just ask this gardening chap out if she liked him?"

"Haah, you know what it's like when you're young and have a crush. All that turmoil of emotion. Does he like you, will he go out for a drink, or will he stand you up? All that agonising over possible rejection. She would only gaze from afar, she'd never make the first move, and in all probability end up with someone like Dave again. I just gave her a helping hand."

"Do you think she'll thank you for it?"

"Probably not." Lily said airily, "But as long as she finds herself a decent boyfriend it doesn't matter."

"I thought you wanted her and Pete to get together though."

"I do. I kept telling Pete that she was an ideal girlfriend for him when he employed her, but there was no way he'd listen to me. Then that strumpet of a thing charged into his life and poor Chloe never stood a chance."

They drove on in silence to the Georgian fronted town hall that dominated Drayton Beauchamp's market square. The clock tower clanged echoed by the parish church peal of bells.

"I suppose we have to go in." Lily said reluctantly as they parked the car.

"Yes we jolly well do." Barbara exploded. "And in repayment you can make mine a very large gin and tonic after the meeting." She added forcefully.

◆◆◆

The Leather Bottle was popular with the locals, it was just far enough off the beaten track not to be spoilt by the onslaught of tourists each summer. Rather than undergo any major redecoration, each subsequent landlord had merely patched up and made do, so that the decoration veered from the original horse brasses through to cutting edge lights by Conran. The huge fireplace which dominated one wall had an array of flowers in the grate to soften the cold bleakness, but without the flickering flames it was as though the heart of the building had been unnaturally stilled. The barman was a ruddy faced chap who still went shooting with the farmers and played cards with the commuting stockbrokers. He had lived in the pub all his life, his parents having been the previous landlords. To Len it was the ideal world, he had never been an early bird, so to have a job that didn't start until mid-morning, gave you time off each afternoon and meant your friends were always calling in for a drink and chat couldn't be sniffed at. He surveyed the pub, the garden was full of people enjoying an after work drink and a quick supper. Inside it was less packed, only the old die-hards who hadn't converted to the idea of enjoying the sun, and associated it with long hard working days in the fields, were scratching around inside. The sound of the latch caught their attention and they watched as Rob and Chloe entered. Len determined they were obviously on their first date, after all the years he had spent behind the bar serving stuttering couples he could spot the signs a mile off, stilted conversation, checking what drinks needed to be ordered, polite vying for paying for drinks. They ordered and headed out towards the beckoning sunshine. He saw them select a central table – well that was unusual, normally the first-daters liked to hide themselves away at the edges so they could selfishly indulge in cutting off the rest of the world. He smiled indulgently, the sun always brought out the romantic in him.

"I'm sorry about this." Chloe apologised yet again. "I don't know what got into Lily. Honestly she can really take the biscuit." Her mood was a combination of excruciating embarrassment and a soaring joy, which wasn't a terribly comfortable combination.
"Don't worry about it, we're here now. So how about you tell me a bit about yourself, after all as my landlord's agent you probably know everything about me already." A sudden image of Rob in his shower popped uncalled into her mind, momentarily she was distracted by the vision.
"Sorry, what were you saying?" She said willing her imagination to stay under control. "Oh yes, about me." She wrinkled her nose as she considered it, causing tiny fine lines to appear on her brow. "I've been working for Lily and Pete for the past three years, I'd been doing various jobs since leaving school and I never thought I'd end up working as a letting agent. In fact if I hadn't gone into Sherborne and Sherborne's offices to plead about not paying my rent when I was made redundant then it might never have happened. As it was they were interviewing for a new agent, and there was a muddle over why I was there, and somehow Lily offered me a job."
"It must be quite interesting looking round all those properties."
"It is." She enthused. "You see completely different sides to people, we have one lady who dresses really demurely and is incredibly shy, and yet when you see her flat it's full of leopard skin and mirrors. And working with Pete is great. He's such an easy going boss. He never complains when I'm late in because I've had a heavy night on the tiles." She laughed and then worrying she was coming across as an irresponsible lush, quickly put her glass of wine down.
"Do you live locally?"
"Yes, here in Drayton Beauchamp. I rent the flat above the office which is really handy."
"And do you live there with your boyfriend?" She shook her head, dispelling thoughts of Dave and his disastrous temporary co-residence.
"With flat mates?"
Again she shook her head. "Just me." Which she thought was the perfect moment for him to suggest pooling resources and moving in together to share the rest of their lives. Instead he

went for the more obvious: "I reckon it's better that way. I'm not sure I could share my space with anyone else now – too many bad habits." He grinned self-depreciatingly. "I bet you feel the same though."

Chloe nodded, a fixed false smiled welded on her face, while inside she screamed 'No, what I really want is too find my soulmate!'.

One of the waiting staff wandered through the tables, a plate of sausages and mashed potato balanced in each hand.

"That looks like ours." Chloe said, grateful for the opportunity to change the subject.

"Two bangers and mash?" The pimply teenager enquired, and placed the plates, complete with a jug of thick onion gravy in front of them with a plonk.

Behind them Alicia and Mavis were getting ready to leave when Alicia spotted Rob. "Don't look now, but your favourite garden designer is sitting over there with a lady friend." She hissed. Immediately Mavis swung her head round and peered through her glasses intently. "So much for subtlety." Alicia murmured as Mavis turned back. "Funny elderly widow." She pointed out, while inside she was trying to quell the growing jealousy that Rob seemed to be able to attract someone, while Zac continued to ignore her.

"No wonder he was so well turned out; I haven't seen him looking that smart for a long time." Mavis took her glasses off and popped them back on top of her head where they nestled in the short grey curls. "So what have you got planned for the rest of the week?"

"Let me just check my blackberry. Oh, surprise, surprise, nothing." Alicia's voice was bitter.

"You wouldn't want to carry on giving me a helping hand would you?" Mavis asked tentatively, watching for the tell-tell signs of rolling eyes, or a smirk that shouted "you can't be serious" but despite expecting a volcanic eruption nothing materialised. Instead Alicia looked thoughtful, pondering the proposal.

"What would I have to do? I don't think I'd be much use with only one hand at any planting."

"Oh no, nothing like that." Mavis quickly assured her. "I thought you might be able to help me sort out my paperwork. I've got the dreaded visit to the accountant soon and I keep putting it off."

"But I don't know anything about running a business." Alicia was horrified. "What could I do?"

"It's simple really, you just need to put all the receipts in one pile, invoices in another and sort by date. That's all I do." Mavis gave what she hoped was an encouraging smile. "It would be a real help."

"Alright." Alicia agreed slowly. "But if I make a hash of it, you're not allowed to shout at me." She made Mavis promise. They finished their drinks and stood up to go.

"If we hurry back you'll be able to watch old Alan Titchy-doda's friend on the tv." Mavis beamed at the thought of a whole hour admiring the physique of the plants. They wove their way through the garden, Mavis calling a cheery 'hello there' which made Rob turned his head so quickly there was an audible crack. "Busy with work still?" Alicia asked in a pointed saccharine-sweet tone. Chloe smiled a polite greeting and Rob, momentarily at a loss for words, stared at the two of them. "Well we'd better not interrupt your dinner." Alicia gave Mavis a little nudge to encourage her to start moving. "Enjoy your meal."

As they crossed the road back to the nursery Mavis demanded to know why Alicia had made her hurry off. "I was hoping he'd give us an introduction. She must be a new girlfriend. I'm just surprised he never mentioned her."

"He's hardly like to is he? You know how difficult it is to have a private life in this village. He probably just wanted to keep it quiet." Alicia hazarded. Secretly she thought they looked the most unlikely couple, the girl had such an open and honest face that it was clear she would never be able to stand up to Rob and his moods. He would walk all over her with his great muddy gardening boots, but then you could never tell what attracted people. She knew deep down that Zac wouldn't ever consider leaving Marcie but she had fantasised he would. Even now she clung to the hope that he would get in contact to see how she was, but he remained obstinately remote. She thought of Matty and Tom wondering if they had managed to sort things out. Everyone seemed to be having problems with relationships at the moment, just occasionally it would be good if life could be a little simpler.

Chapter 11

Matty lay curled up in a foetal ball, her eyes screwed tightly shut so they wouldn't open instinctively when Tom finally came to bed. She felt so alone, cut off from everyone else and bobbing around on a storm tossed sea. She could smell the crisp clean cotton of the pillowcase and tried to force herself back to childhood, to the comforting memories of lying snugly in bed after being bathed on a Sunday evening, but solace refused to come. Below she could hear Tom moving around in the sitting room. Inside mounted a growing tension, waiting for Tom to appear that precluded sleep. There had been a stalemate situation for over a week; pervading the air with its rankled hostility, two hurt people no longer able to communicate. The spark had been an innocent mistake. Like a tiny stone in a puddle, a barely audible plop as it entered, but one that wide spreading ripples reverberating through many lives.

The new assistant at the local chemist, recognising Barbara, and knowing Matty had said she couldn't hang around to collect a prescription, had kindly suggested Barbara could collect her daughter-in-law's prescription for her. Barbara had willingly agreed, and not thinking any more about it, handed it to Tom over the lunch table for him to take home to Matty. Had Barbara handed the innocuous paper bag over directly as intended then life would have carried on in the same rut as before. Instead it become the ember that lit the latent dissatisfaction that had been growing over the past six months, fuelled by undisclosed dreams. For Tom all his hopes of their planned family came crashing down about him as he idly opened the bag. Even Pandora could not have felt such an impact when curiosity had encouraged her to delve into the box. While Tom did not discover envy or greed or famine, he did discover rejection. He had marvelled how the tiny innocent pills could have wiped out his ambitions so effectively. Anger rose up at being the cuckold husband, having his wife pretending to be trying for a family when really she was doing everything she could to prevent it. He had sat at the kitchen table waiting for Matty to come home, oblivious to time, grinding a fist into the palm of his hand. He had no logical thoughts of what he wanted to say, all he knew was that he wanted Matty to hurt as much as him, to feel betrayed like he did. He heard the car pull up outside, the back door open and her cheery voice call out. "Tom, are you here?" She walked into the kitchen with a smile "You're home early. Shall we go for a quick drink at The Kings Arms, I hear Tina's got some new ale in you could try?" Her voice died away as she saw her husband's face, the stony expression. Not understanding, she looked puzzled until Tom flicked the packet of contraceptive pills that sat on top of the table.

"Oh." Matty slumped into a chair, feeling as though she had been winded. "Where did you get those from?"

"That oh-so-helpful assistant at the Chemists gave them to Mum because everyone knows how busy you are these days." There was an uncomfortable silence, the clock ticked in the background as Tom continued to glare accusingly at her, and Matty tried to marshal her thoughts. Eventually he spoke, his voice sounding harsh against the silent backdrop.

"So how long has this been going on? When did you start taking these again?"

"Don't Tom." Matty shook her head, not meeting his eye. He slammed a fist down on the table, making the furniture jump with its ferocity. Looking up suddenly, Matty watched warily, noticing his jaw was clenched tightly causing a small vein to pulse.

"Don't play games with me Matty. I asked you how long you've been taking these."

She dropped eye contact, and after a small pause admitted. "I've never stopped taking them."

He was taken back "But how could you? I'd have seen you."

"I hid them in a box of tampons. I didn't think you'd ever look in there." He turned and went out of the room, wrenching the door open and storming up the stairs to the bathroom, reappearing with the packet of half used pills which he held out accusingly. "How could you?" He demanded. "How could you lie to me? After all that talk of starting a family, of having a baby together. God how could you? You must have been laughing so much at me when I kept asking each month whether you were pregnant. Every time we had sex I kept hoping that this time we would be lucky. Whereas you knew that we wouldn't be – because of you. How could you do that to someone you were supposed to be in love with?"

"Because I'm not ready for a baby." Matty blurted out. She wished she could finds the words to eloquently explain how she felt to Tom, but they refused to come, it had always been the way; articulating her concerns should have been easy, but Tom's assumption that they both wanted a baby had always clouded the discussion. Any words of caution she had made had been brushed aside as natural anxieties, nothing to worry about.

"But we talked about it. We agreed that now was a good time to start."

"No. You decided that it was a good time. I don't want to have a baby yet. I'm not ready. I feel too young. There's so much more that I want to do with my life before I'm tied down looking after something that only lives to puke, scream and eat."

"So what exactly do you want to do with your life then Matty that takes priority over starting a family?" His voice was heavy with sarcasm. "Because the last time I checked you were a farmer's wife with a dead-end job, and no prospects of changing. Or are you trying to tell me that you don't want to be married any more. Is this what's it's all about?"

"No of course not! Don't make this into something else."

"Then perhaps you'd better tell me your grand plan. You've obviously been planning something for a while if you're still taking the pill."

Matty's innards plummeted into a basement of despair. How could she try and explain the tangled thoughts and muddled dreams.

"There isn't, any grand plan I mean. I don't know what I want. I just know I need to be doing something else. Something is missing from my life, I don't know what it is, it just feels like I've lost something in here." She drew her hand to her chest as though to show him a void.

"I don't understand you Matty, I really don't. Most women would kill to be you. To be in what I thought was a happy marriage, not having to go out and work, having the chance to bring up a whole heap of babies and not having to worry about juggling a job with family commitments." Tom's voice broke with emotion.

"But you don't understand." Matty rallied.

"Too right I don't!" Tom exploded. "I don't understand why you've been lying to me for the past six months; I don't pretend to understand why you are constantly discarding everything I want; of why when you are so busy you insist on working when you don't need to…"

"But it's not like that." She tried to interrupt to explain herself.

"Save it. I'm really not interested." And with that he stormed out of the kitchen, slamming the door shut behind him.

He had stayed out to the early morning and when eventually he had come to bed Matty could smell whiskey on his breath. She had tried to lie close to him, her hand tentatively touching his attempting to mend the broken bridges, but he had merely turned away from her, making his feelings clear. Since that point the communication had deteriorated further, so that they hardly spoke to one another. Matty couldn't believe what had happened to them, how quickly everything had fallen apart, and with no obvious way to resolve the problems. It seemed the man she had married had vanished completely leaving her with a distant uninterested stranger. How had it all gone so wrong, she wondered, this was never supposed to happen?

Chapter 12

Lily swept into the office in a blaze of chiffon, scarves trailing in her wake. Brazenly she walked over to Chloe's desk and plopped herself down in the chair. Chloe, having seen her arrive, refused any acknowledgement and simply carried on typing up her property records studiously. After five gruellingly long minutes Lily couldn't contain herself any longer, her inquisitiveness fizzing up like a shaken can of pop.

"Well?" she enquired hopefully but the telephone rang and Chloe smoothly answered in her professional work voice with: "Good morning Sherborne & Sherborne, how can I help you?" She talked away to the potential tenant discussing the properties currently available while continuing to completely ignore Lily jiggling vigorously in her seat. As the call came to an end Lily's jiggling was so intense that Chloe snapped. "If you need to go to the toilet just go!"

"Of course I don't need the loo, silly," Lily said beaming, glad she finally had Chloe's attention. "I just want to hear about last night."

"Huh!" Chloe laughed hollowly. "After your behaviour last night you're lucky you're even allowed in this office."

"I own this office." Lily was calm and poised.

"Well bully for you." Chloe said flicking her hair and turning back to her computer to start typing again.

"Oh don't be like this Chloe." Lily wheedled. Chloe carried on typing as though she hadn't heard her. Deciding there was nothing quite like bribery Lily carried on: "I've booked a table at The King's Arms for us."

"I'm not hungry." Chloe said continuing to stare at the screen.

"But I want to make it up to you." Although her tone was apologetic privately Lily thought Chloe should have been thanking her after all that planning. "I know I behaved awfully last night but I just wanted you to have some fun."

Chloe spun round on her chair so quickly she almost toppled off. Grabbing hold of the desk she managed to right herself. "You made me feel such a fool."

"Sorry. I didn't mean to. I thought I was just giving a little helping hand by organising Rob to take you out. Doing your love life a favour."

"Some favour." But the hostility was draining away, now that she had been able to rant some of her indignation, there was a growing desire to at least recount the evening with someone.

"So it didn't go very well?" Lily was anxious at any embarrassment she had caused.

"Well, it wasn't as bad as it could have been." Chloe said off hand, leaning across for her handbag. "I suppose you'd better take me to The King's Arms; I've got to talk to someone about it." Before adding ungenerously "And you're better than no-one." Lily linked her arm through Chloe's companionably, smiling to herself, it seemed that she could still give Cupid a run for his money.

The King's Arms was filled with ladies lunching with friends. Tina had devised a lunchtime menu that cut out carbs and concentrated on wine. Chloe loved eating here with Lily, she could pretend that she was one of these women with a designer handbag, photogenic children and hard-working husband.

"We'll have two small chicken Caesar salads and a large bottle of Pinot Grigio." Lily ordered as they were seated. "Now, tell me everything. How did it go?"

Chloe tried to look cool and mysterious, but her face broke into a huge cheesy grin which rather gave the game away.

"Oh Lily!" she dreamily recalled the evening. "He's gorgeous. I can't believe he actually went along with your plan. He was such a perfect gentleman. He insisted on paying for the meal. I even got a goodnight kiss."

Lily's antenna started to twitch, this more like it. She fondly recalled her first dates with all their sexual tension and promise.

"So was he a good kisser?"

"It was only a gentlemanly peck of the cheek." Chloe laughingly protested.

"Oh right." Lily tried to keep the enthusiasm in her voice, but her brow automatically furrowed. She had thought there could be deep depths of ardour within the rugged frame, she hadn't anticipated someone who was reserved, Rob had come across as the alpha-male rather than the slow thoughtful type.

"It was only the first time we met up really." Chloe said, desperately clinging onto the vestiges of her dream.

"Of course it was." Lily agreed. "He was probably just acting the gentleman. I bet next time you'll have the full works. There is going to be a next time isn't there?" Surely there had to be a next time after all this planning. "Did he suggest meeting up again?"

"Well not exactly. He said no doubt we'd see each other on rent day, and we talked about seeing that new film that's coming out, but he didn't ask for my number." Chloe dropped her head into her hands. "He's not going to ask me out again is he?"

"Of course he is." Lily lied enthusiastically. "The pair of you looked great together, how could he not want to see you again. You're pretty, and smart, and… and have a great boss."

"I hope so. He is gorgeous in a grizzly bear kind of way." Chloe sighed in ecstasy as she relived the evening yet again like watching a favourite movie, of how he had pulled off her sun glasses looking at her eyes; the gentle hand on the small of her back to guide her as they had walked out of the pub; laughing at a shared joke.

It was obvious to Lily that her young friend was infatuated, now all they had to do was wait for him to call. Jumping into her car preparing to go home, she suddenly remembered the cardigan left behind by Barbara. Winding down the window she pushed the white plastic bag into Chloe's arms with instructions to drop it into Matty's office that afternoon before leaning her head out of the window to also shout "And let me know when Prince Charming calls. I want my commission for this one!"

Left alone on the pavement with the bag clamped to her chest, she thought longingly of Rob. Although she had been enthusiastic to Lily about the evening, a small chill fear sat in her stomach. Would he call? What made it worse was the fact he was the ideal man, all rough and tough, making a girl feel secure and protected. She had even practised writing her name on the steamed up mirror this morning "Chloe Williams", only to blush frantically and rub it furtively away so no one would see, even though she was the only one around. Lily was right, they did make a good couple; they could set up home together – there was a sweet cottage for rent the other side of Drayton Beauchamp, and she could cook hearty stews while he would transform the garden and lug in logs so they could lie together in front of a roaring fire on the winter evenings, the curtains firmly shutting out the drab winter gloom. And they would have a baby, a beautiful baby boy, with Rob's brown and eyes and wiry mane of rebellious hair.

Impulsively she grabbed her mobile and breathlessly waited as she rang Rob's number, defiantly telling herself that a modern woman shouldn't have to wait for a guy to call. No way! In this day and age women could have it all. There were enough magazines spouting girl-power, so she was going to take her future in hand and be in control. If she wanted Rob then she had to make some of the running. As he answered she took a deep breath, thanked him for the great evening, and wondering if he was free for a drink later in the week. It was easy – she had a date with him! She was definitely on the way to becoming an official girlfriend; Rob Williams was going to be hers.

◆◆◆

Chloe walked into Saunders Engineering later that afternoon on a bubble of air, buoyed up by the excitement of the forthcoming date. She was so happy that she decided to ignore the resentful stare of the receptionist, and even to forgive her the fashion faux pas of whiskers and unplucked eyebrows. Cheerfully she asked to see Matty and when the dragon like figure responded coldly that workers weren't supposed to have personal visits during working hours, Chloe had pointed her finger to the clock now showing five:thirty-five and once again requested to see Matty. The discussion had signs of becoming protracted and irascible but luckily Matty had appeared in reception, hurrying to meet up with Alicia.

"Hallooo." Chloe called, waggling her fingers in a friendly wave. Matty looked blankly for a moment then recognising her walked over. "Have you got a moment? I'm returning something."

"Actually do you mind walking and talking?" She grabbed Chloe's arm and wheeled her round to the door. "I really have got to be going; I'm meeting up with someone and I'm already late." Chloe was propelled by Matty through the door and out onto the street before she could answer, whereupon she was forced to half-jog to keep up. "Sorry about this but I thought I'd be out of work by five, so I'm running late as it is."

"No trouble." Chloe panted, gasping for breath, her feet were being pinched by her new shoes and an unbecoming moustache of sweat was beading her upper lip.

"In here." Matty dived off to the left and into the familiar doors of Zanzibar. Chloe hesitate outside, the hip and trendy place, with its crowds of tanned women and arrogant men intimidated her.

"Come on." Matty darted back out and once again grabbed her arm, pulling her through the throng. Slowly the two of them wove their way through the crowd, stopping every so often so Matty could look around for Alicia. They finally met up along the end of the bar where Alicia and a jug of Long Island Iced Tea cocktail sat.

"I hate work." Matty declared as she scrambled onto the bar stool. Pour me a drink – I need one."

Chloe stood self-consciously looking on, now that Alicia and Matty were sitting on the only two bar stools drinking their cocktails she felt like a very awkward spare part. Wondering if they would even notice if she crept away home, she was turning to go, planning to curl up with an episode of Sex in the City and a bar of chocolate when Matty handed her a glass and poured a generous slug of cocktail into it.

"Here you deserve this after that route march. Cheers!" They all clinked glasses, Chloe taking a tentative sip as Matty drained her glass in one.

"Chloe do you know Alicia? Alicia this is Chloe, her boss is friends with Barbara. Alicia's an old school friend, who usually resides in London as an extremely successful lawyer, but who's temporarily staying here because of..." She gave the plaster cast a playful tap. "Chloe was at the office when I was leaving, so I brought her along." Matty explained. ""What were you doing at Saunders?"

"I was just trying to return this." She held up the crinkled plastic bag she'd been holding on to. "Barbara left it at Lily's yesterday, and Lily asked if I would bring it over to you."

"That was kind. Yes of course I'll give it back to Barbara." She took the bag and dropped it down by her handbag.

Chloe became aware of Alicia staring at her, and wondered if the sweat she had tried to furtively wipe away had smudged her lipstick.

"Is something wrong?"

"No; it's just I'm sure I've seen you before." Alicia closed her eyes, trying to recall, then suddenly opened her eyes and clapped her hands. "You're the girl who had dinner with Rob!" Chloe's already red cheeks turned crimson and two dimples appeared. "I recognise you now; I saw the two of you at The Leather Bottle. So you're his new girlfriend." Alicia shook her head. "I have to ask – what do you see in him. He's always so rude."

"He's not at all." Chloe rushed to his defence. "He's kind, and funny and attractive."

"This is Rob Williams we're talking about isn't it? Mr Irritable himself."

"Who is this?" Matty demanded, not wanting to be left out of the conversation, the last thing she needed was to be left along with her thoughts.

"Rob Williams, the landscape gardener who works occasionally with my mother. You met him at the garden open day."

"Oohh yes. The one who looks as though he's carved out of Welsh granite, all hard and craggy." She turned, visibly impressed to Chloe. "Nice one, he's quite a catch." Chloe twinkled at the acknowledgement, ignoring Alicia as she put two fingers down her throat saying. "How can you say that he's the most infuriating, touchy, uncouth, tactless man I've ever met?"

"Oh no!" Matty disagreed. "I think he's like a real life Mellors. I wouldn't mind him tending to my herbaceous borders!"

"Hardly." Alicia retorted. "More like David Mellor."

Causing Chloe to grin and giggle. "Perhaps I'd better order a Chelsea strip then."

Matty looked at her in solidarity and two faces grinned back conspiratorially at Alicia. "Yes;" They agreed, "He's gorgeous."

By the end of the evening all three were propping each other up, giggling wildly at their own jokes and working their way through the complete cocktail list. When closing time came, it took the two barmen ten minutes to persuade the trio to leave, and then only because they bribed a taxi to take them away. It had been a drink-fuelled fest of emotional outpouring; Matty vacillating between wanting more out of life and wanting to go back to how things had been before with Tom; Chloe of admitting how much she wanted to have a baby when Matty retold the story of Tom discovering she was still on the pill; and Alicia complaining about Rob's obnoxious behaviour, of missing London and Zac. With all that anguish it had rather surprisingly not spiralled into a morbid affair, instead it had been riotously cathartic.

The taxi dropped Chloe off at her flat above the office; spilling the contents of her handbag out onto the pavement as she tried to get out, Matty and Alicia had burst out laughing, only to 'shussshh' each other so they didn't wake the neighbours. Chloe happily began picking up items, only to have them fall out of the still gaping bag. With a long suffering sigh the taxi driver sensing this could go on all night, helped Chloe shuffle everything up and clasp the bag shut so she could let herself into the flat.

By the time the taxi pulled up outside Apple Trees Nursery, Alicia and Matty had started to doze. Alicia woke with a start as the car pulled up, a primeval instinct of recognition waking her. Tiredly she hugged Matty goodnight before weaving a path through the headlights to the backdoor. It didn't take much longer to get to the farm cottage luckily; Matty was beginning to find it difficult to keep her eyes open and she desperately needed a wee. Through squinting eyes she fumbled around for the fare and finally she was inside the cottage.

It hadn't occurred to her to wonder why all the lights were on. In her hazy state she slipped off her shoes to quietly tiptoe across the stone floor to the stairs; so intent was she on reaching the bathroom that she didn't notice when the kitchen door opened and Tom stood glowering; illuminated by the light within. She was halfway up the stair when she heard. "Where have you been?" She froze and then cautiously turned round.
"Erm. Out." She offered helpfully
"And you didn't think to let me know?" Matty's brain fuzzily tried to recall the afternoon's events. She could remember being so angry with Tom for his ongoing hostility that she had begged Alicia to meet up after work, and she had planned to text Tom, but she couldn't remember actually doing it. She knew that she had meant to, but it obviously hadn't happened. A small chill of realisation ran through her, but instead of her usual apologetic self, the drink made her defensive. While her apology would have helped to provide a soothing balm, her response was in fact a tart: "Why should I?" that only acted to inflame the situation.
"Because I'm your husband, because it's gone midnight and I was worried about you. Hell Matty, who wouldn't be if their wife didn't return home after work without some prior warning." He took a step towards her. "I've been phoning round our friends since nine o'clock, but no-one knew where you were. What was I supposed to think? So what were you doing?"
"I met up with Alicia."
He thumped the wall. "I should have known that she'd be involved. She's proved nothing but trouble since she came back."

Matty was stung at the attack on her friend, rallying with. "She's a good pal; at least she listens to me. Not like some."

"And what's that supposed to mean?"

"Work it out for yourself." Matty spat nastily and stomped upstairs to the bathroom.

Chapter 13

Chloe looked at her watch again, she couldn't believe that it was only five minutes since she had last checked. Time was dragging by impossibly slowly.

"You're acting like some love-sick teenager. What time are you meeting Rob tonight?" Pete asked amused by Chloe's clock watching antics.

"Six o'clock. We're going for a drink and then driving out to that new restaurant in Upper Norton."

"And how long have you been seeing each other now."

"Four weeks, three days and approximately nineteen hours." Chloe reeled off.

Pete gave a low whistle. "This must be some kind of record for you Chloe. It's a long-term relationship compared to the others."

"What a horrible thing to say;" She screwed up the paper on her desk and threw it at him. "It's not my fault that I kept meeting up with dorks like Dave. At least Rob isn't anything like him."

"Huh!" Pete said darkly, preferring not to go into yet another in-depth analysis of Rob Williams' finer points. Having had an incessant monologue on their every date, conversation, and inner meaning, his feelings towards Chloe's boyfriend were definitely on the shady side of positive. He was starting to wonder whether life wasn't better before Lily had played Cupid; what with Lily crowing about her match-making skills, Chloe acting like an adolescent groupie and Natalia jealous that the focus wasn't solely on the wedding, he was feeling decidedly fed up with his lot.

Ten minutes later Chloe tried another sneaky check of her watch and Pete felt his composure threaten to snap; watching the waiting was becoming unbearable. It was sad anyone could become so obsessed. With a resigned sigh, acknowledging that there would be no work from Chloe for the rest of the afternoon, he bowed to the inevitable.

"Go! I don't think I can take any more of it. I was supposed to take these contracts over to Henry Beaucher and pick up some new shirts. Why don't you do that and then you can go and get ready for your hot date."

"Really?" She grinned wildly, her dimples appearing, realising that she would now have time to buy new nail varnish and do her hair without having to rush. She leant across his desk and kissed him loudly on the forehead. "Has anyone told you what a great boss you are?"

"Yes I am aren't I." He pulled open his wallet and took out a handful of notes. "Choose me three shirts, you know the ones I like, and it's a collar size…"

"I know what size shirt you have. I've done the emergency clothes run so many times it's imprinted on my brain."

"Ohh, right. Here are the contracts and tell Henry to call if there's any problem."

"Will do." She skipped out of the office, her mind already debating which outfit to wear – floaty skirt or little black number. Decisions; decisions.

In the end she went for the floaty rose-pink skirt from Joseph that almost touched the floor and teamed it with flat jewelled flip-flops and sequined top; which was exactly the right outfit Chloe happily concluded as she peeked around at the rest of the diners from over the menu. She could understand why the critics were giving the place rave reviews. With its understated interiors of shimmering greys, sparkling glass lights and dancing prisms from the crystal ware, it was impressive without being oppressive. Just the kind of backdrop for a perfect date Chloe mused.

"Penny for your thoughts?" Rob asked noticing her tiny smile as he put down his menu.

"Just admiring this place, and wondering how anyone can come up with the ideas in the first place. I'd have no idea."

"It was designed by Josie Carrington, you know the woman who owns the design shop on the High Street."

"Oh Henry's fiancée? Henry's firm do all the legal work for Sherborne & Sherborne." She explained seeing his blank expression.

"That's interesting. I was hoping to get someone who could introduce me to Josie. She seems to be building up quite a strong reputation for her interior design business, and I was hoping we might be able to collaborate on a few projects. It would help my business no end to work with some of her clients."

"Lily's good friends with them both, I'm sure she'd be happy to introduce you. I'll ask her next time she's in the office"

♦♦♦

As it turned out no introduction was necessary. Molly approached Rob through Mavis' recommendation to help develop part of the garden where an old pond had fallen into disrepair, looking unsightly and becoming dangerous for her grand-daughter Olivia. It was while he was working there one day removing the old slabs and liners Josie had called in to her mother's, giving Rob the ideal opportunity to introduce himself.

"So you're Mavis' tame garden designer?" She had joked "I've been dying to meet you." She laughed at his surprised look. "Well I had to meet the person who Mavis dotes on and Alicia loathes!" Her teasing tone amused him.

"Are you always this direct?" His tone matching hers.

"Oh no. Usually I wouldn't say 'boo" to a goose'." Her eyes were dancing with laughter, and she pushed her hair back, grinning. "Actually the real reason for wanting to meet you was far more mundane." She admitted. "I've got a number of clients who keep asking about garden rooms, and while I'm fine on the soft furnishing pieces, when it comes to knowing what greenery to use as a permanent backdrop I'm completely out of my depth. It would be good to team up with someone for those types of jobs, and I just wondered if you'd be interested in joining forces occasionally?"

He couldn't believe his luck; having mentally rehearsed all the different approaches, here it was being handed to him instead. "Yes I'd definitely be up for that."

"Why don't you come round to supper next week with Henry and me? We can talk properly then. I can't stop now – I'm just off to Drayton Hall to fit curtains in the Blue Boudoir." She saw his eyebrows shoot up into the furrowed ridges of his forehead. "Yes, it really is called the Blue Boudoir, in case you're wondering." She pulled her blackberry out from her Mulberry handbag, and clicked onto the calendar. "How would next Wednesday suit you? Bring along your new girlfriend; Chloe isn't it?"

"Jesus – is nothing secret round here?" But it was more resigned acceptance rather than anger in his voice.

"I'm afraid not." Josie consoled. "You see Mavis was saying how delightful the two of you looked together, so of course I asked who she was. If you want to know Alicia thinks she must be slightly mad to be going out with you instead of her tasty young boss; so of course I can't wait to meet her as well. Shall we say about eightish?"

He walked over to his discarded sketchpad and scrawled the time and date on a spare scrap before handing Josie a rather grubby business card.

"Sorry about the state of it, hazard of the job. If you need to get hold of me before Wednesday, then my number's there. It'll be easier to give me a call, rather than going through Mavis." She took the offered card, and he added ruefully. "Plus if Alicia answered I'd never get the message."

She slipped the card into the pocket of her bag and studied him. "What is it about you two? I've never known Alicia to be so down on someone before, and you're making her out to be a total witch." She recalled Alicia's response when Mavis had dreamily described him as an outdoor Gordon Ramsey. "I'd definitely use the 'F' word about him – but not in polite terms."

Rob shrugged and turned back to continue working, uncomfortable at the directness of the question. "I'd say that's an understatement. I've never come across anyone who is so spoilt and self-centred. She seems to think the world owes her because she had the hardship of not having anything in common with her parents. As I see it growing up here with a loving family counts for a lot – she should see what most kids have to deal with." He concentrated on pulling up a stubborn rock, as though trying to expel any further thoughts on Alicia.

"I know she can come across as a little bit prickly when you first meet her, but most of it's a front. She's actually incredibly kind when you get to know her."

"Prickly; she's razor wire." He retorted, then realising he was in danger of being rude to a potential business partner, stood up and softened his glare. "Sorry. She's your friend. I shouldn't have said that. It just drives me mad that everyone treats her with kid gloves because they're afraid of her. Especially Mavis, she never points out how wrong Alicia is."

Josie patted his arm, showing that no offence had been taken. "Well at least you can't say you're not telling her! I'll see you and Chloe next Wednesday. Now I really must dash, that Blue Boudoir awaits." And with a quick wave she turned on her heel and trotted briskly down the path, leaving Rob cursing Alicia for being able to annoy his thoughts even when she was absent.

◆◆◆

It was strange having dinner with the company's solicitor, Chloe mused, as the four of them sat round the large kitchen table tucking into boeuf bourguignon.

"I hope you don't mind if we're just in here." Josie had apologised as she'd led them into the kitchen. It's more cosy."

Chloe hadn't minded at all. She was happy to sit and admire the room, she would love to have this kind of room if she had a house of her own; although the chance of being able to afford something as grand as this was very slim, not unless Rob's business really took off. The cupboards were painted a pale green, and a huge old dresser dominated one wall. Instead of the ubiquitous plates and mugs, Josie had filled it with black and white photos, and letters spelling out 'eat', 'happy' and 'laugh'. The floor was a pale bleached wood and the table and chairs were an antique cream, topped with vivid lime green cushions that stopped it looking too washed out. While Henry organised drinks and, under Josie's close instructions, checked the food as it cooked in the Aga, Josie and Rob started to talk business, comparing thoughts on the whole inside:outside concept, mutual clients and opportunities to work together. Sensing Chloe was being unintentionally excluded, Henry offered a walk in the garden so he could let the elderly Labrador, who was patiently sitting by the backdoor, out to have a run.

"What's her name?" Chloe asked as she bent down and stroked the soft golden head.

"Betsy." Henry said, exchanging an intimate glance with Josie, that caused them both to smile at a shared recollection.

"She's a very special dog." Was the only explanation Josie gave.

And now they were finishing the food, Chloe realised that the Henry-at-home was far more jovial than the serious Henry-at-work. He kept glancing across to Josie, as though checking she was really there, and in return Josie would sneak a hold of his hand as it rested on the table. It was apparent how much they were in love; somehow it radiated out, so that everyone felt included within the warmth. Leaning back into Rob's arm she finished her wine and realised how much she was enjoying herself.

Reflecting on the evening as she vainly sought sleep that night, listening to Rob's steady breathing, she suddenly realised that it wasn't something she wanted to analyse too closely. On the surface their relationship was fine, they got on well and had fun; Rob was always attentive, complimented her on how she looked, always paid attention to what she wanted. Yet somehow it felt like she was doing all the running; Rob was always willing to follow on but he never seemed to take charge. It was almost as though part of him always remained detached and unavailable to her; it wasn't anything concrete enough for her to be able to question him on, more a vague feeling that the under the affable façade there was a hidden depth that remained independent. Trying to rationalise it though, Chloe concluded that not all couples were the same as Josie and Henry, openly showing their feelings, willing to be publically demonstrable. She smiled instinctively to herself as a sudden memory popped into her mind, of Natalia refusing to walk with Pete down the high street when he had turned up wearing a Hawaiian shirt and cycling shorts after running out of clean clothes. He'd winked to her above Natalia's head, having earlier predicted that she'd disown him for his outfit. So if was ok for Pete and Natalia not to always be so loved-up, then surely it was ok for her and Rob. Deciding she was worrying needlessly, she pushed away the residue of nagging doubts and settled herself into the crock of Rob's arm to try and get some sleep.

◆◆◆

As the summer continued to heat up, so Rob and Mavis were working later in the evening, trying to avoid the searing mid-day sun, which meant Rob was not only regularly joining the evening meal but preparing it as well.
"Are you taking requests?" Alicia nervously enquired seeing Rob leaning into the fridge examining the contents.
"As long as it's vegetable chilli then yes." He growled from within.
Alicia laughed slightly too shrilly "Ok then – can I have vegetable chilli?" She asked grateful that she wasn't expected to cook. Slipping past him she pulled out the chilled bottle of Sauvignon Blanc, before letting him ease out the cork for her, so she could pour two glasses.
Deftly he prepared the courgettes, onions and tomatoes before riffling through Mavis' scant spices to find the chilli powder and cumin.
"What was the real request?" He asked to break the silence.

"Fresh fish and salad." Alicia admitted not looking at him. "The weather feels like we are in the South of France rather than good old England. I just had a fancy for seafood."

"Maybe next time." Rob sympathised.

"By then it will probably be raining and I'll want Lancashire hotpot or dumplings and stew." She started to gather the plates and cutlery together on a tray. "Mum thought we could eat outside; she's moved the table round onto the lawn so we'll still get the last of the evening sun."

"Good idea; do you want me to carry out the tray for you?" He saw her struggling to try and balance it on the plastered arm.

"If you don't mind but then I will set everything out of the table." She assured him.

They walked out into the garden and down to the piece of grass that acted as the lawn. It stood sheltered by rambling old rhododendron bushes along two sides; away from the house the other opened up to the orchard where the baby apples and pears were slowly ripening. They passed one of the original flower beds planted up by her grandparents that still bore a zany collection of holly hocks and Michaelmass daises clustered around delphiniums and lupins, forget-me-not and lavender. With her good hand she picked off a handful of burnt orange nasturtiums, careful not to damage the petals, as Rob set down the tray on the turquoise painted table and turned to return to the kitchen she held out the flowers in offering.

"I thought you might like to add these to the salad." She said diffidently, self-conscious all of a sudden.

He looked down at the petals in surprise.

"One of those TV chefs was talking about it, using flowers to cook with I mean, and I just thought we could try it." Her voice dried up as he stood watching her.

"Interesting idea." He replied gruffly, scooping up the delicate flower heads. "I remember my Great Aunt using rose petals to make jam, but I never thought to try it."

"It was fascinating reading – there's so many different ones like dandelions and begonias; and apparently marigolds are known as the poor man's saffron. You could read the article if you wanted."

"Thanks for these." He curled his fingers round the petals. "I'd better go and finish the chilli or we won't get to eat at all."

110

The dusky evening light slowly seeped away; the few improvised candleholders threw a flickering light onto the three diners as they relaxed round the table, sipping coffee and enjoying the evening. The warm air carried along the subtle scents of roses and jasmine. For once no-one seemed in a rush to leave, an almost convivial atmosphere had pervaded, and the conversation had flowed like the brook at the end of the fields. Alicia found herself savouring the delights of an impromptu alfresco dinner that London had never afforded. With a curious new sensation it almost felt like this was home.

♦♦♦

They had been planning a day out in London for ages. Alicia wanted to go into the office to see Simon and Matty was longing to look round the shops. They had planned it over the phone, both excited about their day trip out.

"Will you please sit still!" A note of exasperation crept into Alicia's voice as they sat in the deserted carriage.

Matty unrepentantly refused to apologise. "I can't help it. It's been so long since I had a day out in London to look at clothes." She thought longingly of bygone days, when she'd trailed round the fashion boutiques and feasted her eyes on the new season's collections. Where did the time go, she mused, realising just how long ago it was.

"Well you'll have to wait while I go into the office." Alicia reminded her.

"Couldn't I just go straight to the shops – you really don't need me there do you?" She wheedled persuasively. "Plus if you get caught up talking minute details about the States, then we'll never get to the shops."

"I thought this was supposed to be a girls' day out, where we both get to go shopping and have lunch. And knowing you, you'll get so caught up admiring those dresses that you'll forget about the time and I won't even get any lunch."

"Scout's honour! I'll be there for lunch." Matty promised, holding her hand up in a salute for emphasis. "Just tell me the time and place, and I promise I'll be there waiting."

With a good natured shrug Alicia acquiesced, rolling her eyes heaven-wards as she flopped back in her seat.

"All I can say is that you'd better be at Carlo's Wine Bar at twelve, or I'm phoning Tom and telling him to cancel all your credit cards."

The train carried on with its soothingly rhythmic clankety-clank and the two companions fell into private reflections; Matty planning which designers to visit first, Alicia excitedly mulling over her last conversation with Simon. Her work on the Van Plaza Clothing project had impressed Patrick Fernly enough for him to request Alicia be involved in the acquisition project. She wasn't sure what she was expected to do, but hopefully her meeting with Simon would enlighten her on a few more details, particularly the tantalising mention of the possibility of having to go over to New York. She couldn't wait to find out more; maybe George wouldn't be the only one who got to do some pond-hopping this year!

Foot sore, weary, but buoyed up with their lunchtime wine, the two returned home amongst the country commuters. Crowded in between pinstripe suits and whirling laptops they had grabbed the last two seats with the alacrity of fortune hunters on gold.
"I don't know how people live like this." Matty had hissed, peering round at the hordes of travellers.
"This is nothing!" Alicia, the seasoned voyager had scoffed. "You should see the Northern Line — it's far worse than this. You're lucky if you get enough standing room; most of the time there's someone's bag digging in your back and an armpit shoved in your face."
Matty wrinkled her nose in disgust. "Why would anyone want to do it?"
Alicia laughed. "After a while you don't even notice it." She assured her friend. "And living in London has so many benefits over being stuck out here."
"Like what?" Matty challenged.
"It's where the big jobs are, and there are all the clubs and wine bars. There's always something to see and somewhere to go. You're never bored."
Matty looked unconvinced. "Think I'll stick with a nice rural existence and save London for my days out."

"You enjoyed the shops then?" Then seeing Matty nod asked. "So why didn't you buy anything?"

With a sigh she replied "As lovely as everything was, it was all out of my price range. I'd love to have had that purple Mulberry bag and those Marc Jacob boots – but I'm not exactly going to need either on the farm."

"You could always wear them away from the farm."

"Mmm." She agreed non-committaly. "But we could use the money better on something else."

Incredulously Alicia stared at her friend – why did getting married mean you had to give up on life's necessities? If she ever decided to get hitched she'd make sure she kept her priorities in order.

Chapter 14

"I can't go on any more." Matty wailed into her drink. "It's all gone horribly wrong." She was in the morbid phase of becoming drunk and had been berating herself, her life and her choices for most of the evening. Since their day trip out, Matty seemed to have become permanently teary. When she had broken the monologue long enough to stumble off to the toilet, Alicia had taken the opportunity to phone Tom and suggest he came to pick her up.

"I didn't think a taxi would be a good idea," Alicia said apologetically. "She seems quite upset."

Tom's brusque response had surprised her, curtly saying he supposed he had to and that he would be there in twenty minutes.

Alicia had then spent the remaining time trying to persuade Matty not to order another drink and coaxing her into standing up so that they could walk out to the front of the pub and wait for Tom there. She had been careful not to let anyone see what a state Matty was in, particularly when the tears started pouring down her cheeks.

"What am I going to do?" She wailed. "Why can't I be successful like you?"

Alicia felt totally out of her depth, she wasn't used to playing the role of agony aunt to friends. In London Larnie, Nikki and the other girls worked hard to call the shots; they weren't worried about a fulfilling life – just getting on in the firm and where the next party would be held.

"Let's not worry about it now." She weakly suggested, linking her arm through Matty's. "Tom's coming to pick you up, so you'll be able to go home and sleep it off."

"But I don't want to go home." Matty continued to wail, not helping Alicia to comprehend what her friend did want, only what she didn't. "Why do I have to go home?"

"Because Tom's worried about you; and he's coming to get you."

Matty shook her head exaggeratedly. "He's not worried about me, he's just worried about not having someone to give him babies."

They were outside by this point, and Matty collapsed onto one of the benches. Alicia knelt down so she was level with Matty, her friend's eyes were having trouble on focusing on her.

"Matty." Alicia spoke slowly and carefully hoping to break through the drunken fuzz, but with care tingeing her voice. "Why don't you talk to Tom? If he understood why you're so unhappy he'd be able to help you. He loves you, he really does. The two of you have always been great together, you don't want to lose that by pushing him away." But Matty's only response was to thrust out her arm so that Alicia was forced to back off.

When Tom finally appeared Alicia watched as he helped Matty into the Landrover.
"I'm sorry for having to phone." She apologised again. "She seemed to be in such a state." She wrapped her arms round herself; the night air had cooled; matching itself to Tom's frosty exterior. "She's really unhappy Tom." She wondered if there was any way she could try and encourage him to get Matty to open up, but she felt ill-equipped to broach the subject. The sensitivities around married life, family politics and baby talk were laden with emotional dynamite. Deciding that straight talking was the only way she jumped in with: "Perhaps you could get her to try and talk to you."
"Do you really think I haven't already done that?" Tom's voice was loud and harsh, its venom taking Alicia back. "God Alicia you've got some nerve telling me what I should be doing. You go off to London and don't bother to keep in touch with Matty, never email or phone, and now suddenly you're back and her best friend, and you're telling me what I should be doing." He took a step closer, his outstretched finger pointed threateningly at her.

Alicia's comments had uncorked the bottled up frustrations of the last few months and now that he'd started they kept flowing. "We were fine until you arrived back. Now suddenly she's not happy, she doesn't want a family, she doesn't want to be married, she doesn't want to be on the farm." He continued to jab a finger at Alicia and the rage was palpable, her legs buckled slightly and she held onto the back of the bench for support.
Her mouth was suddenly dry. "It's not like that Tom." She began weakly, desperate to put right any inadvertent harm her words may have caused.
"Isn't it? Well from where I'm standing it is! You've been parading how wonderful your life is, with your swanky job and apartment, your expensive designer clothes. You take her up to London and show her all the things that we can't afford. It's no

wonder you've turned Matty against me. Do you get a kick out of it? Knowing there's no way I could ever buy those kinds of things for her."

"But Tom, it really isn't like that." Alicia's denial was almost tearful.

"Stay away from Matty, I'm warning you."

At that moment Rob walked out of the shadows Bertha at his heels; seeing the confrontation he came to a standstill and glanced between the two trying to assess the situation. "Evening." His entrance changed the dynamics, defusing the tension like oil on the proverbial troubled water; Tom turned on his heel concentrating on getting Matty home. Climbing into the Landrover it roared off, gears grinding and the engine over-revving. Alicia dropped to her knees next to Bertha, burying her face into the dog's fur, feeling the warmth against her cheek as a few solitary tears escaped. "It's nice to see a friendly face." She confided to Bertha, her voice muffled by the fur. Eventually she rocked back onto her heels and realised Rob was still standing there watching her. Standing up, she straightened her top, and in an effort to look more presentable, ran her fingers through her hair and under her eyes to remove the mascara-tear-tracks.

"So what was that all about?" Rob indicated with his head the direction Tom had driven off.

"Don't ask." Alicia said wearily. "I made a complete mess of trying to encourage Matty to talk to Tom. She's so unhappy and I just thought if she would tell him what the problem was then she'd be a lot happier. As it was Tom told me it was all my fault anyway." She looked at him intently. "But then I guess you heard all of that." He flushed slightly underneath his dark stubble. He was experiencing an uncomfortable mix of emotions; he had felt vindicated that he wasn't the only one who saw Alicia as spoilt and self-centred; however the strength of Tom's anger and the mis-guided arguments he'd used had initiated an unwanted smattering of sympathy for Alicia. It felt as though something had shifted; an alteration in the landscape that had diffused a different light on things so they didn't seem so black and white. This crushed version of Alicia wormed away at his dislike, fracturing its intensity and melting a little of the aversion. He shifted from one foot to another, not looking directly at her.

"Please keep this to yourself." She continued. "Don't tell my Mum, she'd be upset to know how bad things are between Tom and Matty; I don't want her worried." She saw the deep scepticism carved into his face. "Yes I know that you think I'm an arrogant bitch who doesn't care for anyone, but it's not true. So please don't say anything to her." She turned and started to walk away down the lane, a lone hunched up disconsolate figure.

Rob watched her go, the internal struggle continuing between the deeply embedded dislike and a growing respect; he jammed his hands into pockets and half-glared at her, annoyed that she always managed to create this maelstrom of inner emotions within him. Then suddenly he sighed, expelling some of the stored abhorrence and started after Alicia, whistling softly to Bertha to follow. His long strides allowed him to catch up easily as they became level with his cottage.

"Why don't you come in for a drink?" He suggested. "You look as though you could do with a stiff brandy."

Alicia stopped; surprised to see he had followed her. "I don't think Chloe would appreciate it." She made to continue on into the dark evening, when Rob put a hand on her shoulder and gently pushed her towards the door.

"Come on." He coaxed. "You really do need a drink; and you needn't worry about waking Chloe. She's not here tonight; she was out with her boss on some work function." He opened the door and ushered her in. "Have a drink and then I'll walk you back."

They stepped in, eyes blinking at the unaccustomed brightness of the overhead light, and while Rob found two tumblers and splashed generous helpings of the warming amber liquid of the brandy into the glasses, Alicia glanced round the room, remaining uptight and tense. He handed one of the glasses to her and lightly chinked his against hers. "Cheers." She took a tentative sip, and felt the brandy burn her throat and roll down inside, melting her tension and helping her rigid muscles to loosen, her shoulders dropped slightly and she took another mouthful before finally relaxing. "Besides," Rob continued their previous conversation. "If you turn up looking like that Mavis will definitely know something's up."

She raised a questioning eyebrow at him. "Do I look a real fright then?"

For the first time since she'd known him he broke into a gentle apologetic smile. "I'm afraid so. Why don't you use the bathroom, it's the second door along. There are clean towels in the cupboard."

When she returned he saw her face had been scrubbed clean of any makeup and her eyes had started to lose their redness. She had brushed back her hair and had obviously given herself a quick squirt of the perfume Chloe had surreptitiously left there last week.

"That's better." He told her matter-of-factly, wondering if she was still feeling emotional. "You ok?"

"Much better thank you." She glanced around at the two chairs, one of which Rob was already sitting in, and dropped down instead onto the floor next to Bertha. She stroked the caramel muzzle and the canine stretched out.

"She doesn't normally get on as well with anyone else." Rob complimented. "I always have to shut her up when Chloe stays; she's petrified of Bertha for some reason."

Alicia laughed and held the dog's face in her hands. "How could anyone be scared of you?" She cooed. "You're just one big softie." As though understanding the words, the dog promptly rolled over onto her back, legs in the air, providing a rounded tummy ready for scratching. With a small chuckle, Alicia obligingly started to rub. After a while she stood up and folded herself into the chair opposite the watching Rob. "So how are you getting on with Josie? She said it was going well. Do you have anything in the pipeline yet to work on?" She asked.

"Good I think. We've got some ideas, and we're going to speak to a couple of people, so hopefully something will come out of it. We've had a few good meetings. It's now just hoping for the first commission." He was enthusiastic, but added ruefully. " What I can't get used to though is how everyone seems to know my business."

Alicia shot him an amused glance. "It's the price you pay for being in a small close knit community. Didn't you have the same when you were growing up?"

He shook his head. "Cheltenham wasn't anything like this."

"I can sympathise; I hated it when I was growing up. People always talking about what you were doing, where you were going, how you did at school, which friends you were with. That was one of the reasons I desperately wanted to move to London; so that I didn't have to be part of anyone else's life. I could do what I wanted and no-one would care. But now…" She fell silent and the sentence hung unfinished in the air between them.

"And now?" Rob prompted quietly.

Alicia swirled the brandy around in the glass and stared at it, her head slightly cocked. Then she looked up and shrugged. "Now I'm not quite so sure." She admitted. "Sometimes it's nice to feel included; to be part of something – know that there are people who care." She stopped swirling and drank deeply. "But then again, look at the trouble I've caused for Matty and Tom, so maybe it is better when I'm not part of something. Then at least no-one can get hurt."

She looked down at her glass again and finished the brandy, letting it sting and burn as though to purge her guilt. "But that's far too deep and meaningful for a Saturday night conversation." She concluded lightly, standing up she put the glass down before patting Bertha and walking over to the door. "No don't get up," she assured as he arose, "I'll be fine walking home. Thank you for the drink it was really kind of you." And with that she slipped out closing the door quietly behind her, leaving Rob feeling suddenly very alone.

◆◆◆

Chloe was trying to listen in surreptitiously, but she knew she was failing miserably as Pete's flapping hand shooing her back to work testified. Of course she knew it was rude to listen in to others' conversations, but Pete's raised voice, disgusted snorts and continuous pacing backwards and forwards meant it was hard to ignore. That combined with a glossy brochure being flourished every now and then meant Chloe's interest was not just piqued, it was well and truly caught. She gave up the pretence of working and studied Pete avidly as he hung the phone, slumped into his chair and dropped his head onto his desk with a reverberating 'thud'.

She gave a low whistle. "What was that all about?"

He sat back up and loosened his collar button under his tie. "Remember me telling you that I'd booked a suite at The Oaklands Hotel so that Natalia could have a break from all the wedding preparations? Well apparently this is the only weekend that the Vicar, florist, harpist and wedding stylist can make the run-through preparations. She's refusing to come away. Can you believe it?" Chloe guiltily sympathised with Natalia, if she was getting married then she'd want to get everything right for the day.

"And you can't go away once you've had the run through?" She suggested.

"It's going on all weekend." He started to count things off on his fingers for emphasis. "There's the lighting to be tested for photos, acoustics for the video, placings, flower colours... I bet I even have to fill in a timesheet for the act of consummation on the wedding night just to make sure there's time."

"I doubt that, they won't want Fergus-the-florist getting all hot and bothered at the thought of you being naked before he's done the lilies and pansies." She paused then asked. "So will you be able to get a refund?"

He shook his head balefully. "Nope, it's all non-refundable."

"Well why don't you take Lily, she loves going there?"

He gave her a stern gaze. "I hardly want to be sharing the honeymoon suite with my mother."

Chloe giggled. "Oops, of course not! It's just a shame you can't go." She leant across and picked up the abandoned hotel brochure, flicking through to see photos of luxurious bedrooms, sumptuous sofas and beautiful gardens leaping out of every page. "It's wonderful; I can see why you wanted to take Natalia there." She handed it back to Pete and turned to face her computer. "She's lucky having you."

He pulled a face. "You wouldn't guess it from the wedding grief I'm getting at the moment."

"It'll all be fine once the wedding is over." Chloe assured him. "Just wait and see."

"In the meantime it's in the bin for this." He said philosophically leaning over to deposit the brochure into the waste paper basket and then paused. "Unless of course you want to go?"

Chloe's head shot up and it was her turn to look at him in disbelief, then biting her lip she said self-consciously. "I don't think Natalia would like it if you and I went."

Pete guffawed. "Not with me silly; you and Rob. The two of you could enjoy it if you've not got other plans."

Chloe's face cleared and she stared at him. "Are you serious?"

"Why not? It's all paid for. Someone might as well enjoy it." Then as she hurled herself at him to hug him tightly he managed a strangled "I'll take that as a 'yes' then?"

Chloe's excited chatter reverberated around the greenhouse; Mavis and Alicia exchanged wry smiles as Rob tried to manage the verbal bombardment of lavish hotel rooms, romantic walks they could go on and the famous people who had stayed there. Eventually Chloe had run out of commendations, giving Rob a chance to find out what Pete had kindly offered; then just as they were saying goodbyes, Chloe had mentioned that no big dogs were allowed. Rob's face darkened as he slammed off his phone. "What's wrong with hotels in this country?" He demanded loudly, turning back to Mavis.

"No idea, you'll have to tell us."

Rob kicked a bag of compost in irritation. "Chloe's boss has double booked himself this weekend; he was due to go The Oaklands Hotel but apparently he's got a wedding run through, so he's given it to Chloe."

"The Oaklands!" Mavis was impressed; film stars and models were always staying there.

"Yes but they won't let me take Bertha. I bet if she was some simpering lapdog that lived in a handbag they'd let her in." He glowered into the flower pot he was filling.

Alicia laughed, and Rob transferred his glare to her. "What's so funny?"

"Well I was just picturing you trying to squash Bertha into a bag, and could just see you rolling up with her head sticking out of a suitcase; I'm not sure she'd fit into anything smaller."

"And it would have to be a wheeled suitcase because Chloe would never be able to carry her in the crook of her arm like those models do." Mavis rejoined.

"So if it's a Louis Vuitton trunk I reckon you'll just about get away with it." Alicia and Mavis stifled giggles at the shared vision. Rob turned his gaze from one to the other and shook his head. "You're both mad." He walked over to the plants which were sitting at the far end of the greenhouse pre-selected by Mavis for him, and began piling them into the crates ready for travelling.

"Where do you want these labels?" Alicia called, holding up the wobbly printed care tags she'd written up.

"In the box over there." He indicated a wooden box with a nod of his head. "Then I can attach them once I'm there."

"I hear the gardens at The Oaklands are stuffed full of prized specimens." Mavis restarted the former conversation. "You'll enjoy being able to study those."

"Mum, I think Chloe will probably want Rob to take her on romantic walks, not be giving some lecture on the fauna and flora."

"I still need to think about Bertha, or I won't be doing either." Rob pointed out ruefully.

"That's simple." Alicia dropped the tags into the box and wandered over to where he was standing. "She can stay here can't she Mum?" Two pairs of eyes turned to look at Mavis, and her cheeks flushed.

"Well any other time of course she could. But I'm also away that weekend. It's the WI outing to Blenheim Palace and Molly and I are already signed up for it." She apologised guiltily.

Alicia shook her head. "I didn't mean you'd have to do it!" She turned back to Rob. "I know I'm not much help with this." She held up her plaster cast. "But I can take Bertha for walks and feed her. Plus if Mum's away it will be some company."

"Are you sure?" Rob couldn't quite believe Alicia had been so quick to give him an offer of help.

"Yes of course. It's no problem, she's a darling. Just let me know when you and Chloe are off."

◆◆◆

"Cheers!" Handing a gin and tonic with a refreshing slice of cucumber they toasted. Moving a pile of papers off the bench, Rob sat down next to Alicia. A dish of olives and tapenade sat on the table beside her notebook and pen. Behind them the sun slowly descended across an evening sky that was still as blue as the Bombay Sapphire bottle; occasionally a small lone puffy cloud would saunter across the horizon, but there was no let up on the intense heat.

"It was kind of you to come over and help out on all this." He indicated the papers. "It's a bit of a cheek, but I needed your opinion."

"It's no problem;" she assured him. "And you're definitely right to sort these out now. As the projects are getting bigger, the more money you'll be exposed to if your clients don't pay."

"It was ok in the early days." He agreed. "For the smaller jobs I could fund them and then ask for payment at the end. Now that

I'm doing the landscaping as well though, it's just too much of a risk. So do you think you'll be able to help."

"Oh yes." She assured him with a wave of a hand. "I'll be able to use a standard contract of works. I'll do two for you; one for the smaller ongoing jobs which has a notice period clause and non-payment details included, and the other for the larger projects which need upfront deposits and final payment on completion."

"That would be great. They never teach you about this on a horticultural degree."

"At least you're being savvy. Too many business people put it off until it's too late; and then they have the expense of getting us involved when they should have been more prepared."

"A lawyer with a conscience." Rob teased.

She swatted at him with her notebook. "You know what I mean. It's far better for both parties to know what the position is upfront."

"And the contract between Josie and me?"

"That all looks straight forward. There were a couple of small points I flagged up – and I would suggest Josie just gets Henry to check them. He's made it all equal in terms of risk and input, but it wasn't clear if you do decide to stop working together who can contact the clients in future. I'm sure Henry would be happy to check the other contracts I propose if it made you happier."

"I'm perfectly happy with my original choice." He said smoothly; then rising to his feet finished with: "Plus cooking you supper is far cheaper than Henry's fees!" He went back into the house and through the open window she could hear him whistling as he put the final touches to their meal.

Making a last few notes on the contract, she tidied everything away, clearing the table in preparation for eating. They were sitting in the small brick terrace at the back of Wisteria Cottage. What had originally been two concrete walls jutting out from the house and a brick floor yard, had been transformed. The walls were painted an azure blue, softened on one side by a low wall of piled logs and intensified on the other with three large scarlet abstract wall sculptures. Carefully placed groups of pots gave new colour and texture; in one a group of bronze ferns, in another yellow and orange lilies that pumped out a heady perfume. Beyond two planters held box hedging that framed the view, drawing the eye down to the pastures beyond and the grazing cattle. Bertha lay quietly under the table, tongue lolling out, miserably hot; not even able to raise sufficient energy to seek a friendly pat. Alicia had worn a simple cotton sundress, one of her purchases from the trip into Oxford with Josie. Its cream and biscuit print complimenting her now browning skin. It had felt like an excuse to get out of the shorts she'd been living in, even if it was only to wander down the lane to Rob's.

"Anything I can do?" She called through the door.

"Just clear the table."

"Already done."

He reappeared a moment later, a plate balanced in either hand. As he set them down she saw a fillet of grilled mackerel on a bed of pear and stilton salad topped off with homemade salsa and a drizzle of olive oil.

"You remembered!"

He grinned. "I didn't think your mum would ever get round to buying the right ingredients; hopefully you still fancy this and not Lancashire hotpot."

He opened a bottle of wine; the cork coming out with a satisfying pop. Sniffing it with caution he poured two small measures.

"Try this; it's a Portuguese wine. One of my clients recommended it – said they discovered it while on holiday, and now can't stop raving about it. He gave me this bottle to try."

Alicia sipped it, there was a slight fizz on her tongue, but it was light and fruity.

"It's ok isn't it!" She was surprised, she hadn't expected anything drinkable. Rob savoured and agreed, topping their glasses up to far more generous levels.

The food was delicious; the fish was moist, the stilton and pear a perfect crunchy accompaniment and the salsa gave it a tangy lift.

"This is really yummy." Alicia complimented between mouthfuls. "I can see why Chloe keeps praising you."

"Thanks." He was uncertain how to take the compliment. They chatted companionably as they ate; discussing Rob's business, his latest designs, Alicia's forthcoming trip to the States. As they finished the desert of lemon pannacotta with raspberry coulis, Alicia remembered the article she'd brought. Bringing it out of her bag she handed it to Rob. Its headline '*Just add eggs, flower and water*' leapt out of the page. "I meant to show you this before." He took it and read quickly through. "I thought you might find it interesting."

"It certainly makes you think about our flora and fauna in a different light." He agreed.

"There was another reason for showing you." She admitted. He looked up with interest, and she flushed, slightly unsure of herself. "I wondered if there might be something in it for Mum, to help get more people coming to the nursery."

"What do you mean?" He was intrigued.

"Well suppose she provided the flowers you grew to cook with, not just to look at in the garden. Do you think there would be a market for that? She could give some tips on how to use them in cooking – I'm sure you and I could help her with that if we did some research."

He was flattered at her estimation of his knowledge.

"It's certainly not being done anywhere else that I know of, and it sounds like a good idea. Have you talked to her about it?"

Alicia shook her head. "I thought I'd get your reaction first, if you think it is worth doing then Mum will pay more attention to the idea."

"Why don't we talk to her about it tomorrow? I'm sure she will see the potential. In the meantime, if you don't have to hurry back, we could look up a few other plants online as well if you like, then we'd have a much better list. This only mentions a couple."

"Oh yes! Especially if you can tell her about how people could use them in recipes."

He went inside, returning with his laptop. He sat down beside her so they could both view the screen.

"Come on then, let's find out about edible flowers."

They began trawling through sites.

"Look at this." Rob called up a page. "I never knew that you could use them in brewing as well."

"Carnations are an ingredient in Chartreuse, a French Liquor." Alicia read.

They carried on searching.

"Chrysanthemums are used in Japan for oriental stir fries." Rob was impressed.

"And I didn't realise cornflowers could also be used as a natural food dye; or that angelica can replace liquorice."

"This is fascinating." Rob said, pulling up more recipes. "Here's one for adding borage to make a cheese torta and adding burnet in dips."

The evening slipped away as they chatted about the possibilities for the edible flowers idea, a kernel of an idea building. When he finally walked her home down the lane, Bertha obediently at their heels, they were still discussing their findings with enthusiasm.

"Thank you for this evening." She said as they arrived at Apple Trees. "It's been really good fun."

He kissed her on the cheek. "Yes it has." He agreed with a smile. "I never thought having dinner with a lawyer would be so enjoyable!"

Chapter 15

The early morning sun was beginning to already throw off an intense heat, so that the air appeared to shimmer in a haze. A small production line was underway in the nursery where Alicia, Rob and Mavis were sorting out the final plants for Rob to take to his latest client's garden. Alicia ran through the list of plants required that she had ordered in from Mavis' suppliers, calling out each one in an orderly fashion for Mavis to select the best specimens and for Rob to then load onto the low trailer hitched behind his Landrover.

Even though they had started early in an attempt to beat the burning heat, all three were beginning to feel hot and clammy; tiny dust particles clung to their damp skin and beads of salty perspiration outlined their upper lip. When the final rhododendron had been safely loaded, Mavis disappeared into the house to fetch some chilled orange juice. Alicia slid down onto the dusty ground and sat cross legged on the grass, absent mindedly scratching under her plaster cast with a twig.
"Is it painful?" Rob asked as he lay down in front of her on his side, one leg bent up.
"Not really, it just itches like mad, especially when it's hot."
"I bet you'll be glad when it's off."
"Yes." She agreed enthusiastically, before adding. "Although it will be back to work and no more lazing in the sun."
Rob looked up at the perfect blue azure, without a wisp of a cloud in sight.
"Yep, today is definitely going to be a scorcher. Just what I don't need when I am planting all these up." He indicated to the greenery stuffed trailer with his thumb. "I'd hoped to get some more help to bed these in, but I got let down at the last minute. Looks like I'll just have to be working late."
"I could help if you wanted." She offered thinking of the otherwise long day that stretched endlessly ahead. Rob gave her a surprised look that seemed to say 'thank-you-but-what-could-you-do'. "Oh I realise I can't lift or do anything useful like that, but I could start watering in for you."
Rob tried to keep his expression neutral. "Erm, haven't you got something else planned for today?"
"Nope. I've done Mum's accounts for her, I updated all her supplier brochures and price lists. I even had a go at tidying the

house, although that was much less successful; I couldn't move that much, and everything I sorted out to be thrown, Mum decided she wanted to keep for sentimental reasons!"

Rob wondered what had precipitated this change in Alicia, it wasn't just her attitude, she seemed generally to be glowing. No longer were there deep furrows above her eyes on her forehead from the constant frowning scowl that looked like she always needed botox. Her skin had lost its pasty office complexion, instead it was turning a warm honey from being outdoors so much. Her short severe bobbed hair had started to grow, forming wispy curls around her face and shoulders.

"Well, if you're sure you want to help. It would certainly mean I could get the job done quicker, and the plants will benefit from early watering."

"Fine, I'll tell Mum."

"Tell Mum what?" Mavis asked as she appeared from the house with the tray laden with the juice.

"Alicia's offered to help me with the planting up of Toby and Caroline's garden."

Mavis shot a quick look at her daughter. "You won't overdo it will you?" She chided gently. "The cast is coming off soon, you don't want to risk permanently damaging your arm."

"No, I promise I'll be careful. I'll just help with the watering in and that kind of thing." Alicia assured her.

"Rob, make sure she doesn't do anything strenuous." She warned him, as he stood up and downed the offered juice.

"Don't worry I will." He gave a cheeky cub salute. "Scout's honour."

"I don't know who is the least responsible of you two." Mavis said in exasperation. They drank the remaining juice greedily, quenching their thirst with the tart icy liquid. When the jug was empty, Rob wiped his lips with the back of his hand in satisfaction and suggested they make a move. He held out a large shovel like hand to Alicia, helping her to get to her feet. This time he automatically opened the heavy Landrover door for her, and fastened the seat belt, carefully keeping the pressure away from the sling. Alicia was grateful for his tactfulness; she was increasingly aware of her current limitations, but that didn't mean she wanted huge attention paid to them. He got in the driver side and they moved off.

"So how was The Oaklands?" Alicia was intrigued to know what it was like to rub shoulders with the rich and the famous.

Rob shrugged. "Food was good, hotel was nice, and the gardens were great. They had a first class designer when they came up with that; they've done some really special things playing with space and perception." He heard Alicia giggle and he shot a quick look at her. "What?"

"It's just for someone who was on a romantic break, you seemed to have spent more time looking at the plants rather than relishing the luxury lifestyle. How did Chloe enjoy it?"

"She loved it!" Rob thought back. What should have been a perfect get-away, turned out to show just how different he and Chloe really were. They always had fun together, and he really liked her, but it had become apparent during the weekend that she was looking for more, for a commitment that he just wasn't ready to give. He had realised that he needed to level with her, he didn't want to lead her on to believing there was a future for them. He should have done it at the weekend, but he didn't want to spoil Chloe's enjoyment, but he would need to do it soon, he didn't want her hurt any more than she was already going to be but there was no way of avoiding the inevitable.

The day wore on, getting even hotter as the sun beat down on them working. The rays had dried out the damp soil leaving only dried baked earth. There was no shade for them to shelter from the fierce glare, they were exposed to the searing heat, making their skin feel dry and tight. They toiled in a companionable silence, seeming to work by unspoken communication. Rob would dig in the larger trees, driving deep penetrating holes into the hard unforgiving earth, causing rivers of sweat to pour down his back and stain his shirt. His face, contorted by concentration was, glistening with perspiration and his muscles bulged as they hacked away at the soil. Once the trees and shrubs had been planted Alicia trod down the loose earth, compacting it around the root ball, before lightly dousing the plant with life-giving-water. They followed each other around, and in their wake the garden began to gain definition as the trees provided the height and the shrubs provided boundaries.

They stopped for lunch, leaning against the tyres of the Landrover, thankful for its shade. Rob had bought sandwiches and a bag of oranges thinking he would be on his own. He had divided the sandwiches up between them and peeled an orange, splitting it open so that Alicia could eat it one-handedly. They shared the flask of tea companionably and talked idly about the garden and the village as they munched on their fare.

By three o'clock it became clear that at their present rate, they weren't going to finish that day. There were still the small plants to be dug in, the path to be laid and the lawn to be rolled out into straight parallel lines.

"We're never going to get finished." Alicia wailed looking at the plants and slabs still untouched.

"Maybe it was a bit over-ambitious to think I'd get it done in one day." Rob admitted.

"Can't we do some tomorrow?"

Rob was touched by her use of 'we'. "Afraid not. It's got to be finished tonight, Caroline's holding a party for her father in the garden tomorrow. I don't think they would appreciate us mingling with the guests as we try and plant the remaining flowers."

Alicia whistled. "That's cutting it fine."

"Don't worry, I'll drop you off home and then come back and finish it. Luckily it'll be staying light until quite late tonight."

"I've a better idea. Why don't I start planting up the small flowers? I'm sure I can manage. It might take me a bit longer but at least then you could get on with the path."

Rob looked horrified at the suggestion. "No way! Your mother made me promise to look after you."

"Mum would wrap me up in bedding fleece to keep me safe at the moment. Let me at least have a go, if it's too much then I'll stop." Alicia reasoned, but Rob was clearly unconvinced by her arguments. "It's worth a try isn't it?" She cajoled with a winning smile. "I promise I won't overdo it." Rob felt torn between wanting to accept the offer of help and of wanting to protect Alicia.

"Let me at least try one." She persisted until he reluctantly agreed. With the utmost care Alicia manoeuvred one of the plant pots to the side of the trailer and then transferred it onto her hip so that it was balanced to carry it. Then carefully she let it down onto the earth on one side. Holding it in place with her plaster cast, she tapped the pot with her free hand to loosen the root ball, then slowly eased the plant out of the pot and into the hole already prepared before patting the loose earth back into place. Rob watched, still concerned, but realising it would allow them to work quicker. "Ok," He conceded. "You carry on doing the flowers, I'll make a start on the path."

The afternoon dragged on then became evening, and slowly but surely the garden began to take shape. It was starting to resemble the original designs Rob had so painstakingly sketched months ago. Alicia carried on with the monotonous task of planting the fragrant lavender bushes, the delicate clematis and the vivid oriental poppies with their large fine papery petals. Rob felt the muscles in his back begin to twinge and complain as he laid the last of the path. It wound through the garden leading to the private seating area. There were two side avenues radiating off the path, lined with miniature poplar trees, one leading to a pond and the other to a striking piece of sculpture carved out of granite. The only task left to do was roll out the turf which stood stacked like a plate of swiss rolls. He stood up, and arched his back, hands on hips, trying to free up his tight aching muscles.
"How's it going?" He called across to Alicia; all he could see was her pert bottom sticking up above the sea of lavender.
"Fine." Her voice was muffled by the greenery she was planting.
Walking across to the rolled turf he picked up the first one up and expertly began to unroll it; it was an amazing transformation. As more and more of the turf went down like the final pieces of a jigsaw, suddenly the picture was becoming clearer, showing the final design in glorious 3D. Alicia, having finally finished the planting wandered over to where Rob was fitting the last piece of turf against the path. Wearily he stood up and brushed away the dried mud that caked his hands. He stretched up, then forwards, and then to the side, before rolling his head forwards.
"God I ache."
Alicia used her good hand to rub away at his shoulders and he gave a small moan of pleasure as she worked at his muscles. "It looks wonderful," she enthused over his shoulder. "Just like your original sketches, only better." They stood in silence side-by-side regarding the garden with satisfaction.
"I'd never have managed without your help." Rob complimented. "I'd still have been here at midnight without you."
"If I had the use of both hands I would have been much quicker. Do you think Toby and Caroline will like it?"
"They should do after all our efforts." He said ruefully, running the back of his hand across his sweaty forehead and in doing so left streaks of mud, leaving him looking like an environmentally friendly Rambo. Alicia started giggling at the streaks, spurred on by Rob's furrowed brow questioning the source of her humour.

"What's wrong?" He demanded. "What's so funny?" Still giggling Alicia took a step closer and with her undamaged hand wiped his forehead clean with a handkerchief.

"You should have seen yourself. Just like some sort of eco-soldier." Rob gave a good natured grin, and then, catching sight of something beyond Alicia, bought a finger up to his lips to signal silence, and then placing his other hand in the nape of her neck gently turned her round to face the same way as him. He bent down and whispered in her ear.

"Look over at the pond." Her eyes followed his to the newly created water feature, and there sitting quite comfortably amongst the boulders was a dazzling blue bird, its flame orange breast proudly reflected in the still water. It sat immobile until suddenly it dived into the pond, breaking the glass surface and out again before flying off into the horizon. Alicia spun round, her face beaming.

"I've never seen a kingfisher before; I can't believe how beautiful it was." Rob smiled down sharing the moment with her, aware of how attractive she was without her scowl. Alicia suddenly became aware of how close she was to Rob; of his dominating stature towering above her. She could smell his skin, almost tasting the salt of the sweat in her mouth. Shyly, unexpectedly feeling abashed, she gazed upwards, taking in his heavy features with the thundering dark brown eyes and severe eyebrows. Her skin took on its own sensations; it tingled beneath his grasp where his hand still rested on her neck. She felt a trickle of longing being released inside her, making her breathless. They were so close that he could easily drop his head and kiss her. The thought increased the longing and she felt her knees almost tremble. Their gaze became locked, each seeing the passion flaring up in the other's eyes. The moment was drawn out; Alicia found she was holding her breath in anticipation.

They were unaware of the surroundings, only having eyes for each other. Slowly, almost unbearably so, Rob dropped his head, seeking out her lips with his. As they met the passion inflamed, so that the first gentle brush was followed up with far more intensity as Rob pulled Alicia into him, cradling the back of her head as the fervour increased. Alicia didn't question what was happening; the overwhelming outburst took her breath away, leaving her helpless to the fireworks of feelings exploding inside. The kiss continued neither wanting the sensation to end; they clung together, damp bodies clasped in a vortex of fervour. They pulled away momentarily staring longingly at each other, both unbelieving what had occurred and yet craving more.

Magnetically they were drawn back together; enveloped in their own passionate world, unable to get enough of each other. Her hand held onto his neck, feeling the unruly mane curl between her fingers. He pulled her close into him, so that both were aware of their mounting desire. Her hand worked their way down to the front of his shirt, fumbling inexpertly with the buttons. He pulled back gazing at her with unmistakable intent. His voice husky with emotion declared her beautiful. Alicia started to reply, when suddenly from behind the house someone called out. A voice crashed through their hazy bubble sending it into a thousand shards. Instinctively they stepped apart. As though suspended in disbelief both turned in unison to where the voice had come from.

"Hello! Hello there!" Chloe stood at the top of the garden merrily waving to them. Alicia guiltily withdrew away from Rob and half-heartedly waved back, wondering how she could face her friend. Not noticing that Rob was scowling, Chloe prettily picked her way down the newly laid path, careful not to let her heels become embedded in the fresh soil. She was smiling to herself, so excited by the news she had to tell Rob. "Hi Alicia, I didn't know you'd be here; I was looking for Rob. Do you fancy a drink?"

With an abruptness he pulled himself together. "I'm not really dressed for it."

"Don't worry I'm sure Tina at The King's Arms will be fine. I've got something to tell you."

"What about Alicia?" Unconsciously he caught hold of her arm. As though in a dream Alicia moved away, a false smile fixed in place. "Don't worry about me," she assured him without meeting his gaze as a tidal wave of guilt flooded over her as she thought of how she had cuckolded Marcie in exactly the same way. She couldn't do it again – just taking another woman's man. "I want nothing more than to go home and sleep in a deep warm bath. I've dirt where dirt should never get, and I've muscles that are starting to kill me."

"Why don't I give you a lift home then?" Chloe suggested unsuspectingly before turning back to Rob "I'll meet you at the pub in twenty minutes."

Rob tried to catch Alicia's eye, but she continued to drop her gaze and was already hurrying away to Chloe's car. He strode after her, catching her by the arm. "Where are you going?" He murmured, still dazed by what had happened.

Without meeting his eye, she shook her head. "We have to forget what happened, you've got a girlfriend. We should never have kissed." Then hearing Chloe approach she turned to her friend. "I think we'd better hurry, I'm falling asleep here."

"I'll call you later." He promised. "We need to talk." With a feeling of powerlessness he watched with futility as Alicia left cursing Chloe's timings whilst recognising that if they had remained alone any longer then things would have undoubtedly reached another level. He strode off, confusion muddling his brain as he tried to rationalise what had just happened.

Half an hour later Rob was in the garden at The King's Arms, having washed and changed out of his work clothes. There was no doubt he had to level with Chloe this evening; tell her that this was the end, however hard it was to hurt her. He didn't want to string her along, but that kiss had changed everything. It was as though he had experienced a life-changing revelation, it sounded almost implausible to say he hadn't realised what was staring right at him, but something seemed to just click into place. He looked at his watch and wondered how quickly he would be able to get away. Maybe he would be able to get to Alicia's later, so that he could explain exactly how felt. Although he wasn't sure he could do that, he was never one to discuss emotions, and the turmoil he was going through felt unexplainable; but the one thing he was certain about was the desire to be with Alicia. He downed his pint, starting to feel anxious to see Chloe, to be able to talk to her, so that he would then be free to go to Alicia. He glanced at his watch again, wishing it was all over.

Ten minutes later Chloe leant over and kissed the top of his head.

"You were miles away," she said laughingly "I was waving to you from the car, but you didn't notice. You must be tired after today. The garden looks great by the way."

"Thanks." His voice was gruff, but she didn't notice.

"I'll go and get us some drinks."

"No, I'll go." He went to get up, but she laid a hand on his arm. "You've been working hard, I'll go."

She returned and produced his pint with a flourish. "Tina said you'd like this, it's from the Drayton brewery apparently." She sat down next to him, and played with the straw in her drink, a wry smile tweaking the corner of her mouth. She had spent all day in the same pleasant state; and although she wasn't supposed to be meeting up with Rob until later in the week, she couldn't help but see him tonight. After all it was only fair to share the good news and she couldn't keep it to herself much longer. She almost hugged herself in anticipation.

They both started to speak at the same time; Chloe giggled while Rob said "after you".

"I was saying that I just had to see you. I've got some wonderful news."

"That's great." Rob tried to inject enthusiasm into his voice, hoping the news would reduce the impact of anything he might say.

"I knew you'd be happy as well." She took his hand, and he could see that she was beaming in ecstasy. "I've just found that I'm pregnant."

In that instant Rob felt sick, an abrupt deluge of anger and fear surged through him, as the chains of entrapment clanked shut. He listened disbelievingly as Chloe chatted on about babies. She didn't register his muteness; her exhilaration meant she was floating on a cloud, not taking anything else in. Passively he let her jokingly hold his hand to her stomach, but he couldn't feel anything other than her usual soft roundness. A recollection of a summer holiday at his Grandmother's came into his mind. He had been lying in bed demanding sympathy as he suffered from stomach gripes after gorging himself on her strawberries. She had been pragmatic; her strong Scottish accent unrelentingly reminded him 'ach well you had your fun, so now you'll be paying'. That was how he felt now. What had seemed like harmless fun, was having some very deep consequences. There was no way he could end it now; whatever happened the life he and Chloe had inadvertently created shouldn't suffer. He wasn't in love with Chloe, but he couldn't let her down. So he continued to listen to her chatter about children and pregnancy, his face managing to remain impassive while inside he was raging at the unfairness of life. Somehow just as he worked out who he actually wanted to be with, it had been ripped away. How could this be happening? With a depressing realisation he knew he would have to keep away from Alicia in future; how on earth was he going to tell her that he needed to stay with Chloe? God, that wasn't going to be an easy conversation.

◆◆◆

Alicia realised Mavis had been talking to her only when her mother had turned the TV off.

"Sorry, did you say something?" She apologised, turning to where her mother was sitting in the opposite armchair.

"I was asking how Caroline's garden looked when you finished, but you seemed miles away."

"I think I'm just tired." She tried to reassure with a smile, but it came out lopsidedly. Somehow the caldron of bubbling emotions since the kiss was playing with her usual reactions. While they had been watching some reality show on television, Alicia had watched unseeingly, instead she had been transported back to the kiss; the feel of his hand on her skin and the sensation of his body against hers. She didn't know what to think; she had obviously flung herself at Rob with that kiss, and the poor man hadn't known what to do. Except that wasn't quite right – he knew exactly what to do, which was why little shivers still ran down her body every time she thought about it. No, obviously he had been taken completely unawares; he certainly never struck her as the type that was unfaithful; and it was obviously starting to be serious with Chloe. She didn't know how it happened, just that it had; and it was impossible to deny the depth of attraction. She thought of his promise to call, and snuck another look at her watch. Would he phone? The jitters in her stomach seemed to be increasing, travelling through her body, causing her foot to tap impatiently. How long would she have to wait? What would he say? Gnawing on the side of her thumb she felt the charge of tension increase within her to such a degree that when her phone did finally ring she leapt out of her chair with unprecedented speed. As his number showed on the display she broke into a goofy grin, but the sound of his voice, sombre and heavy was foreboding and instantly she knew that it wasn't going to be good news.

Chapter 16

Matty sat in front of the kitchen table which was festooned with the usual debris that seemed to automatically appear, but she wasn't seeing it. Instead she focused on a spot in the distance, watching the minute hand of the clock monotonously tick. She had been sitting there all morning, numb to the outside world. No longer a functioning human being, instead she had descended into such a pit of despair that she had become an automaton who went through the rituals of brushing her teeth, eating and sleeping but didn't register anything else. She had phoned in sick at the beginning of the week, no longer able to cope with the effort of going to work. Instead she had stayed all day in bed, safe and comforted by the duvet, keeping the world at bay. Today was Friday and finally she had made it downstairs. She and Tom hadn't spoken for over a week, resulting in her voice box feeling cramped from under-use.

The faint sound of the grandfather clock wheezing its chime in the hallway sufficiently roused her to take notice of where she was. Slowly casting her gaze around she saw the ever growing piles of paper, the bills that needed filing, the shirts that needed ironing, the wilting plants and the gathering rubbish. Everywhere were examples of her failure, of her inability to be a good wife, a good housekeeper, a capable human being. Suddenly gripped by fear so intense and overwhelming it flooded through her, her brain began to scream and she couldn't catch her breath, she felt trapped and suffocated by life, as though she was dying. Panic fuelled her actions, fleeing the kitchen with the trophies of failure she ran up to her bedroom, to the safe haven of the bed where she could hide. But as she rushed into the room the unpleasant smell of unwashed linen and the debris of her prolonged stay turned her stomach, making the room into hostile territory and no longer the comforting friend it had once been. Unbidden tears began to fall as the helplessness of her situation drowned her. Hot burning tears scolded her cheeks and filled her mouth, dashing them away with the back of her hand carelessly she felt the need to escape, to get away from everything. Rushing out of the room she looked frantically for the car keys in a bid for freedom.

Looking back Matty could never clearly recall how she had spent the day; they were lost hours, confined to the amnesiac repository of depression. The memory only recalled flashes of a conversation with the Reverend Mother as she had tried to find solace in the church, and ending up at Chloe's flat where she finished off a bottle of wine and immediately started a second. When she questioned Chloe about it afterwards, Chloe had not been able to shed much light; explaining she had popped into Zanzibar for a quick after work drink with Pete, only to find Matty in one corner, nursing a half empty glass of gin and tonic silently crying. Unable to get a word of sense out of her Chloe and Pete had taken her back to Chloe's flat. In an effort to be social, Chloe had opened the wine, avoiding drinking any herself, allowing Matty to promptly polish it off almost entirely by herself before passing out on the sofa.

Chloe and Pete had retreated to the chairs either side of the table; sharing their dinner of cheese on toast. Pete had cast an appraising glance round the flat with an approving eye, Chloe had kept the furnishings to a minimum, but had stamped them with her inimitable style, the walls were a soft pink, the curtains were draped voile with beaded edging and a huge furry cushion sat in one corner. It looked pretty and feminine without being overbearing. "I haven't been in here since you moved in." Pete said in a whisper, not wanting to wake Matty. "You've certainly made it much more attractive than when I lived here." Pete recalled. Lily, unlike most mothers, had insisted that he had his independence and learn to stand on his own two feet. As most of his friends were still living at home with parents the flat naturally became the centre of their socialising and invariably every evening would see at least one mate calling round with a few beers, revving up the play station or listening to the deafeningly loud rock music they were all into. It was probably due to Lily's generosity that none of the neighbours ever complained, but it gave Pete fond memories to recall those early days. Of course the flat had never been as well kept as this; when it had been his there had been discarded cans and half-eaten pizzas decorating the floor, plus an incessant stream of abandoned clothes.
"Actually Lily helped me," Chloe admitted. "I'd no idea what to do until she gave me some ideas. You are lucky having her for a mum."

"Mmm..." Pete said non-committally, uncertain whether having someone larger than life as a mother was a good thing. He thought cringingly of school nativity plays and carol concerts when she would stand up and applaud his one-line input demanding her neighbours follow suit; but he couldn't deny she was also thoughtful. He remembered all the extravagant gestures which meant all his mates thought she was wonderful, and all of his girlfriends felt jealous. Including Natalia. In fact it had reached the point where Natalia was refusing to even speak to Lily, which made his life difficult. "It's a pity Natalia doesn't agree." He murmured without thinking.

"How can she not like Lily!" Chloe demanded in outrage; Pete smiled at the way Chloe always sprang to Lily's defence.

"Isn't that what all those mother-in-law jokes are all about. It's universally acknowledged mother-in-laws are the creatures from hell."

Chloe huffed "Well I don't want that. I want someone who'll go shopping with me, that is happy to gossip for hours on the phone and who loves chocolate almost as much as me."

"And is Rob's mother ready for this new found friendship?"

Chloe wrinkled her brow and shrugged her shoulders. She hadn't actually met his parents, but since they were going to be having a baby together, she'd have to meet them soon. She wanted to tell Pete all about it, of how they were having a baby; but Rob had made her promise not to tell anyone at the moment. So she had agreed to keep it a secret, but it was so difficult not to say anything, after all this was the most exciting thing that had ever happened to her.

It was all very well acting like the good Samaritan to a friend in need, but when that friend seemed to have taken root in your flat with no sign of leaving, surely the good Samaritan had the right to ask 'why'. Matty had been at Chloe's house for three days now. On the second day once she had recovered from her hangover from hell, Chloe had gently tried to broach the subject of what had happened, but Matty had dissolved back into tears and had begged Chloe to let her stay with her for just a couple of days. In the evenings Chloe had missed seeing Rob, staying in eating takeaways and watching all her old movies on DVD. Matty slept on Chloe's ancient sofa. Their conversation was sporadic and lightweight; Chloe was by nature shy and Matty was weighed down by terrible feelings of guilt. Normally Alicia would have brought them together, but she had been conspicuous in her absence, and neither really knew why; but Matty was glad Alicia wasn't there, her friend would have known exactly how to wheedle everything out of her, and actually having to speak her fears and thoughts out loud was just too much at the moment.

In fact everything seemed too much effort at the moment. She had managed to leave a short garbled message for Tom telling him she needed a few days away. She knew it was cowardly to phone when he wasn't there, but she couldn't take the recriminations or emotional guilt any more. She hadn't thought to tell him where she was staying, she'd simply wanted to escape from everything and everyone. People always said you could never run away from problems, but sometimes it was worth a try. She hadn't turned her mobile phone on either, cutting herself off from any contact. She felt like a hunted fox cub, cowering in an earth den hoping that the braying hounds and thundering horses would just pass straight on. Although she stayed holed up in the flat she didn't recall where the time went. The days were the same hazy blur of inactivity. Her eyes seemed permanently red and puffy and her throat felt dry and cracked from her incessant sobs. She had no idea what to do next. All she really knew was that she was clinging onto survival with her fingertips.

Wandering across to the window that looked out onto the high street she pulled the curtain to one side so that she could watch all the shoppers rushing backwards and forwards on their daily routes. Being up above them made her feel remote and removed, away from the crushing mass of reality. She noticed the small trickle of school children, the girls in their summer dresses, the boys in their shorts as they joyfully made their way home as school finished, accompanied by the yummy mummies in their designer cropped trousers and little tops. She wondered about their lives; whether they were as happy as they appeared, en route to school, shopping and discreet liaisons. Her observations were interrupted by the shrill ringing of the doorbell, presuming it was Chloe she hurried across and throwing open the door she saw in shock it was Barbara standing in the doorway.

The previous evening, lying in bed, Barbara had felt the first twinges of guilt. She tried to ignore them and shifted in an attempt to get more comfortable in the vain hope that sleep would come, but it didn't. She lay restlessly awake listening to Joe's rythmetic breathing as he quietly slumbered. For the first time in many years she felt as uncertain as she had done as a teenager. Her previous black and white views had become tinged with grey around the edges. She wished Joe would wake up so that she could get some comfort from him, as they had done in the early days of marriage, when he had been the dashing man-of-the-world and she had been the nervous bride. Somewhere along the lines the roles seemed to have been switched and she had become the power force, wanting the family to be happy and secure. She had encouraged Joe to expand the farm by taking part of the farm tenancy of the Drayton Hall Estate, making sure Tom joined the family farm so that it could be handed down, trying to help Matty become part of the family as a farmer's wife. Except that it hadn't worked. Instead of having a happy family around her she had been forced to spend an evening watching Tom's tortured face as he broke the news that Matty had gone, that she had left him. The desperation in his voice at her disappearance sliced through her maternal heart so severely that she winced with the pain. To see someone you had brought into the world, and so lovingly raised, struck down with such a devastating blow would surely wound the hardest of hearts, especially when she knew exactly where Matty was.

Joe moved slightly in his sleep, turning towards Barbara, and unconsciously sought her out, pulling her close so that his arm lay protectively over her. She returned the hold resolutely, lying immobile waiting for the cold creeping morning light to finally penetrate the room.

There was a silence as Matty stood staring at Barbara. Eventually her mother-in-law asked diffidently. "Could I come in?" Her hands wrung at her handbag nervously. "I realise I'm the last person you probably want to see, but please just let me have five minutes."

Leadenly Matty's arm dropped from the door and she walked heavily across to an armchair, pulling a cushion in front of her, hugging it tightly to her chest as an amulet. Barbara followed and perched on the sofa, her handbag on her knees.

"It's very nice here." Barbara ventured, her mouth felt dry and there was an intense pounding in her ears. Looking at Matty she felt a pang of sorrow at the obvious despair of her daughter-in-law. Matty's normally impeccable coiffure was lank and greasy, her eyes were two tiny slits in a cushion of puffy pink, and her fingers fiddled continuously with the zip on the cushion.

"How did you know where I was?" Matty's voice was dull and listless.

"Lily mentioned it to me; said it was lovely how you and Chloe were getting on, so I guessed you must be staying here."

"Have you told Tom?" Suddenly her eyes were ablaze with terror and concern, and Barbara realised just how upset her daughter-in-law was.

"No." Barbara admitted slowly. "I know I should have done, because the poor man is frantic with worry, but for some reason I decided to come instead, partly because I feel responsible." Barbara felt Matty's gaze fall on her, watching her warily, but she wasn't able to meet the gaze. Instead she concentrated on continuing to battle on with what had become one of the most difficult conversations she had ever had. "I don't know what happened between you and Tom but I can see just how hurt you've become. Tom's my son, and of course I don't want him unhappy; but you're also my daughter-in-law and you certainly shouldn't be feeling like this."

"How can you possibly know what I'm feeling?" Matty demanded in a hoarse whisper. "You've got everything that you want; your husband, your home and your son. How could you know what it is like to feel you have nothing?"

"Don't get me wrong. I know how lucky I am to have Joe; in a way I'd forgotten just how much I need him until this happened. Of course I love Tom, he's my son, and I'm proud of the way he's turned out. It's true, having them around makes my life complete, but that's because without them – what have I got?" She paused before continuing. "When Tom told us he was going to propose, I was overjoyed that finally I'd have the daughter I'd always longed for. Someone I could compare recipes with, someone to go along to the WI with, that I'd have a shopping companion; I dreamt of having lunches while the men worked. The only trouble was after you were married I felt too intimidated by you to ever be able to do any of those things."

Matty stared at her in incredulity. "How could I intimidate you? I'm a big fat failure." Her lower lip began to wobble and tears escaped down her cheeks. Impulsively Barbara leant across and took one of her hands.

"Oh no, you're not. I've never met such a fighter as you." Her voice was firm. "I look at you and see a woman who has got a career and made a life for herself. Someone who has actually done something with her life rather than just go from living with her parents to getting married."

"But all those times you kept making me out to be a failure. Going to the shops when we ran out of things, cooking Sunday lunches every week, doing everything round the house to show that I wasn't good enough." Matty pointed out.

Barbara looked in horror at Matty. "Is that what you thought?" He voice was a motherly mixture of concern and disbelief, wondering how her daughter-in-law could have mis-perceived her motives so dramatically.

"But why else would you do the washing up, or take in the washing, or bother with my shopping unless it was to make me feel small and show Tom what a poor choice he'd made in me." Matty said bluntly, unable to dredge up any vestige of diplomacy.

"Oh Matty," Barbara's heart went out to her. "You really have got it so wrong. I wasn't trying to make you feel worthless. Why would I? And just for the record I don't think Tom could have made a better choice of wife. The only reason I did those things was to help you, because I could see how stretched you were between your job, helping Joe and Tom on the farm and running your house. I couldn't help you with your job, but I could do bits round the farm to lessen the demands on you, and I am certainly qualified in household chores."

"I thought you were pointing out what I should have been concentrating on." Matty said stubbornly.

"I know you probably won't believe me, but I honestly did it to help you. I'm sorry that the way I did it was obviously the wrong way. That wasn't what I meant to do. I meant to help." Barbara's brow was clouded with regret and sorry, deep inside a niggling feeling that had been worming away over the past few months suddenly began to take flight like a flock of startled geese. Guilt transcended through her. She had been aware of the atmosphere that had been mushrooming up within the family, but hadn't tried to resolve it, believing it was a passing phase. Instead she had foolishly congratulated herself on having her immediate family round her and took to making sure Tom and Joe were happy. But all the time Matty was obviously feeling more and more abandoned, deserted by her new family and unsupported by her husband. Thinking about Tom made her remember the stark face, unslept eyes and signs of stubble imploring her and Joe to help him search for Matty. Suddenly she spoke with urgency. "I need to let Tom know where you are!" Matty threw herself back into the chair and wailed "I can't see him."

Barbara moved over and took her daughter-in-law's hand and gave it a gentle squeeze. "Look Matty, Tom is worried sick." Barbara kept her voice calm and rational, knowing that an emotional plea wouldn't help. "If you don't want me to tell him where you are then I won't. But we have to let him know you're safe. The poor man's being envisaging the worst, he's rung every hospital between here and London." Matty was silent. "I think you still love Tom, and I don't think deep down you want him to suffer do you?"

The question prompted Matty to burst into another set of tears. "Everything is such a mess. I've made such a mess of my life."

Barbara leant across and wiped the tears as though Matty was six years old, she recognised the combination of self-pity, emotional exhaustion and physical hunger. She put an arm round the shaking figure until the sobs began to subside, and finally quietened. She stroked the hair away from the face, and dried the tears from the cheeks.

"I think we both need a cup of tea, and you look as though you could do with something to eat. When was the last time you had a proper meal?"

"I had some pizza with Chloe last night, I think." Matty mumbled.

"Come on then, let's go and find something." They went through to the kitchenette where Matty started to fill the kettle. Barbara slipped back into the sitting room and quickly dialled her son, and in a low murmur succinctly explained she was with Matty, but when Tom had clamoured to find out more, Barbara had gently persuaded him to let her deal with it, to encourage Matty to come home without the torrent of emotion that Tom would bring. He finally agreed reluctantly, and her heart went out realising that there would only be one chance to make it up with Matty.

It was ludicrous but the old adage about the English turning to tea in the time of need still held true, Barbara thought. Here they were, two women sipping from mugs of steaming tea, eating sandwiches, and starting for the first time to talk to each other as equals and as friends. Matty was surprised at how attentive a listener Barbara turned out to be; having a deeper perspicuity than Matty had ever given her credit for. Somehow the sad sorry story of how trapped Matty felt by her job; by the demands of the farm; of looking after the house and now Tom's desire to have children tumbled out. Through tears she tried to explain to the other woman how empty her life seemed, how pointless her existence had become; and yet how guilty she felt for thinking this, when in a way she had it all, a loving husband, a job, a nice home. "I don't know what's wrong with me. Why do I feel like this?" She implored, her hands held tightly against her chest as though indicating the source of a very real pain.

"There's nothing wrong with you." Barbara soothed. "I think you've been so busy looking after the rest of us that you just plain forgot to look after yourself. I'll admit I'm no expert, but I think a break away from everything with a bit of space and a lot of pampering wouldn't go amiss. Maybe you should go and visit your parents for a bit? I'm sure they'd love to see you, and you haven't seen them since the wedding."

For the first time that afternoon Matty picked up showing a spark of interest. "But how would I get there?"

"Don't worry about a thing. We can sort it out, if that's what you want."

"What about..." Her mouth went dry with panic. "What about Tom?"

"Leave him to me. I'll speak to him, explain you just need some time to think. Just promise me that whatever you decide you let him know as soon as you can. Whether it's with or without him – just do the decent thing so it doesn't prolong the pain for either of you."

Matty wiped her puffy eyes and blew her red nose into a disintegrating tissue. "Thank you." She said weakly, unable to find any words to express what she was feeling.

Barbara gave her a reassuring hug. "Let's just get you sorted out."

Chapter 17

Lily wanted a party. The summer was morphing into autumnal days and russet sunsets heralding the end of the long sunny days and eternal warmth. All too soon the cold and the frost would be moving in. A rip-roaring party was just what everyone needed to fortify themselves for winter. By this time next year everything would have changed; Pete and Natalia would be married, hopefully Chloe and Rob would be planning a future; and Barbara and Joe would be handing over the farm to Tom and starting to take life easier. In a way all this change made her feel unsettled. It was all too easy to get used to the steady annual rhythm of the rural affairs, so that any variation was deemed unwelcome. Looking out of the window at her immaculately manicured garden, to the lawn where the marquee usually sat but for once it failed to fire up her imagination. It was too tired, too familiar, she wanted something fresh and new, that would get her brain synapses popping and her creativity flowing. Opening the French doors she passed into the garden and wandered aimlessly, seeking inspiration amongst the scented tea roses and blooming azaleas but failing dramatically to find it.

Returning to the house she caught sight of the area she'd asked Rob to look at, and her mind roamed back to the sketches he'd prepared. Hurrying over to her desk she pulled out the designs, remembering his ideas of a brick terrace with tall exotic ferns and feathery bamboo plants hiding the garage wall, and a large triangular canvas sail strung over the area, perfect for shading visitors from strong sun or drizzling rain. Studying the miniature representations she started to see how it could work; tiny white fairy lights strung along the walls and the edge of the sail, flickering tea lights edging the path, ornately decorated box trees in each corner and in the centre would be the bar. She thought longingly of parties when she was growing up, and immediately knew it would be a cocktail bar with a glamorous barman dressed in white to concoct delicious liquid delicacies for the guests. A thrill of excitement ran through her; this was just what she needed; a damn good party to organise. Immediately she phoned Chloe to test out the idea and the ensuing squawks of delight confirmed Lily's suspicion that a party was the tonic everyone needed.

"What a fabulous idea." Chloe gushed, already wondering if her bump would be showing, and whether she would need a new dress. "When were you thinking of holding it?"

"I thought the end of September. Everyone's back from their summer jaunts by then."

"Ohhh it's going to be wonderful. Will I be able to bring Rob along?"

"Of course, and then there'll be Pete and Natalia, Henry and Josie, Barbara and Joe, Tom and Matty..." There was a pause before she added. "If she's back. Have you heard anything from her?" Lily asked tentatively.

"Only a postcard that just said thanks for letting her stay. She didn't put how long she is going to be away for."

Lily shook her head. "It's a terrible business; Barbara's taken it quite hard and poor Tom is wandering around like a ghost. I've no idea how it will all turn out; there seems so much raw emotion there."

"And I'd always thought they were such a happy couple. But it just goes to show you can never tell what really goes on in a relationship."

"You mean in private Natalia turns into a wonderfully warm person." Lily asked waspishly.

"Miaowwww!" Chloe laughed.

"Did I tell you I overheard her deciding which bits of my furniture were worth keeping when I went into a home?" Lily was indignant. "I ask you – what does Pete see in her?" Chloe thought of the slim toned body and decided she could make a good guess. "Anyway I'm going to need loads of help choosing food and drink." Lily continued, her excitement returning. "So make sure you're free and don't let my son overwork you. By the way is he there?"

"Nah, he's showing a couple round that Victorian terrace on the green."

"I bet they say it's too expensive and offer two hundred pounds less a month, the owner will say one hundred, and we'll get them to settle on a hundred and fifty." Lily predicted. Privately Chloe thought it highly unlikely, the house had been on their books for ages. It was gorgeous, three floors with high ornate ceilings and marble fireplaces, the only problem was the high rental the owner wanted.

"I'll let you know." Chloe promised

"And don't forget you're going to be my event co-ordinator."

"Goodie! See you soon."

Chloe smiled to herself, there was nothing like the prospect of a party to put you in a good mood. Then she suddenly realised she wouldn't be able to drink, her dress might not fit, and her ankles might start swelling. Being pregnant wasn't all she thought it would be.

♦♦♦

Pete reappeared later that morning, his tie askew and his top button undone as he wilted in the heat.

"How did it go? Did the Burtons like it?" Chloe asked enthusiastically.

"I finally managed to get them to take it."

"Congratulations – I am impressed."

"It took a bit of haggling. They offered under the rental price, which was too high anyway, but Mr Robson wouldn't accept, so he put forward a figure and they finally settled on taking off £150 a month."

Chloe mentally saluted Lily, there was no doubt she certainly knew their clients. Thinking of Lily she exclaimed. "Your mum's having a party!"

"What's that in aid of?"

"No idea, but she's made me chief event organiser."

Pete gave a low whistle as he lowered himself into his chair and flicked through the viewing diary. "Sounds impressive. So what do you actually have to do?"

Chloe waved her hand airily around. "Oh you know, taste food, try the drink, pick the type of flowers..." She waved her hand again. "Oh lots of things." She said vaguely, realising that she had absolutely no idea.

"Just don't let her take advantage of your time, or you'll end up with no social life."

"As if!" retorted Chloe. Men – didn't they realise life was meant for parties, shopping and chocolate.

"So how are things going with Rob?" Pete enquired waiting for the weekly update.

"Oh fine." She enthused. "Absolutely fine." And a hand crept to her stomach, she couldn't wait to start telling everyone their news. It felt tough at the moment, because the only person she could speak to was Rob, and they didn't seem to be able to meet up all that much at the moment, what with his work schedule and her Agony Aunt stint. Chloe didn't want to dominate Rob's time, but secretly she wished he wanted to see a little bit more of her. He put it down to the demands of his work now that he was linking up with Josie; after finishing late he was only any good for vegging out in front of the TV and falling asleep. Still, she consoled herself, once they were living together she'd get to see him all the time and then she could talk about babies as often as she wanted.

◆◆◆

The party was starting to be the talk of the village; it had grown from a few friends popping by to a full scale knees-up. Lily found her days being taken up trying to keep track of who had accepted, what wines they were having, where to fit all the guests and hoping Rob would be finished on time. She had finally commissioned him to start work on the garden, and they had spent several days working out to how use the space so that it would look spectacular for the party as well as being a useful space afterwards. They played around with various themes from kitsch, complete with glitter balls and mirror tables; through to pastoral serenity with thick rough carved furniture and half sawn log benches, but each time they kept slipping back to something simpler and yet more elegant that was in keeping with the rest of the garden. They chose a wooden decking floor in favour over gravel 'It always ends up getting into your sandals' Lily had complained, and long low planters filled with square cut box; interspersed with tall lollipop bay trees and whispering grasses along the walls as they had originally planned. Instead of the single sail canvas they had opted for a series of three so that it gave the onlooker an impression of rustling fabric overhead, and running along each edge would be the tiny sparkling fairy lights Lily had initially pictured.

Lily had persuaded Chloe to miss a night out with the girls and come over and help with the food tasting, trying out all the succulent canapés and nibbles from the deli. She had organised the tasting at a time she knew Rob would be around measuring up. It was naughty she knew, but having successfully bought Rob and Chloe together, Lily wanted to see the fruits of her hard work start to come to fruition. She had never seen her young friend so happy, and yet she wasn't picking up the vibes of full-flung passion which she herself had experienced in her younger years. Under the guise of party preparations, she had plied Rob with a strong gin and tonic and encouraged him to help with the food tasting. But she felt disappointed, robbed of the intensity that new love brings. Where she had expected half hidden smiles and knowing glances snatched at odd moments there were only casual comments. They appeared like a middle-age couple, not star-struck lovers with passion pounding through their veins. Privately she wondered if Chloe realised, she had assumed her young friend would crave romantic gestures and stolen kisses, but then again as they had commented about Matty, one never really knew what went on in another relationship.

'In a way I should be grateful' Lily thought as the pair concentrated on the food, 'at least this way I have their undivided attention for making food decisions'. The choice of food was spread across the kitchen table, with four or five of samples of each item. Methodically they worked their way through the selection; from the petite quails eggs with celery salt crust; mini Yorkshire puddings with wafer thin roast beef and horseradish garnish; blinis with tapenade topped with apricot slivers; and prunes soaked in wine with belly pork squares. They decided against the miniature chicken tikka kebabs (far too fiddly for finger food), and while the cream cheese vol-au-vents were delicious they squirted everywhere when you bit into them.

"So what do you think?" Lily demanded, after they made a short list of canapés. "Will people approve of our selection?"

"Definitely!" Enthused Chloe, as she pictured her and Rob doing the same for their wedding when he got round to proposing. She wondered idly if it would be before the baby was born.

"Who's going to serve the food?"

"Melissa at the deli, she's got a couple of girls who will waitress, so that everyone gets fed. After all I don't think there's anything worse than going hungry at your own do."

Rob agreed heartily. "I'd better be making tracks though." He apologised to Lily before turning to Chloe. "Do you need a lift life home?"

Regretfully Chloe shook her head. "I drove over straight from work."

"That's a shame. Are you still on for Friday?"

"Definitely; do you want to come round to mine, I'll cook something for us."

"Sounds good." His voice was warm, but the smile didn't quite penetrate up to his eyes as he gave a slightly perfunctory kiss goodbye. Lily walked with him to the front door, watching him drive off before rejoining Chloe. As Lily re-entered the kitchen she caught Chloe sneaking the last cheese vol-au-vent.

"Chloe!"

"Sorry." Chloe spluttered through a mouthful of feta. "But they were so tasty, I couldn't resist."

"So what's Friday night? Anything special?" Lily asked meaningfully, and as if that wasn't enough of a hint, she accompanied it with a large exaggerated wink.

"Of course not silly! We're just meeting up for a meal. It's difficult during the week what with late appointments for me and Rob's shattered by the evening. So Friday's normally good for catching up." Lily's heart sunk a few more degrees this didn't sound like the passionate clinch it should be.

◆◆◆

"Damn!" Chloe put the phone down and swore again. How could it happen? It was so unfair. Pete had known that she was playing Florence Nightingale to Alicia, so how could he phone up to say he was running late showing the Taylors round The Old Rectory when he'd already conscripted Natalia to show Charles Pennington-Smythe round the Old Windmill penthouse? She looked at her watch, in fifteen minutes she was supposed to be picking Alicia up to ferry her off to hospital so the plaster could finally be removed. She racked her brain over who she could call, Mavis was away, as was Lily; Matty would have been the obvious choice, but she still wasn't back. Then with a flash of inspiration she dialled Rob's number.

"What do you want?" Goodness he sounded grumpy these days.

"Good morning to you too." She started brightly hoping that his bad mood wouldn't be a problem. "Would you do me a huge favour?"

There was a sigh. "I'm snowed under Chloe, I'm on my way to a new client and I've got a hundred things to pick up afterwards."

"It wouldn't take long." Chloe wheedled, winding the telephone cord round her finger. "I was supposed to take Alicia to the hospital today, her plaster's being removed, but Pete's just phoned to say he's running late so I'll have to cover his other appointments."

There was a silence on the end of the phone before Rob replied in a low voice. "Ok, I'll go over to her now."
"But what about your client?" Chloe asked guiltily.
"I'll give him a call, hopefully he'll understand."
"Thanks." And then added "See you later?" but he had already hung up. As she put the phone down she realised she'd broken a nail. It looked like nothing was going right today.

"Oh it's you." Alicia said in embarrassment, feeling her cheeks flush at the sight of Rob in the doorway, then suddenly wishing she had worn something a bit more attractive than her old jeans and a slightly shrunken tee-shirt. "I was expecting Chloe, she's picking me up any minute. If you're looking for Mum she's out at the moment."
"I know. Chloe phoned and asked if I'd take you to the hospital."
Alicia was flustered. "Oh, you don't need to do that. I'll phone for a taxi."
"I think we had this conversation when you first arrived." He reminded her gently. "It's not like London, there's only one taxi firm and they're back the other side of Drayton Beauchamp. Even if by chance they're free it'll take them ages to get ready and come over here."
Alicia hesitated, struck by indecision. "Look Chloe feels bad enough about not being able to take you," Rob coaxed. "Don't make her feel worse by turning down her substitute."
Alicia's small anxious frown dissipated and she smiled shyly. "Ok, let me just grab my bag." She picked up the Donna Karen tote and followed him to the car. This time he had already opened the door and was waiting to help her with the seat belt again. "At least it's the last time you'll have to do this." Alicia joked as he carefully belted her in, trying to steer her thoughts away from the last time he'd done this driving to Caroline and Toby's.
"No problem." He assured her, and as he walked round to the driver's side, she was afforded a profile view that crept up into her stomach and gave a tug in the region of her heart. He climbed in. "Look Alicia, about what happened…"
But she cut him short. She couldn't bear to talk about it with him; she didn't want to hear his apologies for a slight misdemeanour when he was still so obviously in love with Chloe. It would be too painful telling him just how she felt. Instead, staring straight ahead she said unemotionally.

"Let's not talk about it. You've got a girlfriend, I know that. Let's leave it there." Then with a false cheerfulness in an attempt to hide the onslaught of confused feelings she urged him on to the hospital.

The drive was steady, the countryside looked shorn and denuded from where the farmers had gathered in the harvest. Anything that was left looked dry and arid, a mixture of golds and russet browns. A haze of hovering heat mist hung in the air causing the horizon to shimmer iridescently. They went past the high street then the green where the Little Acorns were holding a rounders match, and on up the hill. The hospital was a low Victorian red brick building that had originally been designed by the then Earl of Drayton as a nursing home for soldiers returning from the Crimean War, but over the ages small extensions had been added, resulting in a sprawling maze of buildings. Finding a space to park the car, they walked in through the wide double wooden doors of the original entrance, beneath the Latin inscription and carved coat of arms. Alicia felt her stomach contract, the last time she had walked through those doors had been when her father had been a patient, just before he died. For a moment she was transported back to that awful year, to numbly comforting a distraught Mavis while unable to comprehend herself what was actually happening. Blinded to reality, she bumped into a porter as he pushed a trolley down the corridor.

"Ere watch yourself." He called out, snapping her back into reality.

"You ok?" Rob was concerned, he watched the fleeting signs of despair and grief pass over Alicia's countenance without understanding but with concern.

She rubbed her face. "Yes. I was just remembering something." There was a tinge of sorrow to her voice, and in the back of her mind a mirage of a thousand different memories flitted through a kaleidoscope, showing birthday trips, camping holidays and Christmases at Apple Trees, with her mother fussing after them, and her father looking as proud as Punch at her.

Rob slipped her good arm through his. "Come on, let's go and find where you need to be to get rid of that plaster." With a sense of relief, she lent against his strong frame and enjoyed the feeling of closeness it brought.

"I can't wait to be free of it." She confessed holding it aloof disdainfully. "It'll be nice to get back to being normal, getting on with life again."

"You mean going back to London?" Rob's voice was suddenly hollow.

"I suppose so, although I won't be there long. I'm over in New York soon." The excitement crept into her voice. "I've worked hard for this opportunity."

"Of course you have." Rob said with forced enthusiasm, realising that by helping Alicia to keep the appointment, he was helping her to escape. "Do you really have to go?" He suddenly uttered, but Alicia was distracted about what the Doctor would say, and lingering memories of her father's death.

"What was that?" She asked absent-mindedly but his comment passed without her fully registering why he was concerned about whether she would stay.

They made their way through the labyrinth of corridors, the smell of bleach and overcooked food cloyingly filling their nostrils. In distaste she wrinkled her nose, but the smell remained obstinately wedged. They carried on along the rubber floored corridor, their footsteps squeaking, until they reached the nurses' station jutting out beneath the sign that declared 'Outpatients'. Alicia quickly explained why she was there to a chubby faced nurse who stood smoothing her white and green uniform over her ample frame.

"Sit down there and I'll let Doctor O'Donnell know you're here." She indicated a row of plastic chairs with the flick of a finger, and they obligingly sat on the uncomfortable moulded chairs.

"So how are you and Chloe getting along, thinking of moving in together?" Alicia asked idly making conversation as there appeared to be no magazines or papers.

Rob glared at her, wondering if Chloe had broken her promise not to tell anyone about the baby until they had at least visited the doctors. "Why would you say that?"

"Hey don't be like that. I just think in a funny way you're an unlikely couple. I mean I always imagined Chloe going for someone who was far more roses and romance, but you two seem to get on well together, and you've got nothing standing in your way, so it seems only natural that you'll start living together."

He had to acknowledge her logic, but a small chilled hand grabbed at him as he realised that they would have to start living together soon if he was going to take responsibility for Chloe and the baby. He wished he could talk it through with Alicia, hear what she thought he should do, but he and Chloe had agreed not to tell anyone at the moment. So he sat and silently waited as Alicia was called by Doctor O'Donnell.

◆◆◆

It had been a long week. As well as putting up with Lily's caustic remarks about the forthcoming wedding, Pete had been covering for Chloe who seemed to have lost contact with earth and was floating along in a separate galaxy. He had finally found a property for Charles Pennington-Smythe in a converted windmill with views across the neighbouring vales. After his initial insistence for a large detached house, he had ended up with a penthouse apartment. But at least he had picked the keys up at the beginning of the week, so he should be fully ensconced in his new apartment by now.

As Pete let himself in the house, calling out a cheery hello, it was eerily quiet. Used to Natalia's pop CDs battling against the sound from Pete's News 24, it appeared a ceasefire had been called. In fact judging from the state of the house it looked like there was going to be a permanent resolution to the warring factions. With slow faltering steps he crossed the living room half-sliding on the discarded magazines under foot. Pictures had been torn off the walls, unwanted photos lay abandoned so that a montage of the couple's memories lay scattered, grinning ironically up at him. The cushion pads – stripped of their lacy covers lay exposed on the floor and the curtains hung lopsidedly where Natalia had tugged off the decorative tie-backs.

Hours later Pete was still slumped in the armchair, a half drunk can of beer in one hand, the other covered his face. He couldn't bear to sit looking at the room, but neither could he summon the energy to move. The whole house resembled a scene of destruction, home to a whirling dervish who had swept through each room leaving chaos in its wake. No room had been left untouched, drawers wrenched out, contents spilt as they were rummaged through. When Pete had first walked in his immediate concern had been burglars, then as he noticed that the TV was still sat in the corner he slowly began to reassess the situation. It was the curt note on the table that confirmed his second thought – that Natalia had left him. Walking from room to room, each one resembling a bomb site, his brain tried to register the note Natalia had scrawled. It appeared that she had discovered that she wasn't after all in love with Pete, that she was leaving him and moving in with Charles Pennington-Smythe. Ironic really; having found Charles the perfect love-nest, Charles then completed it by installing Pete's lover. What had enraged him most though was the way Natalia had decided to leave, surely he deserved a little more than a scrawled note telling him she had left to be with someone far more suitable.

He was still sitting there in his office suit, his tie loosened as the light moved from the bright afternoon sun through to the molten dusk and finally to the inky blackness of the night. His neck felt stiff and cramped, and his eyes were dry and gritty, but still he continued to sit, caught up in the thoughts and reflections of the past two years. An immense sorrow filled him, but if he was honest he couldn't tell if it was an intense grief at the loss of Natalia or the shame of having to admit publically that his fiancée had run off with another man. Being with Natalia had always been complicated; he'd enjoyed being the main provider and alpha-male protector – a role he always felt that he had failed with his mother, but Natalia's obvious material desires had recently begun to irk him. It wasn't that he minded spending money but Natalia didn't share the same ethos of linking earning to spending. She still believed that money would always flow freely for her and that there was no need for her to concern herself with earning it. He knew he was going to have to eat a large slice of humble-pie to break the news to Lily, he could already hear her cackling laugh as she declared '*I told you so*', with evident delight '*I always said she was a gold digger*'. It was more wounding though to have to admit she was right rather than hearing her crow. He tried not to think about the money he had already shelled out for the wedding preparations and vaguely wondered whether he could claim on his insurance for desertion by a fiancée. With a huge effort he finished his beer, crumpling the empty can and dropping it on the carpet in disgust.

He felt chilled, even though the night was itself warm, and his stomach gave a deep rumble as he realised he hadn't eaten since breakfast. He moved into the kitchen, stepping over the strewn CDs and discarded books, not bothering to turn on the lights. As his eyes became accustomed to the duskiness he saw the cupboards were bare and sighed in exasperation, Natalia had never enjoyed looking after the house and rarely had she bothered with grocery shopping. In the fridge he found a wedge of brie and a half-eaten can of baked beans. Pulling them out, he cut the rind off the oozing cheese and microwaved them together. It formed a congealed mess on the plate; tentatively he prodded it with a fork and dubiously tasted it. It stuck to his teeth and coated his tongue but as his stomach rumbled again he persevered until it was all gone. The unappetising smell lingered and he realised he'd need to start taking control of his life again or he'd end up eating meals like this every night. He'd teased Chloe often enough about her bachelorette days living off take-aways, now she'd be returning the mocks. Thinking of Chloe gently ribbing him made him feel better, plus if Natalia wasn't around he could abandon his diet and start stealing Chloe's Rolos again.

Chapter 18

On the other side of the globe an equally emotion-riddled storm was occurring. It seemed time and space really are salves for wounded lovers. Matty sat looking at herself in the mirror, amazed at how externally she had changed, turning from a wane scarecrow into a bronzed butterfly; her skin was beginning to freckle from the sun and her stands of hair were lightening from sitting outside on the balcony of her parents' apartment. It had been strange being with them again, but somehow their reserved manner was just what Matty needed, she didn't require the pained enquiries of overly concerned parents. She just wanted to know she could just sit and retreat into herself to think. It had been a week after Matty's arrival that her mother had finally broached the subject of Tom, asking in a casual manner whether Matty intended to start divorce proceedings. The shock of realising just what was at stake made her start rationally analysing her life with Tom. Being away from the farm, the house and her husband allowed her to objectively assess her life with a detached air, unpicking the gathers and folds of the patchwork squares making up her world, so that she could view them from all perspectives. The main thing which became apparent was that it wasn't Tom who made her unhappy, but the way he had assumed she would give up her job to be like Barbara. True they had never really discussed it, but she had kept the job at Saunders as a defiant stand, like a wayward teenager. It had been a bid for maintaining some independence, but it wasn't the job that she really wanted, it was something she could do with her eyes shut. What was missing was using her brain, of feeling stretched mentally and creatively, of having challenges thrown her way. She thought wistfully of lost dreams, of her plans; of being involved in fashion, of working with clothes, and wondered whether it was too late to try and turn back the clock. She had lain awake that evening, the gauze fabric of the mosquito netting dancing in the slight breeze from the fan. The air was hot and humid and Matty shifted trying to get comfortable. She pictured Tom back in England, lying in their bed, wondering if he ever thought of her; a slow hot burn ran over her skin as the realisation of what she had actually done penetrated her brain; a sense of guilt and shame flushed her cheeks. Almost in bewilderment she recalled her actions, how had she let things get so bad? How could she have been so uncaring to abandon her husband without even saying goodbye? Then a surge of panic replaced the reproach, as she understood what she had to lose. The clock on the cabinet ticked slowly through the night, on into the early hours of the morning, their hands slowly moving round.

At half-past four she gave up all pretence of sleep and got up, the stone tiles felt cool against the skin of her bare feet. Wrapping an ancient silk kimono around her she walked out onto the balcony, staring out at the dawn drenched horizon, watching the sea become a cauldron of molten lead, coloured by the glowing fireball of the sun. When her parents' maid appeared to start preparing the family's breakfast she found Matty deep in concentration, pouring out her feelings onto sheets of thin airmail paper by way of commencing her penance. Matty had no idea what the future would hold for her and Tom, but honesty compelled her to admit that she had probably well and truly burnt her boats there. The one thing that she needed to focus on therefore was trying to rebuild her life; starting with a job that she would enjoy and probably somewhere to live, especially if Tom didn't want her back. Hopefully Chloe would be able to help her find something though. She finished the letter with a heart-felt *'my love as always, Matty xxx'* and held it momentarily aloft, weighing up the consequences of sending it, hesitant to bring about a final decision from Tom before holding her breath and deftly folding the letter into the addressed envelope. She slipped into a pair of cotton trousers and shirt and made her way to the post office, anxious to start understanding the remnants of her marriage.

Over breakfast she raised the subject of her future. Her father listened politely, one eye on the clock to make sure he wasn't late leaving for the office, the other giving small encouraging looks. Her mother sat perfectly still listening, no emotions registering on her face until at half-past eight she reminded her husband it was time for the office. The two women watched him straighten his tie in the hall mirror and plump the dandily placed handkerchief in his blazer pocket, before he bid them a jaunty good-bye.
"Dad looks a lot happier these days." Matty commented, contemplating her father's springy step.

"He is, being here in charge of the office has given him a new lease of life. I'm not sure what would have happened if we had stayed in England. Poor chap would probably have pined away.
"It must have been difficult for you both when he left the Army."
"It was! You give over half your life to the Forces, and they then cast you off without a second thought. Poor Roger had never known anything outside of the Army, he was used to following orders, he just couldn't cope with the change to being unwanted and idle. That's why this job is such a blessing. He still gets to work with some of his old pals over here, so at least we've got friends round us again. And he likes being busy, being part of a team."
"Do you think you'll ever come back to England?"
Emma shook her head. "Probably not. The change in lifestyle, the climate and the price of property. No I think we'll see our days out over here."
Matty picked up her coffee cup and finishing the strong bitter drink, stared at the grouts and asked. "So what do you think I should do?"
Emma was flattered that her daughter was seeking her opinion, but felt ill-placed to advice. "I'm not really the person to ask. I've always been an Army wife. I've followed your father wherever the Army decided to post him, each time setting up a new home and making new friends. Moving here was the biggest decision of our lives, and that wasn't very difficult as there were no other jobs and we couldn't afford to stay in England."
"But do you think Tom will forgive me?" Matty's voice caught slightly as she vocalised her greatest fear.
"I don't know. I've only met him when we came over for the wedding, but I do know that he seemed a genuinely honest man. Whatever he decides, I don't think he'll play games."
Matty silently agreed.
"And what should I do?" she asked miserably.
"Now that I do have an idea on! As soon as we're finished here we're going over to The Club. There's someone I think you should meet."

'The Club' was an old colonial building erected by Victorian traders who had built their wealth in spice and silks. Its chunky white washed walls and crenulated roof gave it the impression of having been uprooted from the English countryside and the ex-pats had continued to congregate there ever since. Large oil paintings and sturdy dark wood furniture decorated with current copies of Country Life, Vogue and Bling & Boudoir made it a replacement for a missed bygone England. Matty had been there a couple of times with her parents for cocktails, but she had studiously avoided the eager Club secretary who wanted to pair Matty off for the weekly tennis match, and involve her in the panto preparations. "I'd love to." Matty had lied, a smile plastered on her lips. "But I'm only here for a short holiday."

They walked up the short drive and into the cool interior where a gate boy, resplendent in crisp white uniform, grinned widely and held the door open with a small gesturing bow.
"Come on it's up here." Emma pointed to a smaller spiral staircase that Matty hadn't noticed before. Following her mother up into the upper room, which although by no means as grand as the public rooms below, were still of graceful proportions. The floor was a dark oak that was almost covered by a pretty china blue rug. On one side were two comfy armchairs, and on a low coffee table lay various fashion magazines. On the other side of the room were two rails running the length of the walls, holding ball gowns and cocktail dresses, a myriad of colours each shimmering in the light like preening butterflies. Bemused at what her mother was planning, Matty watched as a well dressed lady of her mother's age appeared and warmly greeted Emma with a kiss on the cheek.
"Simply super to see you. How are you doing darling? It's ages since you've been to see me." She scolded.
"I know, but I haven't needed anything. We don't have any invitations until Christmas now."
"And this is your daughter?"
"Yes, Matty this is Elizabeth." Matty's mother proudly turned to introduce her daughter.
"Well come and sit yourselves down. I've got some tea organised." She ushered them into the two armchairs and bought across a footstool to daintily perch upon. A diminutive Asian woman carried in a tray laden with teapot and set it down on the table for them.

As they sat sipping the delicately flavoured liquid, Emma and Elizabeth outlined the story of how Elizabeth had set up her dress agency. "But what's this got to do with me?" Matty politely questioned, not comprehending why they were telling her this.

"Because you could do this!" Emma enthused, holding her hands out towards the rails. "You could set up your own business, running a dress agency."

Matty stared at her mother as though she had gone mad. "But what do I know about clothes."

"You know your Marc Jacobs from your Marks & Sparks." Emma pointed out, and Elizabeth corroborated with.

"Which is more than I did when I started." She grinned conspiratorially at Matty. "But sometimes that's a blessing. It means you aren't corralled in by all those rules of what one should and shouldn't do. Instead you just give it a go."

"But I live..." Matty inwardly gulped at the thought of Tom and their cottage, and wondered just how badly her bridges were burnt there. "... I live in a village, it's not exactly Carnaby Street."

Emma flapped her hand as though swatting away her daughter's negativity away. "From what I saw at the wedding there are plenty of Farmers' Parties, Hunt Balls, local business functions and all those commuters' Christmas drinks."

"Darling, I bet you'd find loads of women who want to exchange things they never wear," Elizabeth concurred. "There's not one woman who doesn't have at least one thing in their wardrobe that wasn't a bad buy, unwanted present or simply no longer fits, that they'd prefer to swop for something else." She took another sip of tea before continuing. "And it's so easy. All you have to do is sell things for people. It's easy-peasy. No need to buy stock up front, or worry about what's going to be this season's must have. You just agree a price for each garment and then keep your percentage when it sells."

The opportunities began to open up in front of Matty's eyes like bursting rosebuds unfurling with potential, the latent possibilities of having her own business. Whatever happened she would need to have an income, particularly if her worst fears about her marriage were realised and Tom demanded a divorce – not that she could blame him if he did, she was fully aware that her behaviour had been unforgiveable. With a rising sense of excitement her voice trembled slightly as she said. "I suppose it would be something I could do. Although I'm not sure there really is enough demand for just ball gowns though in Drayton Beauchamp. Maybe I could look at smart outfits as well, you know suits, that kind of thing." She mused, now starting to picture herself setting up her own business, being able to work with clothes every day, keeping up to date with the latest fashions.

Elizabeth and Emma exchanged discreet congratulatory smiles at Matty's response. "Just remember the two golden rules, don't go cheap or you'll end up like a charity shop and no one will want to buy from you."

"And the second?" Matty enquired.

"Always make sure everything is dry cleaned before you take it. There is nothing more off putting than the smell of someone else's sweat when you are trying things on." Elizabeth grimaced. "Believe me I had a few whiffy things in the beginning." Emma and Matty looked horrified. "But that doesn't happen now." Elizabeth quickly reassured them. "Why don't you have a quick peak at what we've got; you never know you might spot something." She stood up, and led them over to the rails. "I'll leave you to browse, just give me a call if there's anything you want to try on."

The two women slowly and methodically worked their way down each rail, looking at the collection of Chanel, Vera Wang and Prada, hanging with Ralph Lauren and Marc Jacobs. It felt like being let loose in a wonderful calorie-free candy store, all the potential held within the shimmering skirts, asymmetrical hemlines and embroidered bodices. Emma gave a muffled laugh and pulled out a Vivienne Westwood creation of banana yellow frills and ruffles.

"No!" Matty exclaimed as her mother held it admiringly against her. "You look like a luminous canary."

"But it's so cheerful." Emma protested.

"No it's so awful!"

Reluctantly Emma replaced it on the rail before quickly pulling out another garment, a deep scarlet, cut in the Chinese style with a high mandarin collar and three tiny seed pearl buttons on one side. It was tailored to fit the body and the straight skirt came just to the knee. It was piped in a contrasting blue that softened the edges. "That's more like it." Matty said visibly impressed; Emma held it up against her daughter so they could both regard Matty's dressed image in the mirror.

"Go and try it on." Emma urged. "There's a pair of Karl Lagerfeld heels over there as well which would look great."

"But I don't have any money." Matty protested.

"Think of it as a present from your Father and I. Go on, the changing room is over there." She gave a small gentle push and propelled her forward. "I'll just wait here for you."

Matty stood looking at her reflection, the dress fitted to perfection, just catching in the right places, emphasising her womanly curves. The tall heels, gave her legs added length, and her newly acquired tan was further enhanced by the scarlet silk. Although she had poured over designer clothes in Harper, Vogue and the fashion supplements, she had never actually worn them before. Pulling back the curtain she stepped out and paraded slowly in front of her mother, before stopping and grinning.
"It looks as though it was made for you." Emma's voice was warm with admiration. "We're definitely going to take it."
With a sudden rush of gratitude Matty leant across and kissed her mother on the cheek before adding ruefully. "Now I just have to find an excuse to wear it."

◆◆◆

As it was the excuse came sooner than she had imagined, and in a way she would never have been able to predict. Five days after posting the letter to Tom, Matty had still heard nothing, despondency and rejection had begun to set in. She couldn't blame Tom for being angry, but it didn't stop any of the hurt that gnawed away inside her. The tears that had flowed so freely in the lonely hours of the morning were testament to that. She had been late out for breakfast and had opted for strong coffee on the balcony instead. She sat morosely watching the world go by on the streets below, wallowing in self-pity. The scent of the bitter coffee filling her nostrils as she cradled the cup. She realised that she needed to start making some decisions about her life. She had been living off her parents since arriving, not having brought any money with her. She didn't know if she would be entitled to anything from Tom if he did want a divorce, after all she had given him more than enough grounds for demanding a separation. Her eyes glazed over with unshed tears, missing the exotic lush vista that stretched across to the calm azure sea. Instead of inspiring wonder and curiosity it merely emphasised the loneliness she felt, of the longing to be back in England, in the cottage with Tom. Idly she wondered whether to email Chloe to find out about a place for rent, but then there was the larger question of how she would pay for it. The tantalising thought of her own dress business floated through her mind again; she could envisage the racks of clothes, the shelving for accessories, the display area with soft spotlighting. Then the phantoms of cash flow, shop leases and bank managers would rear their menacing heads and chase the dream away.

The sound of her mother's footsteps roused Matty from her unhappy dwellings; wiping her eyes quickly to remove any signs of tears she composed herself, wringing out a small bereft smile for the benefit of Emma.

"There you are! I wondered when you would surface."

"I didn't sleep very well last night." Matty mumbled apologetically, moving up on the bench so her mother could sit down, but Emma waved a vague hand.

"Actually I just came to let you know that we've all been invited out to dinner tonight."

Matty wrinkled her nose. "I don't really feel like it."

"Nonsense." Her mother briskly chided. "It's just what you need. You never know who you might meet. Anyway it's an opportunity to wear your new dress."

Matty belligerently agreed like a sullen teenager, but Emma chose to ignore it. Instead she continued upbeat with. "And I've arranged for us to go and visit a hairdresser after lunch. It's always such a treat to get one's hair done." Gently she pushed a loose curl off of Matty's face and looped it behind her ear. "I know it's tough on you at the moment," Maternal concern ringing through her voice. "But things will get better, you just have to be strong for a bit longer."

Matty took hold of her mother's hand and held the palm against her cheek, feeling the soft skin moulded against her face. "Thank you for everything." She mumbled.

"Darling, it's nothing. Honestly it's been lovely having you here. I'm sorry it's been under such rotten circumstances."

"I feel like I've made a mess of my life." Matty's thoughts ricocheted back to her conversation with Barbara all those weeks ago when she had broken down in front of her at Chloe's flat.

"There's a local saying out here that reminds us the darkest moment always comes just before the morning sun. Somehow things always turn out ok."

"I hope you're right." Matty replied morosely.

◆◆◆

165

The evening air was scented with lotus blossom and jasmine, it hung about like an invisible cloud, enveloping everyone in its warm sweet embrace. They were walking across the town square towards the smart hotels that sat back along the road leading up to the hills. In front of her, Matty watched her parents, her mother's arm tucked comfortably into the crock of her father's. They were quietly talking, their heads turned in slightly to each other with a familiarity and contentment that only heightened her own loss. Self-consciously she touched her hair, feeling the sticky sculpture unforgiving under her fingertips. Gone were her normal carefree curls, instead her hair had been teased and sprayed back to form an elegant French pleat. To soften the overall effect a few kiss curls had been left seductively loose, framing her delicate features. As the trio reached the grand glass slab front doors Matty noticed her father peel off and slip quickly aside to speak to the concierge.

"Is everything ok?" Matty whispered to her mother as her father signalled a nod to her mother.

Emma patted her daughter's hand consolingly. "Of course it is. Let's go and get a drink." They walked through the pale marbled corridor, along to the bar area where the views gave a panorama of the dusky rolling lush hills and inky blue sea. In the distance tiny lights twinkled giving the impression that troupes of fairies were flitting around.

"Sit yourself down." Her father ordered as though she was one of his squaddies. "We've got to nip off for a moment, go and see where our guests have got to. No, no, you stay seated." He held out a halting hand as Matty made to rise to go with them. "Take a look at the drinks menu and we'll back in a mo." She watched their retreating figures before picking up the leather bound drinks menu and idly began to read through the concoctions that the hotel offered. Behind her people milled about meeting up with friends, ordering drinks and chatting loudly above the pianist's gentle jazz melody. One of the waiters glided over and silently set a glass of fizzing champagne down in front of her.

"I haven't ordered anything." Matty protested, but the waiter merely grinned at her with his slanting eyes and murmured it came with the gentleman's compliments. Intrigued, Matty started to look round for the gentleman; it had to be one of her parents' friends, but in a moment the faint but unmistakable whiff of Calvin Klein scent assailed her, transporting her back to the cottage, and setting out to the Drayton Hall fete. A steel band tightened round her heart almost causing her to cry out in sorrow, but a discreet cough from behind her made her head spin round and suddenly she was face to face with Tom. In disbelief she simply sat and stared at him, unable to say a word, expecting him to vanish before her eyes. Incredulity swept through her, how had he found her? With a trembling hand she gingerly stretched out a finger towards him, slowly extending until she touched the sharp crease of his trouser, the fabric soft under her finger. Then a tsunami of emotion erupted within, and tears began to cascade uncomprehendingly as she tried to work out what was happening. In an instant Tom was crouching by her chair, cradling her sobbing form in his arms, gently soothing her. Matty's hands had flown to her face, her cheeks burning with shame and wet teardrops running through her fingers and down the back of her hands The shock of seeing Tom in the flesh when still so afraid about the future caused a massive sentimental overload. She had imagined their meeting to be so different; she had planned to be witty and vivacious, with a subtly seductive aura to tempt and tease him back. Instead here she was a crumpled mess, tear stained, gasping for air, hardly designed to attract anyone back.

Around them people stopped their conversations as the sound of crying filtered through the room, turning to stare at the couple. Concerned waiters flapped around them enquiring what was wrong, Tom tried to shoo them away with a wave of an arm, but they honed in like a swarm of wasps attracting even more attention. Finally the Maitre d' worried about the commotion hurried through, and in an instant assessed the situation. With a few quiet words and selected calming motions the hiatus was forgotten, the staff melted away and the stares of the other guests were coyly lowered.

Matty's sobs subsided to a small occasional whimper and Tom carefully removed her damp hands from her face; her puffy eyes now smeared and tear stained remained lowered, avoiding any contact.
"Darling." Tom's voice was low, and he gently turned her chin towards him, forcing her gaze to meet his. Looking at her red puffy eyelids, encircled by blotchy mascara, the ruffled hair escaping from its pleat and the bottom lip that had been chewed anxiously, he was aware just how desirable she still was to him.

He almost felt as though he had forgotten just how beautiful he found her, and for a moment he feasted his eyes on his wife after the prolonged absence. He pulled out a handkerchief and fumbled inexpertly at wiping away the black mascara stains, and smoothing back her hair. Still she sat immobile just looking at him as though in a state of shock, her hands clenched tightly on her lap, her knuckles straining white through her skin.

Picking up the glass of champagne he offered it to her, holding it to her lips. She mechanically took a sip, feeling the need for some assisted courage, and as the bubbles skipped round her mouth and down her throat, she found her voice and almost fearfully asked. "What are you doing here?"

Tom picked up one her hands and dropped a kiss into the palm. "I thought I might visit my wife." He answered lightly, aware this wasn't the time to launch into a deep and meaningful discussion, but he felt her jump as she heard the words '*my wife*'.

"You actually came all this way just to see me?" She was incredulous. "But what about the farm?"

"Matty, do you seriously think you don't take precedence over everything else? There was only so long I could go without being with you."

"How can you even bear to talk to me?" Her voice sounded miserable and confused, the earlier tears threatening to return. Tom put his forefinger against her lips and stalled her.

"Let's not discuss it now. We'll talk later when we're alone." He leant across and kissed her slowly and firmly, enjoying the familiar sensation that absence had made even more desirable, and felt her respond with the same depth of feeling. Pulling away he cradled her face between his hands. "I guess your parents will be wondering what's happening."

"Do they know you're here?" Any rational thought had long since evaded her.

"They helped to organise it, I'd never have managed it on my own." He admitted.

"But what does it mean for us?"

"I don't know, but we do need to talk, and I promise we will do. For the moment though let's go and find your parents." He took her hand and chivalrously helped her to her feet. Self-conscious now of her sodden state, she wiped her cheeks and patted her hair into place.

"You look beautiful by the way." He murmured in her ear as he led her through to the dining room.

◆◆◆

The evening seemed suspended in jelly; while the others chatted and ate, Matty felt as though she was an ethereal spectator. She didn't know what to think, the fact that Tom was here was surely a positive sign, but her behaviour couldn't be ignored. What would their discussion involve? Was he trying to be nice to her, let her down gently, so that he could get on with his own life and find someone a little less emotional? She drank heavily from her glass and pushed the food round her plate, the small filo parcels of crab in pernod had been cooked to perfection, but however hard she tried to chew a mouthful, it was impossible to swallow the tasteless lump. Every so often she would turn to look at Tom, studying his profile with an agonising familiarity as he discussed the state of the world with Roger, the dismal England rugby team performance in the latest match and the forthcoming cricket tour. Emma squeezed Matty's arm and gave an encouraging smile, but when Matty tried to return it she found that apprehension had deadened the nerves, so that it ended up as a frightened grimace. When the meal finally came to an end and her parents had stood up to go, Matty had been filled with an intense panic, what would happen now? Would Tom come back with them, or would he be going back to England. She started to rise from her seat, anxiously looking from her parents to Tom, not sure what they expected of her. She didn't want to stay if Tom had no plans for them spending the night together. In the end though the worry was futile, Tom calmly detained her with a lowered whisper of "Please stay behind so we can talk." causing her knees to give way so she dropped back down into her seat.
"Would you like another drink?" Tom hospitably offered once they had bid goodnight to the other two. Matty nodded, she didn't really want one but hopefully it might give her a little more courage than she was currently feeling. Two brandies appeared and tentatively she sipped the liquid, not used to the burning sensation as it rolled over her tongue and down her throat.
"When did you fly in?" Matty asked, feeling like a gauche teenager and fearing what the silences in conversation meant.
"About five o'clock this evening."
"And are you staying here?"
"Yes, for tonight at least."

"All the guidebooks say it's one of the most romantic hotels in the town."

"I'm sure it is."

"Who's looking after the farm?"

"Mum and Dad."

There was a small silence before Matty said quietly. "That's kind of them."

"Actually they've been incredibly supportive." Tom agreed and Matty felt a death knoll sounding in her head. This was yet another example of her failure to be a good wife. "It hasn't been easy without you there. God knows the worry you put me through. You didn't even tell me where you were going Matty. Didn't I at least deserve that?" Matty's head hung forward and two fat tear drops trickled down her cheek, she nodded her head mutely. "You must really hate me not to even want to be in the same house as me." The weeks of worry and concern came out in a flood. "What did I do that was so wrong that couldn't even speak to me? Did you just stop loving me?" The anguish in his voice caused her to sharply look up at him with her large brown eyes.

"No never." She whispered vehemently. "It was me that I stopped loving. I got myself into such a mess that I couldn't get out of it. I felt I had to literally run for my life. I wish I hadn't gone off like I did; I wish I hadn't been so awful to live with; I really wish I hadn't made such a mess of everything. But the fact is I did. I screwed up big time. I know that. I can't expect you to forget everything that I've done. I know I'm to blame for it all."

"No;" Tom's natural fairness wouldn't let her shoulder all the blame. "I should have been more understanding about you wanting a life outside of the farm, of not wanting a baby. The truth is I kept pushing for it, because deep down I was afraid I would lose you." He ran a finger down her cheek. "I could never believe how someone so beautiful and intelligent could ever be interested in me."

Matty caught his hand in hers and dropped a kiss into the palm. "I'd never stop loving you." She vowed, and summoning all her courage, she leant across and kissed him on the lips. There was a momentarily hesitation before he responded ardently, returning her kiss with a passion that sparked a mutual desire alight. Dimly aware they were in a public place, Tom pulled back slightly, feeling Matty's breath against his neck. They were grasping each other's hands so tightly it was as though they never wanted to be parted again. A huge wave of longing swept through him and he knew they needed to retire somewhere more private.

"Shall we go up to my room?" He spoke suggestively into her ear; the mirrored desire was written across her face as she coyly smiled up at her husband.

"If we don't, I'm going to have to demand my marital rights right here."

Pulling her up so that their bodies slotted together he held her close, "I'm so glad I found you again." and taking her hand he led her up to their room.

◆◆◆

The next morning Matty arrived at her parents' apartment, shattered from the lack of sleep, aching from the passionate reunion, mentally exhausted from the emotional roller coaster, and yet glowing with contentment and jubilation.

"I needn't ask how it went." was Emma's greeting, noting her daughter's expression.

Matty beamed back as she started to tell her mother about the previous evening. "We talked and talked, you know about everything, even the awful bits. How dreadful life seemed for us both, and why it all seemed to happen. Having had some time here, I could talk to him for the first time about what I really wanted out of life, and he was honest about wanting a family, but may be not yet." It seemed so hard to get across the hours of conversation they'd had, sitting together in bed, Matty lying in the crook of Tom's arm as he held her close. "He's asked me to go back with him when he flies back to see if we can work through it."

"And are you going to go?"

"Oh yes." Her voice was adamant, knowing that she wanted to be with Tom above everything else. "But of course it's all going to be different. We did talk about a future, about making changes to our lives. He agreed that he would speak to his parents and make sure we had time to ourselves, but without excluding them of course." She added quickly. "And I told him about the dress agency idea. He really liked the idea of us setting up something together, he even suggested we look at maybe using one of the old barns and converting it into a showroom. As Tom pointed out, if it doesn't work out as a business for us, we could still rent it out to make money."

Emma was secretly amused at how Matty was deferentially referring to Tom. "That makes sense. And what about Tom wanting a family?"

"We agreed to wait for a year, so that we can get ourselves sorted, or as close as normal as we can get after all this, then we'll see. But this time it will all be different; and if it all works out then there's no reason why I couldn't have a baby and keep working if it's at home."

Emma could see the zeal of conviction shining in Matty's face, obviously convinced there could really be a happy-ever-after. She hugged her daughter briefly. "I'm so glad you two have managed to work things out. I can't think of a more suitable couple. Just don't forget about your father and I when you go back." She pleaded with a light laugh. "We've really enjoyed having you here."

"Oh Mum!" Matty felt a prickle in the back of her throat, she smiled encouragingly at her mother. "You can come and stay with us, you'll be able to see the shop and maybe Tom can take Dad to Twickenham to see a match; and we will definitely be back here when the rain and the farm get too much for us – you just see."

"I can't wait!"

Chapter 19

Rob rustled the paper as he turned over the page, moved from the local WI updates to the sports section, his eye was flicking down the league results to see how the Drayton Beauchamp team were faring in the competition when he became aware of a restless bustling to his right. Lowering the paper he saw Chloe fidgeting with the cushions. "Sorry; I'm ignoring you." He apologised, folding the Drayton Chronicle up neatly and replacing it on the table where he'd found it. With a small recognition of sympathy he realised Chloe was obviously having to summon up courage for something, but he'd no idea what for though.

Ever since she had announced her pregnancy they seemed to have inhabited separate universes. Not that there had been any arguments or cross words; they hadn't deliberately decided to seek any division, and yet subtly their relationship had changed. As Rob had thrown himself into work with a zeal unfamiliar even to him, so Chloe had pulled a soft comforting blanket around herself, retreating into dreams of her baby. There was certainly no fault, or recriminations, but Rob realised if they were going to build a life together for the sake of the baby then they needed to become much closer. He pushed away the memory of Alicia knowing that any chance had been lost and concentrated on all the positive things about Chloe. It wasn't difficult, she was warm and funny, kind and generous – the sort of partner most men would be proud of.

He noticed that Chloe had styled her hair and worn make-up, obviously trying to make an effort and he cursed himself for turning up in old slacks and a Ben Sherman shirt that had a hole in the elbow. He needed to think about being here for Chloe. The trouble was it just wasn't part of his natural behaviour. 'You've got to give it time,' he silently instructed himself 'surely we'll be able to make a go of it'. So turning on an encouraging smile designed to put Chloe at her ease and began to tease out what was on her mind. It took a few tentative starts, before Chloe finally took a deep breath. She had been practicing the sentence for weeks, not wanting to sound too demanding, and yet desperate to have Rob more involved.
"I wondered if you would come to the Doctors with me; you know to get the baby checked out."

A shot of guilt ricocheted around his rib cage; he felt like a total cad. Having been so caught up in his garden work he hadn't even spared a thought for how Chloe was, other than a slightly perfunctory enquiry when they spoke on the phone. He covered her hand that was still fiddling with the cushion, with his large calloused one and squeezed it warmly.

"Of course I will Chloe."

She visibly relaxed. "Are you sure? I know how busy you are with work, but it would be so much nicer if you were there."

"Of course I'll be there." He repeated firmly. "Just let me know when." He watched her walk over to the table and pour two coffees from the cafetiere she'd obviously made before he arrived this morning. She had a faraway look about her, almost tempting him to ask why, but deep down he already knew. She was picturing herself holding the baby.

Taking the offered cup he savoured a mouthful of coffee. "I'm sorry I didn't think to offer before; it can't have been much fun worrying about it." He took another mouthful. "I guess I had presumed you had already been before you told me." He gave a bear like shrug. "I know – that's men for you." He was self-effacing.

Chloe giggled, not offended by his honesty. "I couldn't envisage myself going alone. It just wouldn't seem right, after all the man is as involved as the woman, so she shouldn't get all the fun bits alone." Privately Rob didn't see any fun elements, but he could see her point of view about both parents being present.

"So when should we go?" He tried not to let his heart sink as Chloe pulled out the largest pregnancy encyclopaedia he'd ever seen. She flicked through a couple of chapters until she found the page she wanted.

"In here they recommend seeing the Doctor at eight weeks."

"And when's that?"

Chloe's brow furrowed. "I'm not really sure."

"Well when did you take the test?" Rob had some vague notion that the tests only worked from four weeks, so they should be able to do some rudimentary maths to establish how many weeks pregnant she was.

Chloe's cheeks sizzled red and she averted her gaze. "I didn't do a test." She admitted.

Rob was confused. "So how did you know you were pregnant?"

She looked at him squarely with a 'how-do-you-think' look. "Because I haven't had my period, and I am never late.   So obviously I'm pregnant."
"But you haven't done a test?"
Chloe shook her head. "I didn't need to, I already knew." She told him, although in reality that was only half true but she was never going to admit to Rob the real reason.   Having gone shopping the week before pay-day, she had fully intended to buy the pregnancy kit, but on finding out much they cost she had hastily retreated and instead used the money towards a pair of Ted Baker shoes in the sales instead.   Now, wiggling her toes in the beloved shoes, she felt uncomfortable at Rob's thunderous stare, and wondered whether it had been the right choice.

◆◆◆

Chloe looked at herself in the mirror; never a boastful person, even she admitted though that she looked radiant.   Her cheeks were peachy pink, her hair was glossy and a small playful smile seemed permanently attached to her lips.   She couldn't wait to update her FaceBook page tonight; she would show everyone just how lucky she was.   Pregnant with a gorgeous boyfriend, maybe she'd be able to sneak a photo of Rob to put up on the page.   Now she never need be envious of all those school friends with their endless children and perfect marriages, she was officially joining the ranks of the successful people, and leaving behind her sad singlehood.   In her hand was the pregnancy test Rob had promptly bought, now she just need to get the proof.

Sitting down on the toilet she held the stick in position and waited; and waited.   She couldn't believe how long this was taking.   Finally in exasperation she turned on the tap and willed herself to wee, she wanted to present Rob with the proof of the pregnancy.   His look had turned from confusion to disbelief at the situation; she wanted to show him that she had been right.   At last she finally felt herself going, and she wiggled the stick around. With excitement she started the long two minute wait; it was hard to believe that sitting on the loo, knickers round her ankles, staring at a pseudo-lolly-stick could make the butterflies in her stomach do the aeronautics they were currently practising. One minute and counting; her feet started to do an involuntarily little jig in anticipation. She checked her watch, yep two minutes was up. She looked back at the stick, expecting the two red lines to appear, but stubbornly they were absent. She shook the stick like a thermometer, waiting for them to emerge, but it still remained clear. She tried again. Nothing. A feeling of loss and disbelief descended on her; she couldn't believe it, the test must be faulty. That was it, she decided robustly, time to go and tell Rob he'd just have to go out and buy another.

An hour later and it was official; her life was falling apart. She'd been so happy this morning waiting for Rob to arrive, tidying the flat, making coffee for them, sneaking a look at all the baby outfits she'd bought. Now it had all dissolved into a soggy grey mess. She was sitting on the sofa, Rob was holding her hands, and he was being sympathetic and consoling; but he'd dropped the final bombshell leaving her now without a baby, a boyfriend or a dream lifestyle. She'd never be able to update her Facebook page at this rate.

"But we could always try for another baby." She had protested as Rob had kindly but firmly told her that they didn't have a future.

"Chloe; you need to have one with Mr Right. You deserve to have the whole dream; the white wedding, the adoring husband, and a whole gaggle of cheerful children."

"But you're Mr Right." She had persisted.

"I think we both know I'm not. We have had lots of fun, and I really like you, but we aren't going to be walking off in the sunset together. You're worth so much more, someone who is going to shower you with roses and romance; who will whisk you off your feet and take you to Paris for a weekend, share midnight walks and want to set up a home with you forever."

Chloe recognised the truth of Rob's words, but tried one last time. "You could do all that."

Rob grinned, causing his face to crease even more. "I can't, and you know it. I think more about work than I do about anything else. I can talk about acers, hellebores and tender herbaceous borders, but I'll never do tender declarations."

Chloe wiped away her tears and ran her hands through the hair she had so carefully prepared this morning. "So there isn't anyone else?" Her voice was timid; half-afraid of the answer.

Rob's mind flew back to Alicia but he knew he had well and truly burnt that bridge. "No," he responded truthfully. "There's no-one else."

She nodded satisfied at his answer, and he saw her face suddenly fall again. "What it is?"

"Lily's party; I'll have to admit to everyone I'm single there." She thought of having to face Pete and his comments about her failure to keep any man. Rob took her hand once more.

"Do you want to go as friends?" With relief she threw her arms round him, and he gave her a quick squeeze back. "Come on," he encouraged. "You never know, you could meet Mr Right there."

♦♦♦

The excitement must have been evident to everyone; she found it difficult to contain; it kept leaping out unexpectedly so that one moment she caught herself smiling gleefully for no real reason and the next it felt like a fizzing soda stream inside her. Sitting in business class Alicia affected to appear like the sophisticated professional she was; while an inner child pointed out the complimentary wine list, was dying to try out the new sleeper seats and had already eaten all the offered canapés. It had seemed to take forever to reach today; always looming in the distance. Now finally she was onboard the plane all ready for her big American experience. She had spent a short time in the London office finalising the other projects and preparing for the trip. Simon had prepped her, setting out the plans for the client's work, introducing her to colleagues in the New York office, assuring her he would be out shortly to help finalise the details. The project had grown, as well as acquiring the Brand XF distributor; they were picking up several smaller companies who were struggling to get their ranges out across the high street stores. It promised to be an intense few months. The pace and complexity of the deals meant living and breathing it every day and almost every night. In her briefcase, alongside her laptop, were the client files carefully outlining the target companies and the due diligence required. Even Zac had deigned to make time to take her out for lunch, reminding her that a good performance out there would reflect favourably on any Partner application and promising to spend more time with her when the assignment had finished. Now, sipping the champagne, half listening to the obligatory safety talk, she was already imaging being there. Only seven more hours and finally it would become reality.

◆◆◆

Finally after weeks of anxious preparations, the party was really going with a swing. Everyone had complimented Lily on the fabulous new garden, and rightly so. The bamboo grasses hid the ugly garage brickwork; the decking concealed the dead balding grass and let people circulate so much easier. The box trees were decorated with silk cream garlands and the sails which were hung suspended overhead had Moroccan lanterns at each point throwing jewelled light onto the revellers. Along the path were burning torches, lighting the way to the party. A makeshift bar had been set up in one corner, constructed by Rob out of logs and railway sleepers, and now held a variety of cocktails. The five piece dance band were set back on the lawn, so that their music gently wafted over the guests as they chatted, mingled and drank.

As the party stepped up a gear revellers would use the decking as an impromptu dance floor, with the lanterns forming ornate glitter balls. Waitresses dressed in navy and white uniforms wove their way expertly through the throng, topping up glasses and handing out canapés; in the middle of it all was Lily resplendent in a Vera Wang dress that carefully hid the slight creping around her neck, but showed the slenderness of her calves. Everything had gone to plan, and now she was amongst her friends celebrating. But celebrating what? It seemed a bit pompous to suggest they were celebrating her garden, instead she decided they were simply here to celebrate friendship. Glancing around the sea of animated faces she knew all the efforts were paying off. She spotted Chloe chatting to some of the neighbouring farmers who were friends of Tom, obviously confident in her new Whistles outfit, and enjoying the end of her self-imposed abstinence. It was a shame that she and Rob weren't still together; Chloe had reticently told her everything over lunch as they had shopped for her outfit, but deep down Lily hadn't been surprised. They had lacked the spark that passionate love brought. It was sad, but she had to admire Rob for his honesty, he had obviously tried to do the decent thing standing by Chloe, but coming clean about the lack of future at least meant Chloe hadn't been kept hanging on. He had acted as the perfect chaperone all evening, but you could tell they needed different things. Further round she saw Josie and

Caroline catching up; Josie was worrying about the hours Henry was having to work, and Caroline was talking about Max's return to school antics. Henry, Pete and Toby were talking to Tom and several others of the commuters about the cricket season. Barbara and Joe were talking to Tina from The King's Arms; members of the Drayton Beauchamp WI were admiring the plants and in the distance Matty was talking to Mavis and Rob about gardens. She noticed every so often Matty and Tom would exchange a shared smile; touching really. Barbara had been quite emotional on the phone, as she had retold how Matty had phoned from her parents to apologise to her and Joe for putting them through the worry, and that Matty wanted them to be able to find a way of starting again. Barbara admitted to promptly bursting into tears at the relief, and having to be comforted by Joe.

Breaking off from the conversation about the need for new practice nets for next season, Pete walked over to where his mother was standing alone by the bar. He had seen Chloe and Rob arriving together, and as he hadn't been into the office for several weeks, had presumed they were still together; he had nodded a quick 'hello' but avoided any conversation. Picking up two glasses of champagne cocktails he held one out to Lily; his face flushed from a few drinks, but these days now looking far more relaxed.

"I just wanted to say 'congratulations' – the party's going well."

"That's kind of you. I can't believe we have so many guests. I thought loads were bound to drop out."

"And miss one of your infamous parties – hardly! They've become the social event of everyone's calendar." She laughed at his blatant flattery, throwing back her head and letting out a throaty chortle. "You're a born charmer; but I'm glad to have a moment with you; I just wanted to say how much I love my present. It brings back so many happy memories of you growing up." She patted his cheek tenderly. "Now go and take that charm and rescue Chloe. There's only so much chat about sheep shearing and foot rot that she can take." Pete hesitated. "Please Pete, you know what she's going through."

"What?"

"You and Natalia. You know the whole breaking up thing." Lily looked questioningly at her son, but she could see he wasn't following. "You did know that Chloe and Rob have split up didn't you? She's worried about not having anyone to talk to here, so go and look after her for me." Registering this new piece of information with alacrity, he decisively picked up another glass of champagne and headed off to where the Young Farmer contingency were flocking. Deftly he touched her elbow and with a smooth apology appeared to extract Chloe effortlessly. Lily felt a flush of maternal pride run through her, somehow since splitting up with Natalia Pete had gained a confidence and stature she hadn't predicted, if anything she had been concerned about how he would take Natalia's desertion. It had been such a shock the way her daughter-in-law-to-be had just taken off like that. So thoughtless; such a coward's way out. Lily had been so angry when Pete had told her, that she had started to think about hiring a private detective to track Natalia down, just so Lily could have the pleasure of giving her a piece of her mind. But Pete had restrained her calmly telling her he knew exactly where Natalia was, who she was with and suggested they let the matter rest. "What!" Lily's face had been purple with indignation. "You can't mean that; she can't just go." She had ranted at his son. Pete had simply smiled.

"Yes she can; she has. And if I'm truthful I'm pleased she has. You were always telling me Natalia was no good for me. Turns out you were right after all." Lily had been left, spluttering incoherently, unable to argue against Pete's logic but futilely wanting some kind of revenge for her son. Then tragically Lily had flung herself into an armchair with the instruction. "You'd better pour us both a drink, I think we both need it." The wind well and truly removed from her sails.

Now here he was, the perfect guest, leading Chloe past the crowds to sit and chat, no sign of heart break or regret. In fact Lily had never known him so buoyant. Perhaps he was turning out to be a chip off the old block after all.

"Hadn't you better go and talk to Chloe. You don't want to be stuck talking to us all night." Matty suggested to Rob. "Plus I want an update on how Alicia is getting on in New York, and whether her rich lawyer has left his wife yet; and I bet you don't want to have to stay and be bored by that. Did she make it back ok?"

"Oh yes, a very nice young man collected her." Mavis began to update Matty and reluctantly Rob moved away, part of him wanted to know how Alicia was, even it was to masochistically hear about her rich lover. He knew that he needed to forget about her, that he had lost any chance of reconciliation but he still found himself expecting to hear her demanding tones when he called in at Apple Trees or phoned the nursery; the silence only added to the feeling of abandonment that swept through him like a heavy sea mist. Seeing Chloe's profile amid the throng he dutifully made his way over, before realising she was with Pete.

"Everything ok?" He politely enquired.

"Oh yes thanks." Chloe gushed. "I'm having a wonderful time." She clinked her glass companionably with Rob's. "I can't believe the garden, you've done such a good job."

"Yes it's wonderful." Pete agreed, his tone warmer to Rob now that he was no longer Chloe's boyfriend "It's always been a bit of a waste land before, but you really have made it work." Rob felt embarrassed at their praise, and with a sudden perspicacious insight realised he was de trop. Making an excuse he moved off, leaving the pair together.

"It is a lovely party." Chloe said dreamily sipping her drink, glad that she could enjoy alcohol once again. "Do you think we should go and talk to everyone else?"

Pete shook his head. "I've got a far better idea. Come with me." He took her hand and led her away from the party, past the band and towards the inky blanket of night. Chloe felt the slight tug of her high heels as they went across the grass; the spikes puncturing the turf and she tried not to think of the damage her Ted Baker's may be suffering. "Hold on! I can't go that fast." She laughingly protested.

Pete turned towards her. "Sorry." He slowed the pace but kept hold of her hand, enjoying the warmth of it in his.

"Where are we going?" Chloe was intrigued.

"Wait and see!" Pete teased.

"Is it much further?"

"No, just round here."

"Where?" All Chloe could see was the night-cast shadows of the garden, and then suddenly they rounded a corner and there in front of them was a delicate Chinese bridge. Along the handrail were twinkling lanterns, the fret work was interspersed with tiny bells that tinkled as the soft evening breeze caught and toyed with them.

Chloe clapped her hands together. "Where did this come from?"

"It's my present to Lily. We used to have one here when I was a child, but it had rotted away. I thought it would look wonderful in the new garden once the party's over."

"What a great idea. She'll love it! How did you get it delivered without Lily seeing it though?"

"With difficulty. That's one of the reasons I haven't been in the office all week – trying to work out when we could get it finished. It was eventually smuggled in between the caterers setting up and her hairdressing appointment."

Chloe giggled and wondered over to the bridge, running her hand over the glossy paintwork appraisingly.

"Go on try it out." Pete encouraged. With a sexy sashay Chloe gingerly stepped onto the construction and walked half way before stopping and leaning on the rail, calling for Pete to join her. Casually he stood by her, both looking out into the night, the stream bubbling away beneath their feet and the soft sounds of the band floating across the still air.

"So it's all off between you and Rob then?" He tried to keep his voice neutral. Chloe sighed. "Yes. I've yet another failed boyfriend story. I don't know what's wrong with me."

"From where I'm looking there's nothing wrong with you." Chloe swatted at him. "Don't try using your charm on me Pete Sherborne." She warned.

"Why? Is it starting to work?" He asked playfully into her ear. She turned to him. "You forget - we've shared an office for three years. I've heard all your charm before."

"Then perhaps it is three years that we've wasted." Pete's voice was so calm and collected that Chloe had to replay it in her mind twice to try and register it. She waited for him to crack a joke, but his profile remained impassive; when he didn't she spluttered out. "What? You've never said anything."

"Actually I don't think I realised until Natalia left me; we've known each other for so long, and we've always been best buddies that I've never thought of anything else. Then after Natalia left everything seemed to get even more jumbled in my head, and I just kept looking forward to catching up with you in the office and being free to go for after-work drinks. Then tonight you turn up with Rob, looking absolutely stunning, and I realised that I wanted you more than anything else in the world." Chloe was stunned, she had always thought of Pete as her boss, and therefore off limits on the boyfriend front.

""But we work together; it would never succeed. Think how awkward it would be if it doesn't work out and then we have to share the office." She realised she was rambling with nerves. "And what would Lily say..." The rest of her sentence was lost as Pete leant across and kissed her longingly. There was a fractional hesitation as Chloe's brain computed the situation; after all this was Lily's son; her boss; her best buddy; and yet even as their lips touched she was aware strange things seemed to be happening to her. Pete ran his hands along Chloe's bare shoulders, causing electric shocks to be set off under his touch. Flickering flames of desire began to leap up and nibble away as she began to return the embrace, passion sent tiny bubbles of insanity cascading through her brain. Goodness where had he learnt to kiss like this?

Eventually they pulled apart; dazed by the onslaught of emotions, Chloe collapsed against Pete, her head resting on his shoulder, her mind was in a whirl.
"Wow. What just happened!"
"I kissed you."
"Yes, I know that – but when did you turn out to be such an expert kisser."
Pete smouldered modestly. "I've always been a good kisser." He dropped a sensual kiss on her neck, sending a trail of goose bumps across her skin. "So do you think you would consider going out tomorrow?" Pete whispered into her ear.
"Would it involve more kissing?"
"Definitely; in between some smooching that is."
"Then it's a yes!" She snuggled closer. "But it's quite a long time until tomorrow. Do you think I could have another one just to keep me going?"
Pete began to kiss her plump lips. "I'm sure I can arrange that."

The party was changing mood; its vibrant energetic charge had been replaced by a slower, languid pace. The band had moved onto the melodic dance pieces, and on the dance floor couples were swaying, their bodies forming a bobbing throng. The lights above threw dancing silhouettes onto the floor that moved in time to the music. Every so often a couple would realise the time and bid Lily farewell, returning to babysitters, feeling old age, or in preparation for an early start.

Henry and Josie were swaying, arms locked around one another, occasionally sharing whispered thoughts; Rob had left, escorting Mavis home, and Barbara and Joe were thinking about morning milking. Lily's eye alighted on Pete and Chloe's dancing figures. That was certainly unexpected! And yet, the spark between the two was almost tangible, the electricity that was being emitted like a force field separated them from the other revellers. Lily was impressed by her son's behaviour. It looked like Pete had finally become a man.

◆◆◆

It was almost twelve hours later before Lily resurfaced again. Pulling on an ancient, but beloved, silk dressing gown, she wandered bleary eyed downstairs, desperate for a thirst quenching glass of water. As she filled her glass and took a satisfying gulp the telephone rang; leaning across the vast worktop, Lily jiggled the wire, causing the phone to clatter onto the granite surface, before tugging it towards her.

"Hello?"

"Lily, it's Barbara. I just wanted to let you know what a fabulous party it was."

"That's kind of you."

"We all had a whale of time; although my feet are suffering from all the jiving, and I think Joe's back is twinging a bit. Trouble is you forget you're not as young as you think you are!"

Lily cackled. "Tell me about it. I used to party all night and go into the office the next day without a second thought. Now I'm thinking about going back to bed!"

"Sounds a good idea – in fact Joe told Matty and Tom to take the day off so they wouldn't have to rush round the farm."

"That was kind of him. Those two seemed to be getting on well though."

"Yes, I think they are definitely going to give the marriage another go. What about Pete and Chloe though!" Barbara's voice was tinged with amazement, and Lily's majestic bosom again puffed with maternal pride.

"I know who would have guessed it! I mean they've always got on really well, but I never thought they would actually get together."

"Just goes to show that you can't tell."

"I know." Lily wondered if there would be any work done in the office tomorrow; she felt pangs of pity for any prospective tenants that called in hoping to find properties.

They carried on chatting for a few minutes longer about the party until Barbara heard Joe coming in for his lunch. Lily put the phone back down and went outside to survey the scene of mass post-party destruction, wondering what devastation she would find. Instead, as she rounded the corner, she was met by a subdued but busy group tidying up. Pete, spotting Lily, called to Chloe and waved Lily over, pulling up a couple of chairs for them to sit on.

"What's all this?" Lily demanded, pulling her dressing gown round her and wishing she had at least brushed her teeth.

"I asked Melissa if she would come back this morning and tidy up so you wouldn't have to; and I went and picked Chloe up so we could help."

"That was very thoughtful of you."

"I also organised for them to bring over some brunch for us all so we wouldn't have to worry about food. Chloe and I were just waiting for you to wake, before we started on it. I'll go and let Melissa know we're ready." He walked away to one of the helpers and they disappeared into the house, leaving Lily and Chloe alone.

"Let's walk." Lily commanded. "We need to talk." Chloe trailed behind, worried about what Lily would say, knowing how protective she felt about her son. They reached the bridge, Lily walked ahead before rounding on Chloe.

"So!" She demanded "You thought you'd seduce my son did you?" Lily asked stony faced. "Is that all the thanks I get for giving you a job? Saw your chance to be another gold digger did you?"

Chloe blanched, she'd never considered how this would affect her and Lily. "Well... I mean... no...." Chloe stuttered, her mind racing into overdrive trying to work out what to say without angering Lily; her hand clung to the delicate handrail, which had witnessed such joy only hours before.

"Have you nothing to say?" Lily stated again but this time faltered as she interrupted herself with a huge cackling laugh and clapped her hands together. "Honestly Chloe your face was a picture! " She laughed again. "Did you really think that I'd play the Victorian Matriarch?" She leant across and squeezed one of

Chloe's hands. "I can't think of anyone better." Chloe let out a huge sigh and visibly relaxed, relieved Lily had only been joking.

"I'm not sure how it all happened, but suddenly it feels just right." Lily smiled to herself, that episode with Natalia must have helped Pete to understand what he really needed in a woman.

"I'm sure the two of you will be very happy together, at least you know that you're already friends. That makes a big difference. It's all very well having someone that makes the heart strings zing – but they need to be able to pick you up in the tough times as well. That's something you and Pete already have."

"Taking my name in vain?" Pete called, valiantly carrying a tray laden with bagels, smoked salmon and scrambled eggs; in the middle three glasses of sparkling Bucks Fizz.

"Now that is just what I need." Lily exclaimed as they clinked their glasses together.

"To Lily's party." Chloe said, looking lovingly at Pete.

"Mum's party." Pete echoed back, returning the longing look.

Chapter 20

Chloe gave a small satisfied sigh and reclined once more onto the pillows. The floor around the bed was festooned with coloured tissue paper, glitzy shopping bags and trails of clothes, so that the antique Aubesson rug was totally hidden from view. Her hand crept up to the small silver chain hanging round her neck, a Tiffany's heart lay cold against her skin. Pete had presented it last night after they had arrived at The Oaklands for dinner. It was ironic really how different this visit to the hotel was to her last one. It wasn't just that the person was different; the whole thing of being with Pete was totally different. It had the unusual combination of feeling exciting and new while at the same time there was a serenity and familiarity that made her feel secure and certain. All the old persistent worries of whether this was Mr Right that she usually experienced simply melted away. No longer was she trying to sift through conversations for deeper meanings, trying to read more into them, or acting as she thought was expected rather than being natural. Instead she could just be her; after all Pete had seen every side of her (and after last night's passion – had studied every part of her in great detail); there was no point in pretending to be anything else.

The first few weeks at work had been tentative, as both adjusted to working and playing together, but far from causing problems Chloe felt as though life had bounced into glorious techno-colour; they retained their usual professional personas, but every once in a while Pete would drop a kiss on her neck as he passed to collect a tenant's keys or draw a heart in the froth of her cappuccino, reminding her just how lucky she was.

There was a soft knock at the door and a liveried waiter entered with a large silver platter bearing a breakfast extravaganza.
"Breakfast Madam." He announced, and as Chloe leant on her elbows and cast around for a free surface, he deftly crossed the cluttered floor. "Shall I place it here?" He shifted the glossy ensemble of magazines and placed it on the mahogany table by the window. He retired quietly, leaving Chloe eying the food, suddenly ravenous after another night of nocturnal activity. She'd never get to start her diet if they continued like this, she mused.

Pete appeared, a towel slung round his hips, giving Chloe an expert view of his trim toned body, with its small blonde tendrils across his chest, his hair glistening, still wet from the shower.

"Did someone knock?" He asked bending down to kiss Chloe as though he hadn't seen her for months, rather than a few minutes.

"They bought breakfast up for us." She indicated the silver tray. "It smells delicious. There's croissants new baked rolls, and fresh coffee. Are you hungry?"

He leered vicariously and waggled his hips in a provocative manner. "I certainly am." He declared "But not for food." He added with great innuendo, and dropping onto the bed beside her, drew back the covers to marvel once again at her body.

"And I thought you might be too exhausted after last night." She coyly fluttered her eyelashes. With a practiced air he pulled her towards him so that she could feel his damp skin against hers.

"Definitely not." He gave her a long lingering kiss sending excited ripples through her veins. Breaking off he carefully brushed her fringe off her face. "They may be tasty rolls, but haven't you heard the saying 'man cannot live by bread alone'. I'm definitely partaking in something else first!" And with a flick of his hips she ended up underneath, happily looking up, wondering just how she had managed to bag the jackpot. With another contented sigh she returned his embrace, all other rational thoughts draining away. Ever since Lily's party life had become a whirl; occasionally she would guiltily think about her abandoned FaceBook, knowing she should be keeping everyone up to date with the romance. Somehow though it just didn't seem nearly as important as just being with Pete; maybe all those friends who kept tweeting about their perfect marriages and idyllic children weren't quite as happy with their lives after all.

◆◆◆

Time passed in a blur; settling into the hotel, meeting up with Patrick and Michael Fernly to discuss the strategy for the deals and meeting up with colleagues from the New York office. Alicia was slowly finding her feet in this strange city but having George there was a blessing. He had already worked out the best places to eat, where to go for drinks and the most happening clubs in town.

She also made an effort to stay in contact with Mavis, but the time differences and her erratic schedule meant they only really spoke on Sundays when Alicia had finished a workout at the hotel's gym and Mavis was settling down for a Sunday snooze. She found the link with England strangely comforting as though she had roots to return to; she had never envisaged missing home before. Now with the hope of garnering any news about Rob it took on an extra importance. It was during one of these calls, as the autumnal leaves turned gold, that Mavis mentioned the latest exciting village revelations.

"You'll never guess what's happened!" Mavis declared sometime after Lily's party. Alicia shuffled on the bed, getting comfortable for a lengthy update from Drayton Beauchamp. "Tell me all." She instructed.

"I forgot to tell you at the time, but Chloe and Rob split up." Alicia sat bolt upright, her grip on the phone tightening, causing her knuckles to protrude. Mavis continued oblivious to her daughter's reaction. "Apparently they ended it ages before Lily's party, but I didn't realise. Turns out he went along so she wouldn't have to go alone."

'That was typical of him', Alicia thought, 'quietly considerate'. "So why did they break up?" Alicia's voice sounded high and strained from her inner tension, but Mavis didn't notice.

"No-one's said, just they ended up more as friends, but I did wonder if Rob had found someone else."

"Oh?" Her voice was a hollow whisper as a death toll sounded inside her head, clanging so loudly she felt her ears were ringing. "Why do you say that?"

"He hasn't been himself over the past few months. Call it female intuition, but he is very pre-occupied so something, or someone, must be keeping him busy." Alicia digested the uncomfortable thought; when Mavis had mentioned the break up her heart had leapt at the prospect that Rob unencumbered by a girlfriend may well get in touch, but Mavis' revelations burst the tiny bubble of hope outright.

"So how is Chloe taking it? She hasn't been in contact at all. Is she devastated?"

"That's the funny thing. She got together with Pete at the party."

"What; Pete her boss?" Alicia was incredulous.

"Yes I know, that was my reaction, but actually they are so well suited you wonder why they didn't get together years ago."

189

They carried on chatting about mutual friends and village happenings, of the Little Acorn's unfortunate harvest festival and the nursery's latest customers.

"So are you coming home soon?" Mavis asked wistfully. A guilty rush ran over Alicia.

"I'll be home for Christmas." She promised.

◆◆◆

"So?" Lily demanded "How is it going?" She had managed to wait a whole month before interrogating Chloe; if that wasn't a test of real maternal devotion she didn't know what was. She had been astute enough to recognise that if the happy couple felt any outside pressure it would only end up damaging the fledgling relationship. So she had bided her time, using her army of eyes and ears to watch, digest and report back on how things were unfurling romantically; and it wasn't disappointing. It seemed that on the face of it Pete and Chloe were becoming inseparable, but she had to make sure, after all the fall out of this relationship failing would be catastrophic for all concerned.

They were lunching at The King's Arms, Lily's treat, ensuring delicious food and tasty gossip away from the office and Pete's delicate ears. "Come on," Lily continued. "I'm dying to hear everything."

A playful smile flitted across Chloe's lips, leaving in its wake a deep glowing happiness.

"Oh Lily, I don't know where to start." She gave an inadequate shrug of the shoulders and continued to fiddle with her wine glass. "It's just so..." She cast round for a word that could describe exactly how she felt; but she couldn't. Happy was too simplistic, besotted was too intense; contented was too mundane. It was as though she was floating along in a wonderful heavenly bubble; yet what was exciting and thrilling also felt strangely familiar and comfortable. She gave up searching and finished lamely with "Sooo.... perfect."

Lily clapped her ringed hands together in excitement; she could sniff out a heady passion from ten strides away. "I know! I remember when I met my third husband, the Australian explorer, I felt like I was on a constant bungee jump, either I was happily bouncing up or I was in a free fall of heady emotions."

"That's exactly it!" Chloe clamoured, glad of a fresh audience with whom she could revel in the wonderful minutiae of the relationship She was sure Matty was bored with her repetitious raptures, and Alicia had even laughingly begged for a little respite from the love-fest recollections on the phone last night. However here she was with a soul-mate who was only too eager to share in the glorious self-wallowings of early love.

"It feels like it is some wonderful dream that I can't believe it's really happening to me and any moment I'm expecting to wake up with a huge crash and be back to the sad singleton I was before the party."

Tina appeared and cheerfully served their lunch; a tempting concoction of duck confit and avocado within a filo basket. Lily clinked her glass with Chloe's. "Well here's to you!" She took a sip, savouring the cool gooseberry taste of the Chenin Blanc. "I have to tell you that I've never seen Pete so happy."

Chloe blushed. "And you really don't mind?"

Lily threw back her head and cackled with laughter, causing several diners to look across with interest. "Haven't I been encouraging the two of you to get together for the past three years? My attempt at being Cupid might not have worked for Rob, but I think this time I've come up trumps!"

The sound of Chloe's mobile trilling caught their attention, and she picked up the prized Louis Vuitton tote bag, plucking out the ringing phone from within. Seeing Pete's number on the display she blushed with pleasure and enthusiastically answered it. Lily picked at the food, adroitly watching Chloe in amusement as she whispered sweet nothings back at Pete. There could be no doubt about their intentions. As the call finished Lily pointed to the bag. "So you're still enjoying it?" Chloe ran a loving hand over it. "I can't believe you're letting me use it."

"Oh phewey!" Lily waved the appreciation away with a smile. "It was only gathering dust – anyway isn't that what boyfriend's mothers are supposed to do? It's lovely having someone to go shopping with and share things with. I didn't exactly get the chance with that Mexican Minx."

"Have you heard anything from her?"

Lily shook her head. "No, she's had the good sense to stay out of my way. Pete might be happy to just forget everything, but I am more than willing to share a piece of my mind."

"At least it's all turned out ok now."

Lily smiled indulgently at her. "Yes it has."

191

◆◆◆

Autumn rolled into winter with worrying speed; all over the city Christmas had replaced Thanksgiving. Sitting at the window in one of the small coffee shops just off Times Square, Alicia sipped her latte and gazed unseeingly out at the throngs of shoppers and multitude of brightly coloured lights and decorations. London was tame in comparison with its Oxford Street festivities. New York certainly had the edge on being big, bold and brash, not having planned on being away so long she had blitzed her Amex in Bloomingdales on a winter coat, the softest cashmere jumpers imaginable and a necessary but unflattering bobble hat and gloves.

There was never been a dull moment. When she wasn't working, she was out sightseeing; enjoying the staggering view from the Empire State building, taking a leisurely stroll through West Village, successfully navigating the odd intersections of West 4th and West 10th to find the Magnolia Bakery and its heavenly cupcakes. Friends of George's parents had invited them both over to their weekend home on Manhattan Island for Thanksgiving. In the middle of the festivities, having eaten the turkey and about to start on the pecan pie a small knot of home-sickness had formed in the pit of her stomach. She suddenly missed being part of a family recollecting the alfresco suppers at Apple Trees and the Sunday morning strolls to pick up a paper. Alicia realised with a jolt that Drayton Beauchamp now felt far more like home than London did. It was strange how things turned out. Even having Simon giving an update on London life, and Larnie regularly sending her news it now felt distant and cold.

Simon had been out several times, but as the deal had now been concluded he was heading back to the London office to deal with another client crisis. Her return next week would mean that at least she'd be back in the UK for Christmas, not that she would have been alone had she stayed. George was planning to stay over until New Year, but there was a hankering to go back which she had never anticipated.

As the nights began drawing in and mornings remained dark Alicia felt as though she lived in a world of eternal gloom as she went to work in the half-light and came back to the hotel in the orange street light haze. When they spoke on the phone Mavis began mentioning how cold it was; and Alicia worried that her mother was feeling her age. It was nothing new, since her father had died she had often considered how her mother would fare, but being so far away a whole plethora of questions uncomfortably raised their heads now about her mother's future. How much longer would Mavis be able to cope on her own, especially if she had an accident; did she have any savings or was the nursery her only asset? She hadn't raised it with Mavis before, but maybe they could talk about it at Christmas. She was looking forward to getting back to the village for the festive break, any furtive thoughts about seeing Rob again were kept firmly locked away. The last thing she needed was to go making a fool of herself. However the prospect of seeing Matty's new shop and Chloe with Pete were helping to ballast her ebbing spirits, and Josie had promised to find one of Henry's eligible friends to take to the Christmas Hunt Ball. A bonhomie of gratitude filled the spaces left by Rob's absence. She counted down the days left before her return.

◆◆◆

As a '*thank-you*' to all the team who had been working on the Van Plaza deals, Patrick Fernly had made a reservation at the Eleven Madison Park Restaurant. "It'll give everyone a chance to let their hair down a bit." He had explained. "We've all been so damned caught up in these transactions that I reckon we need a bit of fun!" He had squeezed Alicia's shoulder slightly too hard, so she was forced not to wince out loud. "Don't you reckon Ali?" Alicia bit back the retort that her name was actually 'Alicia' and instead fixed a disingenuous smile on her face.
"Sounds wonderful." She agreed.

The table sat in the balcony, overlooking the crowded dining room below; the large windows overlooked Madison Square where the trees were decorated with lanterns. It was sophisticated and luxurious, deep red roses adorned the cream and gold tables; over head the chandeliers sparkled. Everyone it seemed was in the mood for some serious partying. Patrick demanded to see the wine sommelier, then showing off dismissed all of the sommelier's recommendations and loudly ordered the Krug Grande Cuvee. Alicia watched with disgust; working in close proximity with Patrick over the past months she had found him overbearing and bombastic. The work itself had been interesting and totally absorbing but she didn't like Patrick's attitude. She fought to stifle a yawn, she hadn't been sleeping well for the past week and felt both mentally and physically exhausted. Her case was sitting packed, complete with brightly wrapped presents for everyone, ready for her flight home tomorrow. She regarded her menu and with a sinking heart realised she wouldn't just be able to order. The restaurant specialised in giving four key ingredients which each diner then discussed individually with the chef to create a tailored dish. She wished she was here with Rob; it would have been great fun having him suggest dishes for her to try but instead she simply asked the chef for his recommendation and agreed to it immediately. It took ages to go round the table getting the individual orders. In the meantime glasses were emptied and rapidly filled, large volumes of alcohol were being consumed on very empty stomachs. Standing up to make her way to the ladies, Alicia felt her legs wobble slightly as the champagne took hold; she would need to slow down a bit if she wanted to last the evening.

As the evening wore on all inhibitions were lost; the talk became raucous and loud, voices were strident and language was argumentative. With an enforced discipline she kept her eyes from continually straying to her watch. The time was dragging by. Eventually the desserts arrived, and Alicia felt a sense of relief. As soon as everyone had finished she would be able to make her excuses and escape back to her hotel.

When Patrick ordered cognacs for everyone, Alicia held up a surrendering hand and politely declined.
"I'm wacked, and if I don't go soon I'll be falling asleep here. It's been a great dinner Patrick." She complimented him insincerely. "Really enjoyable. Thank you."
There were a few calls of "light weight" shouted but she ignored them and retreated, heading down to the cloakroom to retrieve her coat. She was half way down the corridor when she felt a heavy hand on her arm arresting her.

"Aren't you going a bit early Ali?" Patrick's eyes were glinting, slightly unfocused from all the Krug. His fleshy face was reddened with drink and he leaned in menacingly as he spoke.

"Patrick you're hurting me." She tried to move his hand, but it dug in deeper with a vice-like grip.

"That's not a nice way to speak to someone who managed to swing the whole States thing for you." He was mocking her.

"What are you talking about?"

He regarded her with a blatant hunger that sent a chill of horror through her.

"I had to threaten to take my business over to Crawdons and Farlison before Simon saw the sense in seconding you out here."

"But I thought it was because of my original ideas for the acquisition."

"Don't be naïve. I can buy any smart lawyer I wanted, but there's not many that have your looks and provocative Ice Queen act. I've seen you giving me the signs."

"You're mistaken." She started to protest, but he brushed them away, brutally grabbing the back of her head and pulling her into a rough kiss, his teeth and lips grinding away at hers, while his other hand grabbed hard at her breast. For a moment she was pliant, shocked by the ferocity and violation, so markedly different from the passion Rob had kindled.

"I suggest we go somewhere more private to continue this." Patrick said forcefully as he pulled her towards the private rooms. She struggled against him, her heels slipping on the stone floor but he clung roughly onto her. They came to the door and she increased her struggle, panicking at what he obviously intended to do. As he turned the handle he had to let go with one hand she snatched the opportunity to push him away, fear galvanising her, tears smarting in her eyes and anger welling up inside. She slapped him with the full force of her weight, screaming at the top of her voice. A red welt appeared; yelling in pain he shoved her away. "You've just made one big mistake Ali." Spittle flew from his mouth as he began his threatening tirade. "No-one ever does that to me and gets away with it. No-one. I'll make you sorry for that. Just wait and see. You'll regret it, believe me."

She fled out of the restaurant, feeling sick, not even bothering to stop for her coat, bumping into unseen passers-by, wanting to put as much distance as possible between her and Patrick. Falling into a mercifully free taxi she couldn't stop shivering with shock – how could Patrick have tried to force himself on to her? This wasn't how her glorious adventure was supposed to end.

◆◆◆

Christmas finally arrived. Having returned to London, she had found life curiously flat. It was as though she had entered a half-way point; after the buzz of New York it felt quiet and restrained, and she missed the village camaraderie of the summer, she just didn't seem to fit there anymore. Once more counting down the days, Alicia at last set off to catch the train home, her bag bulging with clothes and presents. She was due to get in just after two o'clock which would give her enough time to relax and prepare for meeting up with Matty and Chloe for a Christmas Eve drink, the first time they had been able to have a girlie catch up since the summer. They had planned Christmas Day to be totally self-indulgent, just Mavis and herself eating the huge turkey they had ordered, drinking plenty of red wine, watching old films and scoffing the boxes of chocolates generous customers had given. Boxing Day on the other hand though was due to be a riotous affair. Barbara and Joe had invited everyone over for a party and it was strange to think her social calendar was now fuller than if she had stayed in London. Alicia couldn't remember being so excited about being at home since her father had died and as she watched the scenery race by she idly wondered if finally time was healing some of her unacknowledged grief.

The train journey sped by, helped no doubt by the two miniature bottles of red wine purchased from the buffet bar. They slipped down a treat, getting her firmly into the party spirit. Half-heartedly she picked up her book, but her attention was diverted by the passing scenery; the changing panorama of the suburbs opening up to the villages and the expansive fields and countryside. She recalled the journey home with her mother that summer and was astonished to realise that it had only been six months ago. It felt as though it had been another life. Now she was looking forward to going home. The familiar hills and buildings of Drayton Beauchamp came into view and as the train pulled into the station, there was Mavis wearing her combat trousers and boots, stamping her feet against the cold, anxiously scanning the carriages for her daughter. With a rush of filial love Alicia shot off the train as soon as it had stopped, lugging her luggage behind her as though it was an errant child, her hands juggling the other bags. Hugging and chatting they made their way to the car, both pleased Christmas was finally here.

While Christmas Day was the lazy self-indulgent day they had planned; Boxing Day was a riot of fun. The whole time seemed to be filled with drinking, eating, catching up on gossip and noisily playing the various board games that appeared. The party atmosphere was heightened by a self-conscious Chloe sporting a glittering new ring, and a self-satisfied Pete who proudly pointed it out to everyone.

In the afternoon Joe, Barbara, Lily and Mavis lolled in the comfy armchairs by the fire, listening to music while the others donned thick coats and pulled on their wellingtons for a bracing walk. Pete and Tom strode manfully ahead, throwing sticks to Tagger who bounced around expectantly in between collecting and returning. Matty, Chloe and Alicia followed on behind, arms linked companionably together.

"So what's it like having Lily as a potential mother-in-law?" Matty joked.

"Oh great!" Chloe enthused. "It's like having a cross between a fairy godmother and Margaret Thatcher. You can't believe how lucky you are, until you remember how frightfully efficient she is at getting things organised, and then it's frightening if you get in her way!"

"And how's Rob taking it?" Matty carried on.

"I haven't seen him for ages; he sent Pete and me a text wishing us a 'Happy Christmas' which was sweet but that's it. Have you heard from him at all Alicia?"

Alicia looked up startled. "Why would I have heard from him?" She knew her tone sounded unusually defensive.

"Only because he works with your Mum. Nothing else."

"Of course. No I haven't."

"I think he's planning to move on." Chloe continued. "He was asking about giving up the tenancy of the cottage with Pete, so I guess there's nothing to keep him here anymore."

"What a shame," Matty's voice was gloomy. "I was hoping he would be able to help us with the landscaping round the new shop."

Alicia felt her stomach plummet, and she stumbled slightly across the mud; she had never considered that Rob wouldn't always be around.

"You ok? You've gone very pale." Chloe asked with concern peering into her face

"Of course, it's nothing." Alicia quickly assured them. "Let's catch up with the boys."

♦♦♦

Later on that evening as they made their way home, Alicia quizzed Mavis over Rob.

"I thought I'd told you about it." Mavis said absently.

"No you didn't." She tried not to sound petulant. "So what's he doing?"

"He's buying a nursery near his parents in Gloucestershire, so he can grow the plants he needs for the garden designs. It means he's not so reliant on just the design work then." Alicia could see the sense; it would boost his business, it was just a shame it meant that he would move away. "But what about the work with Josie?" She persisted.

"I expect they'll still work on projects together. Josie's work is growing, so they will probably find more clients in Gloucestershire anyway."

"Won't you miss him though?"

"Of course – it's been good for business working with him, and I've enjoyed the challenge of the new plants he uses, but I can't stop him wanting to get on building his business."

"So when is he going?"

"He's already given notice on the bungalow, so it must be soon. I don't know what's got into him. He seems to be working himself too hard. He's out all hours; never seems to have time for a coffee and chat anymore. He's really throwing himself into finding new clients and helping out here, plus all his usual gardening jobs.

Alicia, impressed, raised her eyebrows. "Why's he doing it?"

"I wondered if he was trying to mend a broken heart, you know since he split up from Chloe, but apparently not. Josie's seen them chatting a couple of times and it looks like they're just friends. So I don't know why he's so driven. All I know is that I'll miss him when he's gone"

They pulled up outside Apple Trees and they scrunched their way across to the house.

"And I miss not seeing him now." Alicia thought silently wondering when the pain would start to lessen.

The New Year's Eve party was spilling out of the house and into the garden. Music was pounding away in the dining room, which had been transformed in a disco. People mulled about in the sitting room, getting drinks from the vast array of bottles littering the central island in the kitchen. Chloe and Pete were dancing energetically, encouraging others to join in, imbibed with the party spirit, Matty took Tom's hand and they succumbed as well.

Alicia leant against the wall, watching the scene unfolding, she couldn't get into the party mood, despite wearing her favourite Stella McCartney dress and Josie finding an entirely eligible friend of Henry's to act as her escort. Part of her regretted not seeing Rob this holiday; somehow she been half-hoping, half-dreading meeting up, anxious at the prospect of seeing him, whilst still looking for any vestige of hope. He obviously had his life planned, upping sticks and moving out to Gloucestershire; and a sudden treacherous thought darted into her mind, maybe there was another woman involved as her mother had suggested. Involuntarily she refused to dwell on that possibility, it was far too uncomfortable to consider. She drained her glass and looked sadly into it, thinking how the remaining dregs seemed to represent her life at the moment. She pulled out her blackberry, checking whether George had sent a cheery message from across the pond, but it remained obstinately blank apart from one message from Zac wishing her and half the office a perfunctory happy new year.

"Expecting someone special to call?" A deep bear-like voice asked behind her. Spinning round she saw Rob standing there; for a moment she could only stare, taking in the well-tailored suit and shirt that emphasised his height and breadth. She had never seen him so smart and somehow it only heightened his tall craggy looks, like a carefully groomed grizzly bear.

"What are you doing here?" She finally asked

"Josie invited me and I thought it would be good to see everyone." Alicia studied his face, the cold weather had dried his skin and he had lost weight; the gauntness emphasising the craggy cheek bones but still looking attractive. She was glad she was still leaning against the wall; it gave support to her now trembling knees.

There was a small silence, her brain refusing to cooperate, but her fear that he would suddenly go made her blurt out: "How was Christmas?"

"Quiet – I spent Christmas Day with Mum and Dad, but I've been working most of the time."

There was another tangible silence. Around them the revellers were chatting and singing.

"Did you hear about Chloe and Pete getting engaged? Isn't it wonderful!" She enthused, and then realised belatedly that it wasn't the most tactful comment she could have made.

"They make a good couple." He nodded.

"So you weren't too upset then?" Alicia asked tentatively.

Rob looked at her in surprise. "Why would I be upset?"

Alicia was surprised at the directness of his question; she remembered only too well how Chloe had been his first choice last summer.

"Well as I recall you certainly didn't want to break it off with her before." She snapped.

A look of thunder rolled across his face, and sensing she may have triggered an argument, hastily changed the subject, the last thing she wanted was to fall out with him.

"Are you really setting up in Gloucestershire? It sounds like a good plan for you if you want to grow your business."

He stared at her intently for a moment as though about to say something, then the moment passed. With a suppressed sigh he replied. "Yes that's the plan. I can't afford to buy a nursery around here, but if I move back there I can live with my parents while I get the business going. Your mother's been very helpful, giving me advice, putting me in touch with her suppliers, and what to look for. You two certainly seem to be getting on much better these days." He complimented.

"We are." Alicia agreed. "It's funny really, but now we spend more time on the phone chatting than we ever did when I was at home."

"How's London after the heady heights of New York? Enjoying being back in the bright lights of the city?"

Alicia started to give her standard answer when something sagged within her and her shoulders shrugged, she turned to face him, looking up at him with her large almond eyes.

"Actually it wasn't everything I thought it would be." She admitted. "I really thought that it was going to be the answer to everything – my big opportunity to make my mark in the firm. But it turns out I was wrong. I'm not even sure I'm cut out for it."

Instinctively Rob knew something was wrong. "What happened out there?" He asked with concern.

A memory of Patrick mauling her flashed into her memory and shame ran through her. She wanted to throw herself into Rob's arms and sob her heart out; tell him how awful it had been, how scared she had felt. But how could she? He would think she had gone mad. Instead she lied. "Oh nothing, just the cut and thrust of business." He gave a low growl of sympathy. She changed tact. "I'm still worried about Mum being here. It's as though she's suddenly getting old. I'm not sure how much longer she'll be able to be on her own."

"She's hardly infirm!" Rob protested. "I can't see Mavis wanting to give up yet. Have you spoken to her about it?"

Alicia dropped her gaze and shook her head, and Rob noticed that she had allowed her hair to grow so that instead of short severe hairstyle it had become a soft mass of waves framing her face.

"It might be an idea." He suggested, hoping to calm her worries. "I've got a feeling she has no intention of hanging her gardening boots up yet."

"It sounds silly, but I don't want to raise it in case by doing so I prompt something to happen and I'm not here." Rob went to touch her shoulder in solidarity but stopped himself.

"I'm sure you'll find the opportunity." He started to move away. "I'd better go and find Josie to say 'hello'." As he moved Alicia wanted to grab hold of his arm and keep him by her, so they could go somewhere and just talk. She wanted to be close, to hear his reassuring tone. She wanted to sit and talk about his latest designs, ask how Bertha was keeping, whether the Landrover was still playing up, and tell him about how she thought of him every time she bought herbs or flowers but he was already engulfed into the party throng. A feeling of total abandonment descended on her, she felt undesirable and unattractive; any half-formed day dreams of Rob being interested in her were shattered into tiny shearing fragments.

"Was that Rob I saw you talking to?" Mavis asked later in the evening.

"Yes." Alicia's voice was dull and listless.

"You don't sound very happy. Don't say you and Rob are squabbling again. I thought you had got over all that."

Alicia shook her head. "No; it's just he didn't seem very interested in talking to me," Then added as a mock-joke. "Not even to argue."

Mavis studied her daughter; seeing a very different woman to the one she was last year. Her mind flicked into over-drive through searching for explanations, and suddenly everything became crystal clear. The caution in Alicia's voice whenever Rob was mentioned, the tentative questions Rob had asked over Alicia's departure, the fact neither of them now seemed to be speaking. Jumping in with both muddy feet she asked curiously. "Do you have feelings for Rob?"

Alicia felt her face burn crimson; vehemently she tried to protest, but there were no words, her tongue refused to deny it, and she couldn't even turn to anger. Mavis smiled knowingly "Does he know?"

In a small voice she admitted: "He's not interested, he's made that much clear."

"Are you sure?"

"Oh yes." She retold the sad sorry tale, ending with the final phone call when he had explained that he needed to stay with Chloe.

Trying to conceal her incredulity and surprise that it had all happened without anyone else being aware, she gave her daughter a quick hug. "Goodness." She said finally. "Whoever said living in the country was boring!"

"Ten, nine, eight, seven..." The New Year count down had begun. "Six, five, four..." Everyone was squashed into the living room, champagne ready for the stroke of midnight. "Three, two, one! Happy New Year!" Couples everywhere were kissing and hugging. Caroline and Toby were laughing, Matty and Tom were holding tightly onto each other, clinched in a passionate embrace; Pete was romantically kissing Chloe's hand; Josie and Henry were toasting each other. Mavis and Alicia hugged and wished each other all the best for the coming year.

"I'm rather glad you broke your arm." Mavis said slightly tipsy from Henry's generous hospitality. "It was lovely having you to stay over the summer." Then seeing Alicia's raised eyebrows. "Well most of the time anyway."

"Are you worried about staying there on your own? Should you be thinking about retiring and taking it slightly easy?"

"Of course not. I get a bit lonely but I'd never want to lose the nursery. It means I'm still close to your Dad. I realise you don't want to come back, but I do enjoy you being at home, it's nice having you around."

Alicia waggled a finger. "Now I know you're drunk! You'd hate having me around all the time, hogging all the wardrobe space, cramping your style, stealing all your drinks and using all the hot water. Plus I work in London."

"You could be like all the other commuters and use the train." Alicia shook her head, she could tell Mavis had obviously started scheming. They were interrupted by Rob looming over. "Happy New Year!" He kissed Mavis on the cheek and clinked his glass against hers. "Thanks for everything you've helped with over the past year." He turned to Alicia, going to kiss her as well, then fractionally pausing, a flash of remembrance leapt into his memory of their previous kiss. He looked momentarily awkward at the recollection and the disparity with the situation now, but Alicia misread the signs and ducking her head murmured an excuse and strode away.

"What's wrong with her?" He growled, upset that she couldn't even bear to be close to him. "Something I said?"

"More like something you didn't say." Mavis pointed out ironically. "You two really take some beating."

Chapter 21

"Come and sit down." Simon pointed to the seat but avoided facing her directly; he swung his chair at a angle so he was facing towards the side window; his hands pressed together, his chin resting on the fingertips. Alicia warily recognised the stance and immediately was on the alert.

"You wanted to see me?" She tried to keep any emotion out of her voice.

"Yes, I'm going through the projects the team are working on and I think we need to make a few changes. I'm going to ask Larnie to head up the Van Plaza project; I'll handle the Winterson business and you can work on the Ferguson Property contracts."

Alicia gasped. "But why? The Ferguson work is just run of the mill contracts; there's no real legal input required. Why can't I do that and the Van Plaza work? I know they are planning to look for companies out in Asia."

Simon cleared his throat awkwardly. "They've asked me to remove you from the team."

"What!" She leapt to her feet, every nerve in her body taut with anger and indignation. "Why? Is this Patrick's doing?" Simon shifted, uncomfortable at her intense stare. "Do you know what happened out in the States? Did he tell you that?"

"Alicia, you're a bright woman, you're not some country bumpkin. You know the way of the world. If the client expects you to smile you do, when he tells you to jump you ask 'how high'. Van Plaza are a valued client to the firm."

"You mean they are spending lots of money with us." She retorted with a hollow laugh. "Did you know he tried to force himself on me?" She demanded, annoyed that Simon was still refusing any eye contact. "Don't you care about what happened?"

"Not really." Simon said simply. "I think Patrick may have had a little too much to drink, but you certainly over-reacted. I expected far better of you."

Tears stung her eyes. The unfairness of the situation would have been laughable if she hadn't felt so let down by Simon's refusal to even hear her side of the story.

"So if you could do a hand-over to Larnie please. We have a client meeting next week and I really do want her to be up to speed." He was dismissing her without a fair hearing. She stood for a moment, silently pleading with his profile for justice, but realising his mind was already decided, shook her head in sorrow and walked out head bowed.

Seeing devastation written across her face as she walked out of Simon's office, Zac propelled her into one of the empty meeting rooms and sat her down. He perched on the table, a look of amused concern playing round his lips.

"You've just heard about the Van Plaza project I take it?" Mutely she nodded. "Oh come on Alicia. There's no need for all this doom and gloom act. These things happen. Do the work on the Ferguson Properties and I'm sure I'll be able to swing another big project your way. This time next year, no-one will remember all this." He put his finger under her chin and lifted it so he could see her face. "You really are going to have to toughen up a bit if you seriously want to make Partner." He counselled. "This isn't like you. Everyone knows what a hard nut you are."

She regarded him with disbelief; for someone who had shared her bed for the past two years, he had absolutely no idea who she was; so different to Rob's instinctive understanding.

"Look I know it's not easy at the moment." He sympathised. "Marcia's away this weekend; why don't I take you somewhere special for dinner and then we can go back to the flat and work out which projects to work on."

She marvelled at his approach; that he would seriously consider dinner and a quick jump into bed would solve anything. Sitting there, so self-assured with his classic good looks and expensive tailored suit; she thought with sadness how much time she had spent longing for him to call so they could grab an evening together. All that yearning had drained away, observing him now she saw he was a distant stranger. Realisation dawned that she could never bear to be with someone who wasn't totally committed to her, as she was to him.

The realisation shifted her whole world a few degrees; forcing her to reassess her life. Was that what she still wanted? Reduced to sharing a man, having to despise herself while pandering to men like Patrick Fernly; turning off all her emotions so that she was deemed to be the right candidate for the role? Would she look back in twenty years' time and wonder if she had made the right choice.

"How about it?" Zac was urging.

Suppressing her desire to simply put her head in her arms and sob her heart out, she sighed heavily.

"Not this weekend thanks. I think I'll go home instead."

◆◆◆

The February air hung heavy on the wet branches; dewdrops glinted like diamond necklaces around the discarded Christmas tree. Outside Mavis' plants looked cold and bare, the only sign of any life were the shy primrose pushing their pale yellow faces up towards the weak sun and the holly, looking as though it had all the necessary vigour with its glossy green leaves to let it stand dominantly against the elements. In the greenhouses though there were a riot of colours, leaves pressed against the damp panes, the early flowering daffodils and crocuses which were being brought on in preparation for the Easter period.

Nestled away from the dank dreary atmosphere, Mavis and Alicia sat huddled round the log fire sipping morning coffee; in the background the local radio station played a selection of golden oldies.

"I'm glad you decided to come down last night – although we might have to go shopping for some food. I've got nothing in." Alicia grinned. "I realised sitting in the office that I just couldn't take another night in London; so I grabbed a bag and phoned you in the taxi."

"Have you thought any more of moving back here?" Mavis asked nonchalantly.

"Mum!" Alicia was shocked that Mavis had raised the topic of her coming home again; but not as shocked as she was by the realisation that it might be something that she would consider. In fact in a moment of idleness, she had checked out how much her flat was worth, and whether there were any local jobs but there didn't seem any jobs which didn't entail driving to Oxford, Bath or Cheltenham. Her mother might be keen for her to move down, but Alicia wasn't so sure that fate was.

"Josie was saying Henry might be looking for someone; he's really over-worked at the moment."

"I'm not sure Henry would want to take on someone who hasn't any experience of the rural affairs of clients."

"But you could ask him, couldn't you?" Mavis persisted.

"I suppose I could." Alicia reluctantly agreed, and she could have sworn Mavis had almost rubbed her hands in glee.

"Well things in life change don't they. They don't always stay the same."

"What are you trying to say Mum?"

Mavis fiddled with her pruning knife. "Well take me. Here I am, living here in the house your Grandparents had, working in the nursery, with only memories of Bill and occasional visits from you, and maybe I feel like I'm missing out."

"Do you mean that you want to get married again."

"Nooo!" Mavis chortled. "Bill was the only man for me, you know how much I miss your Dad still. No, what I meant was that I want a bit of time to try a few new things. Start a hobby, meet a few friends, join in the WI a bit more – but without having to worry about work."

"You mean give up work?" Alicia could see how her mother was entitled to some 'me' time after all the work she had done over the years, but she wasn't sure if she could help fund Mavis' retirement.

"Nooo!" She said again. "Maybe just cut back a bit here and there."

"How would you do that."

Mavis' eyes twinkled. "Well I've had a few ideas." She confessed, and Alicia knew that Mavis had definitely started scheming. The sound of a car pulling up outside interrupted them.

"Are you expecting anyone?" Alicia asked and was intrigued to see a faint blush stain Mavis' cheeks. The visitor knocked on the door, and suddenly in walked Rob calling out *Morning Mavis* as he rubbed his hands together trying to get some warmth back.

"Hello Rob; we're through here." Mavis called, avoiding Alicia's interrogative stare. "Do you fancy a coffee?"

"Sounds good."

He walked in, and then realised that Alicia was there as well, and half froze.

"Sit yourself down near the fire." Mavis busily instructed, giving up her armchair and hurrying off to make coffee.

"How are you?" He gruffly asked Alicia.

"Fine. Desperate for a bit of country air, so I came down last night – however I haven't quite had the courage to step outside yet."

207

Rob gave a low chuckle. "It's certainly cold out there. I've been wrapping your Mum's potted trees up in bubble wrap to keep them from freezing."

There was an awkward pause both wanting to ask questions but not daring to. The pause lengthened into deadly silence, waiting despairingly for Mavis' return.

"Have you had much luck finding somewhere to buy?" Mavis asked having handed a steaming cup of coffee to them both. Rob grimaced and shook his head, and Mavis felt a small fluttering of excitement inside her. It looked like her plan could work; although she couldn't really claim the credit for it. It had all been Josie's idea. So simple really; it had been staring them all in the face and no-one had seen it. It had started with Josie demanding to know why Alicia had seemed so upset at the New Year's Eve party. Unable to prevaricate and thinking that maybe Josie would be able to help, Mavis had told the whole sorry tale. And she was. After some deep pondering, a few phone calls and a shared bottle of wine, Josie had come up with a plan. Now it just needed Mavis to see it through.

"You know the solution has been staring us all in the face."

"It has?" Rob wasn't sure; he'd tried looking at places near here.

"Why on earth move away, when you could be staying in Drayton Beauchamp."

He sighed and ran his hand through his unruly hair making it stand up even more. "But I can't afford anywhere round here." He admitted sadly.

"You could if you went into partnership." Mavis told him, remembering the words Josie had so carefully coached her in.

"Who would I go into partnership with?"

Mavis stared incredulously at him; wasn't it obvious?

"Me of course!" she cried. "It would be perfect; you would be able to do all the design and client work; I could do all the plant husbandry side and we could employ someone to help out on the general gardening and lawn cutting jobs. Plus, I've been talking to some people about the edible flowers idea. One of the local supermarkets likes it, and the Drayton Chronicle want to feature us in a series of articles. So we could do more on that as well. Don't you think it's a great idea Alicia!"

There was a stunned silence as Alicia and Rob stared at her, taking in the news from their own perspective.

"You mean buy into this?" He indicated the nursery through the window.

"Why not? Look both of you come with me." And she hurried out of house, leaving Alicia and Rob to exchange puzzled looks and follow furtively after her. They walked through the cold air and across to the long low barn that usually housed the old lawn mowers, discarded plant boxes and general packaging. It had been cleared, the joint efforts of Josie and Molly, leaving a clear open space, and for the first time ever, Alicia could see what a large area it was. The floor was patterned by the dancing rays of sun infiltrating the now clean window panes, and the walls had been swept clear of cobwebs.

Mavis turned to them, her arms outstretched into the space. "If you were happy with this, then we could convert it into a flat for you. Of course it isn't large, but at least you'd be on site and you wouldn't have to worry about renting anywhere." She took a pile of rolled up plans from off the window ledge and handed them to Rob. "We drew up some plans so you could see what it would be like." Fascinated Rob opened up the drawings and saw a large living area with kitchen, a study to one side and a smaller bedroom and bathroom at the end.

"It certainly looks like you've thought of everything." He agreed slowly.

"Doesn't it just!" Alicia concurred and suspiciously wondered why her mother hadn't thought to mention any of this before. Mavis walked over and put an arm around her daughter's shoulder.

"And Alicia and I would live in the cottage still, so you'd get to see both us all the time."

"I didn't know you were moving back." Rob was shocked.

"Neither did I." Alicia replied through gritted teeth; she hadn't appreciated how far her mother's scheming had gone. Mavis gave her a quick squeeze.

"Don't be like that darling. You know you hate London; and I'm positive Henry will offer you a job. This way you can come back home." She turned to face Rob again, realising that both he and Alicia were struggling to keep up with events. "Look, I know it's a lot to take in, but I've been thinking about it, and I reckon it makes perfect sense." Her eyes twinkled benevolently at them. "You talk it through; I'll be in the house if you want me." She disappeared into the misty day, leaving Rob and Alicia alone; they stood staring at each other, neither moving, neither daring to consider it.

Eventually Rob asked. "Did you know about this?"

"Of course I didn't." She snapped. "It was the first time I had heard anything about it. I knew my mother was up to something, but I thought she wanted me to move back to the village, I didn't realise that what she was really planning was for me to move out and you to move in."

"I think she was planning for us both to be here." Rob pointed out softly.

"Well that's hardly going to happen is it? Despite what Mum thinks, I don't think Henry will give me a job so I still have to work up in town; and as much as I love my mother, I don't think I could go back to living with her full time. No, the way I see it, is if you go into partnership with her, then at least she'll have someone around so she won't always be alone."

"So that's all you see me as? Someone to act as your mother's companion!" Rob was stung at her insinuation.

Alicia dropped her head, so he couldn't see the confusion and longing in her eyes.

"No of course not; I didn't mean it like that. I do worry about her being on her own."

"And there's always your lover to consider." Rob snapped, thinking back on all the details Chloe had inadvertently shared.

She flushed, uncomfortable with the memories of Zac. Defensively she replied. "That's all history. Anyway, it was only ever a bit of fun. It wasn't as though anyone got hurt."

"Is that what his wife thinks?"

Guilt rushed up; when she and Zac had been together she had never bothered to consider Marcie; but since she had stopped seeing him she felt uneasy about their behaviour.

"Marcie knew what he was like when they married. I wasn't the first and I'll bet I'm not the last."

"Oh, so that's ok then." Rob said sarcastically. "You can take what you want regardless of the other woman."

"Like it was with you and Chloe." She retorted, needled by his accusations, even if they were true. "You didn't even bother to get in touch once you two had split up."

"You know why."

"No I don't. All I know is that I stupidly kept hoping you'd call. But you never did. Did you?" She ranted. "You can't have been quite so infatuated as you made out that day in the garden if you couldn't even be bothered to phone me."

"Well neither did you." He shouted back

They were both glowering at each other, tempers raised, ready to go into battle.

"So it's starting all over again is it? The old Alicia is back." He snarled. "The arguments, bickering and the snide remarks – just like before."

She sneered at him, turning to go. "I thought I knew you; thought you were different from this; that I meant something to you. I must have been mad. How wrong could I be?" She went to leave, but he grabbed hold of her hand as she passed him, wanting her to stay.

"Don't walk out on me." He yelled.

"Why not!" She retaliated, but her shouts were muffled by his proximity as she was swung round to face him. Any anger suddenly disappeared. They were standing close, close enough to breathe in a familiar scent and be transported back to a hot summer day, the shared intimacy that couldn't be found anywhere else; captured so firmly in both their memories. Flowing images of those previous highly-charged embraces heightened their sensitivities, igniting the unbidden latent desires.

Involuntarily their lips longingly sought the other's as they relived the moment; at first tentative and testing, afraid after the long wait that it would prove to be only a dismal replica. But the feeling only intensified, declaring the end of a lonely journey. As the urgency grew, so did the passion and force. She ran her hand up his neck and through the thick unruly crop, pulling him closer. Feeling as though she had finally discovered what she really wanted she held onto Rob with such ferocity it felt like she never wanted to let him go.

The time went by unheeded; as the months of loneliness and separation were erased. Finally, they broke apart, only to stand looking at each other in wonderment, afraid of the moment breaking. Taking hold of her hand he pulled her back into him, feeling their bodies slot neatly together so that her head rested on his shoulder, his chin on her hair, dropping a kiss onto the tousled waves. "I've missed you."

"I thought you had someone else." Alicia admitted. "I thought that's why you wanted to move away."

"No, after that kiss there could never be anyone else. I just couldn't take being here, and knowing that I'd ruined any chance of being with you. The situation with Chloe was... complicated;

I'll tell you all about it sometime, but everything took so much longer to sort out, and by that time you were away in America starting a new life. I couldn't see how you'd ever forgive me for what had happened."

She stroked the side of his face tenderly. "So will you stay?"

"I'm not sure if your mum's really serious, or if she was just hoping to act as Cupid. I guess I'll have to talk to her properly."

"You could go and talk to her now."

"Oh no that can all wait. I've waited long enough for this." He declared, kissing her once again with renewed fervour. "I want to concentrate on this rural affair right now."

Chapter 22

Slowly it was all coming together. All their late night planning over a glass of wine was now becoming reality. As soon as permission was granted by the Council, Mick had started work on the barn, patching up the roof and putting in oak framed windows and new doors to make it water tight. Joe had spent a week ferrying out the mud and muck that had accumulated within the barn over the years, using a wheelbarrow to shift each load and clear the space for the new floor Mick was due to put down. When the new lights had been fitted Tom had spent the evenings with supplementary spotlights painting the internal walls and hanging gold metallic wallpaper. Barbara also chipped in, spending weeks scooting round the countryside collecting designer clothes which Caroline and Josie had chivvied friends to find, ferrying them back to the barn each evening. Popping over for a quick respite to Lily's she had been choked with thanks as her friend had simply opened her vast wardrobe doors and told Barbara to take what she wanted to help Matty get started. Alicia had rallied her friends in London, getting George to drive down with a car full of suit carriers full of the latest once-worn-forever-discarded labels.

Now all the clothes sat in neat piles on the oak floorboards, just waiting for Matty to hang them on the sumptuous velvet hangers she'd discovered online. Standing in the middle of the space, with the sun slowly setting behind the ancient oak trees that sat proudly on the crown of the hill and Rob just visible through the window finishing off the planting, Matty felt a thousand tiny bubbles of excitement fizzing up inside her. The dress agency would soon be ready for business. Josie had suggested she think about a special opening event; and the idea of a charity fashion show had been floated. Tentatively Matty had mentioned it to Tom, uncertain if he would really want so much razz-ma-tazz for their business, but to her surprise he had really liked the idea, even suggesting that Barbara might be able to get the Drayton Beauchamp WI to help with some of the organising. Sceptically she had watched, ready to step in to pick up the pieces; however the efficiency the WI ladies had displayed would have put the military to shame. Their attention to detail and network of contacts (everything from a PA system through to a catwalk stage had been 'borrowed' from husbands, friends and neighbouring WIs) was awesome.

"Penny for them?" Barbara asked, walking in with several Lulu Guinness outfits she had picked up from Edna Hawkes' daughter.

Matty spun round. "I didn't hear you come in." She apologised. "I was just thinking how exciting this all is." She gestured with her hands to the converted room. "It all looks so wonderful, and you've all worked so hard to help get it finished." She felt choked with emotion. "I'm just so scared that it will be a flop and I'll have let everyone down." Barbara put down the pile of clothes on the chaise longue.

"Nonsense." She said briskly, not wanting to get caught up in the stress of emotions. "You're not going to fail. Joe and I are proud of what you and Tom are trying to do." She put an arm round Matty and gave her shoulders a quick squeeze. "So no more doubts. This is going to be a great success."

"Do you really think so?" Matty asked, still feeling the pangs of uncertainty within.

"I know so." Barbara declared drily. "After all, Lily's wardrobe alone will keep you in clothes for a year!"

"Are you coming?" Matty had demanded the previous evening.

"I told you I'd be there." Alicia had laughingly reassured her.

"You'd better; I've sorted out just the right outfit for you!"

"As long as I look tall and glamorous in it. You're not palming me off with any old rubbish."

"Hah!" Matty had rejoined wickedly. "It's a beige crimplene granny skirt with a matching brocade waistcoat and flat lace up shoes!" Alicia sincerely hoped her friend was joking – she didn't want to commit social kamikaze. "That should serve you right for never coming back to see me."

"This is the second time I'll have been back this month. That's a record for me!"

"Ok." Matty conceded. "It's just fun having you here. I can't wait for you to move back."

"You won't have any time for fun when you get the dress agency open." Alicia told her with pseudo sternness.

"I know." Matty sounded down. "That's what Josie keeps warning me as well." She reverted back to her excitement. "Which is why this weekend's got to be such fun!"

◆◆◆

As Rob drove up to the barn, he pulled in past the newly painted gate, and Alicia noticed it now proudly bore the sign 'Dress to Impress'. Along three sides a new hedge had been planted so that the showroom was tastefully screened from the working farm and fields. The barn lay long and low along the remaining side; its golden blocks and ancient oak beams glowing benevolently in the late morning. Either side of the door stood two spiral topiary box trees planted in terracotta pots. The old double doors that had allowed entry to carts had been replaced with glass, tempting visitors to press their noses to the panes and revel in the textural delights. For a moment, after Rob came to a stop, Alicia just sat taking in the remarkable transformation.

"It looks good doesn't it?" Alicia gushed and then coyly added "And of course the plants really make the difference."

"Be careful, or I'll be forced to reprimand you for those impertinent comments!" Rob leant across and pulling her towards him felt a sudden rush of desire and yearning. He stroked the lob of her ear and warm downy skin of her neck. "Do you really have to be here today?" He whispered. "Because I reckon we could just sneak back to Apple Trees and nobody would know."

Alicia leant into him, breathing in the heady scent of soap, grass and compost, severely tempted by the offer, but knowing she would never be forgiven. "You know I can't let Matty down," Regret ringing in her voice. "But hopefully from next month it will all get a bit easier."

"I hope so; it's getting fairly lonely here without you." He kissed her, and she enjoyed the floating sensation which never failed to occur. "Now, get going, or I really will end up taking you home." Laughing she climbed out of the car. "I'll see you later."

Walking inside the transformation was even greater. Gone were the flaking brick walls and mud floor she had seen at Christmas, replaced with oak floorboards and soft cream walls and gold wallpaper panels which bounced off the light from the overhead lanterns. At the far end a set of dressing rooms had been incorporated; each one fully decked out with angled mirrors, padded armchair, black and white photos of vintage clothes and large ornate hooks. The walls had been left clear of any fixings so the dresses were arranged on free standing oak rails that allowed Matty to move them around as required. There was a hive of activity already underway. In the centre of the room a small catwalk had been set up, so the 'models' could strut their stuff in helping a good cause. The charity Tom had suggested was the Drayton Beauchamp Rescue Centre, and several of their posters lined the entrance. In one corner Barbara and her WI army added the final touches to the canapés, squabbling over whether to add tarragon to the salmon rolls, if more dill was needed as a garnish and castigating a dejected Edna Hawkes for not thinking about celery salt to go with the quails' eggs (so de rigeour nowadays). To the left Derek and Shane, the photographers, were setting up, ready to capture the big event for posterity, and in the centre Matty was organising her conscripted models, mainly recruited from the Drayton Young Farmers. Noticing Alicia, she beckoned her over, kissing her warmly on the cheek.

"This looks spectacular!" Alicia congratulated her friend noticing the new haircut and expertly applied makeup.

"I know! But I can't take the credit really, Barbara and the WI fairy godmothers conjured up most of this, and Josie persuaded Derek and Shane to venture out of London once more – helped I'm sure with promises of lunch at the Deli!"

"Where is Josie; I thought she'd be here, and Chloe come to that."

"They're coming later. They organised a girls' get together, starting at Josie's with a champagne reception and then they're all coming on here afterwards. She reckoned a few glasses of fizz before they got here would help everyone be far more extravagant when it came to buying clothes."

Alicia grinned. "She has no shame at all."

"Come along and meet the others, then we can get the outfits organised. I've got some really stunning bits saved for you."

"If they're that stunning you know I'll end up buying them."

"That's what I'm counting on!" Matty replied wickedly.

◆◆◆

The barn was packed; ladies from all over the county had turned up in force to enjoy an evening of food, fizz and fashion. The temptation to pick up a designer snip bought out the best in everyone; and the Mulberry purses and Donna Karen clutch bags were rapidly opened to buy yet another bargain. Everyone seemed to have acquired multiple 'Dress to Impress' stiff embossed bags with their gold cord handles and green glossy lettering. The cameras flashed as each model in turn sashayed down the catwalk, cheered on by friends, boosted by the high heels and buoyed up on Matty's generous servings of booze. Matty sparkled in the spotlight, appearing friendly, natural and informed as she outlined each outfit, talked about the designer and suggested accessories for day and evening wear. The canapés circulated successfully, despite the missing celery salt, and everyone enjoyed the night.

The men had wisely stayed out of the way, knowing full well that tonight was a testosterone-free zone, but Tom and Joe wandered past on their way to The King's Arms, stopping to look in the brightly lit window at the festivities, each proudly intent on their wife.
"Reckon they're getting on much better now." Joe sagely declared, nodding his head towards Matty and Barbara who were giving a vote of thanks to the Young Farmers. "Hopefully they've sorted everything out; you know your mum didn't mean to make trouble. She was just as pleased as punch when you got married to Matty. It's not been a happy time, but happen everything's turning out alright now." As though sensing they were being watched, both women instinctively lifted their heads and spotting the friendly voyeurs gave encouraging waves. "Reckon you can rest easy now son." Joe said patting Tom on the back before turning to walk on. "They're doing just fine; and it's time for us to get that pint you promised me earlier."

People were starting to leave, reluctantly looking at watches and remembering baby sitters, husbands and lovers who all needed to be attended to. Small groups drifted off, discussing the bargains they'd found, congratulating Matty on the opening; trickles of happy revellers spilling out into the dark inky blue night. The few that remained regrouped and refilled, emptying the last of the bottles. Josie walked up and hooking a friendly arm through Alicia's congratulated her on her successful modelling debut with a gentle squeeze.
"You looked fantastic in that Armani jumpsuit; very Michelle Pfeiffer *Cat Woman*. You're lucky having such a great figure; mine's going completely to pot living with Henry." She pulled a face. "Every time I try and start a diet he keeps buying chocolates to celebrate. Trouble is I can resist most – but those

ones from the Deli are to die for. So of course I end up eating them and then I'm back to square one."

"I'm sure Henry's not complaining." Alicia knew how he doted on her friend.

"Hah! He's never around at the moment to complain. He's having to work all hours at the moment, which is no fun. Poor man is exhausted, but he hates letting clients down, so he's rarely getting home before nine o'clock most nights." She took a sip of wine. "He really needs someone else in the office; he can't keep going like this. I keep telling him to get someone in, but he says he's too busy to find the time." Alicia smiled. "Yes I know – ironic isn't it! So when are you coming back here for good? I miss not catching up for lunches like we used to do in town."

Alicia gave a wistful smile. "The buyers on my flat want to exchange at the end of next month; so hopefully I'll be back here from then on."

"I can't wait. Rob is a real bear with a sore head when you're not around. But he said that the plans are progressing well for the nursery."

Alicia nodded. "Although they've changed slightly – Rob and I are going to live in Apple Trees and Mum's going to have the annexe, she said it would be much easier as she got older, although I can't see that happening for quite some time. With the money from my flat we can get Mum's annexe converted, and then Rob and I can redecorate the house so that we can make a few changes. I don't know how Mum ever managed without a power shower, and she's agreed that the kitchen definitely needs updating. It feels a bit odd though; Mum and Dad had the house from Granny and Gramps, and now Rob and I are moving in. It'll be a bit of a squeeze all three of us in the house until Mick can get the annexe work completed, but at least either Mum or Rob will be cooking when I get home from the commute."

Josie rounded on her. "So why haven't you contacted Henry about working for him? Why ever not! He'd love to have someone like you, who's young, enthusiastic and full of energy. You have just the right experience to be able to help him and you both know you get on." Alicia started to refuse, after all why would Henry want her to join his practice. "No I mean it Alicia, give Henry a call tomorrow." She told her friend sternly. "I'll speak to him tonight, and let him know. It would be a great solution, you get to work locally and Henry doesn't have to work himself to death." Josie could see Alicia wasn't fully convinced.

"What is it?   Why aren't you jumping up and down with excitement?"

"It doesn't happen that easily." Alicia was wary of believing there could be a job for her in the village.

Josie squeezed her arm. "Trust me. Maybe this once it does." She turned and saw Rob's car pulling into the drive.   "Look talk to Rob and see what he thinks – but for what it's worth I think it's the perfect solution."

Alicia walked out into the blue-black night on a cloud of euphoria, excitement and hope; behind her Matty, Josie and Chloe were swopping stories of the night, three good friends. Ahead of her Rob stood tall, solid and steadfast, with quickening steps she left the light of the barn and sprinted over to him, feeling his arms pulling her into a warm embrace. Maybe, just maybe everything was coming together.